DEEP STEALTH

T.J. McCandless

HELLA BOOKS

New York London Sydney

ISBN 978-0-9863957-1-0

Printed in the United States of America

Rev. 1.27

Acknowledgments

A certain place in cyberspace,
and those who dwell therein

C.C. and B.K.,
sharp of eye and tongue

Cover photo by Radley Balko

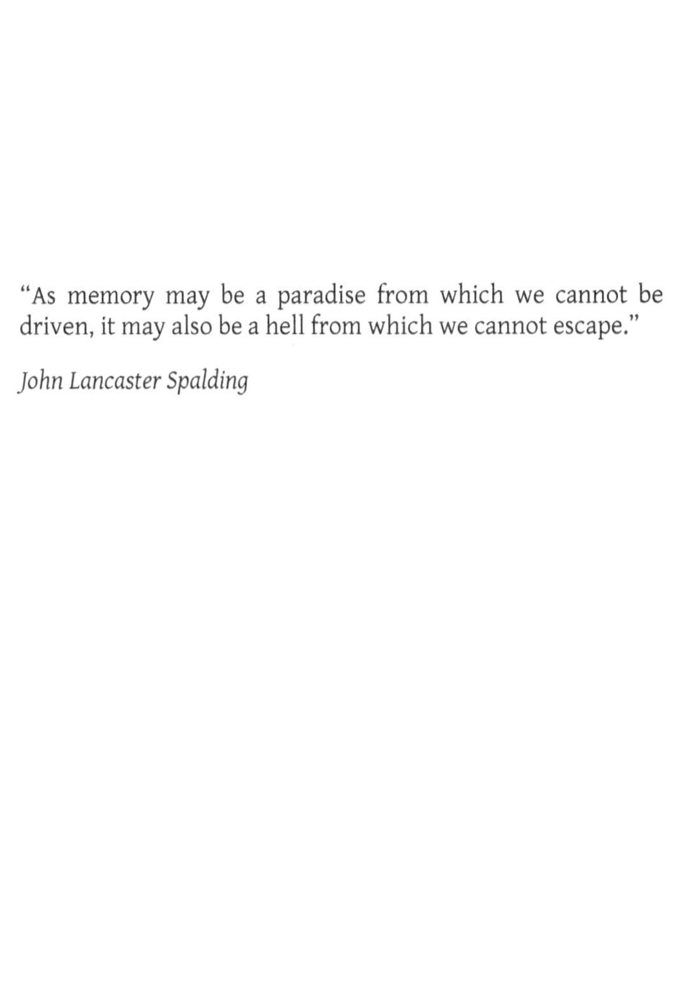

"As memory may be a paradise from which we cannot be driven, it may also be a hell from which we cannot escape."

John Lancaster Spalding

DEEP STEALTH

1

It was a place for screaming, but she had no mouth. No mouth, no body, no physical form of any kind. She was adrift without form or substance in a boundless void, a vast gray sameness that seemed infinite. She had no idea how long she'd been there. Maybe forever. Time was a meaningless concept in that eternal nothingness.

Perhaps she was dead and the void was purgatory. If so, she had no memory of the sins she was there to atone for. But she knew suffering—soul-crushing loneliness and unrelenting boredom were always with her. Sleep provided an escape, if only temporarily. When she woke she was still in the void, still trapped in a dream without end.

This had been the sum total of her existence, for countless sleep cycles of unknown duration at unknown intervals.

When the manifestations began, she rejoiced. Anything that broke the monotony was welcome. She first became aware of a soft beep, as regular as a heartbeat. A recurring light, painfully bright and mercifully brief, was next to appear. But of most interest to her, sometimes she could hear people talking. She would listen closely, but their voices were indistinct, like faraway echoes. However, they seemed closer each time she heard them, and her hope grew that she could find a way to communicate with them, ask them questions. Starting with, where was she? And who was she?

She waited. There was no alternative.

The orderly entered the room pulling a cart behind him. He walked over to the basin and flicked on the light above it. The room had two beds, but only one was occupied. The patient, a young woman, was unconscious. She was intubated and catheterized, connected to an IV pump and a monitor that emitted a steady beep. The orderly stood beside her bed a moment. The brief visits with her had become the high point of his shift. Sometimes he'd talk to her, tell her how pretty she was, even with all the tubes sticking out of her.

He turned away to attend to his routine tasks, glad that the room, his last that shift, would be quick to knock out. The sink needed a once-over, and the soap and towel dispensers refilling, and the waste basket emptied and relined—a sequence he carried out on automatic pilot, stealing occasional glances at the coma patient.

Tough break, sweetie.

In his fantasy she would wake up and realize immediately that he was her soul mate. And overlook the fact that he was a good ten years older, overweight, and balding prematurely. As fantasies went, it was a good one.

He sensed an impending sneeze and reached for a tissue from the box on top of the cart, inadvertently nudging an empty stainless steel pan with his elbow. The pan teetered on the edge of the cart for a breathless moment and then fell to the floor with a resounding crash that echoed off the walls, a ringing metallic cacophony. The orderly lunged for the pan, but the clangor subsided before he could get his hands on it. With any luck, they hadn't heard it at the nurse's station at the far end of the hall. He was in their crosshairs already for chronic lateness. Several tense minutes passed and no one came in to investigate, so he figured he was in the clear.

Hope I didn't disturb your sleep, honey.

He switched off the light over the basin and jockeyed the cart through the doorway, eager to punch out for the night and get the hell out of there.

The young woman in the bed stirred.

An undertow was trying to pull her back down, but she fought her way upward, toward the source of the sound and the light, fearful she wouldn't have enough strength to make it.

But at last, like a swimmer breaking the surface of a dark sea, she was awake.

She moaned, but the only sound that came out was a hollow wheezing through a tube in her throat. Entirely by reflex, she grabbed the tube and yanked it out. A long, thin tube in her nose came out with it. She gagged and coughed and then lay panting with exhaustion. After a while she felt strong enough to raise her head and take stock of her surroundings.

In Oregon Medical Research Institute's hospital cafeteria, Dr. Aaron Lachmann was about to take his first bite of coconut cream pie, his favorite, when his pager vibrated. He ignored an impulse to hurl the device at the wall like a baseball, shatter it into a dozen pieces. For reasons he couldn't fathom, the medical profession continued to cling to the archaic technology, even in the era of the smart phone. He laid the fork down, fished his phone from his coat pocket, and punched in the number. The voice that answered belonged to one of the evening shift nurses at the neurology ward nurse's station. He identified himself.

"Dr. Lachmann," the nurse said, "I thought you'd want to know right away—our Jane Doe regained consciousness just a short while ago. The ventilator alarm went off when she pulled out her trach and gastric tubes. When we got to her room we found her awake and alert."

"On my way," he said, standing up.

He was almost to the exit when a resident he knew entered the cafeteria. Lachmann pointed to the untouched pie on the table where he'd left it. "Yours if you want it," he said. The resident demonstrated his appreciation with an exaggerated bow.

During the elevator ride to the third-floor neurology ward, Lachmann marveled at the unexpected development. "Awake and alert," the nurse said. Go figure. The smart money said she wouldn't suddenly regain consciousness after being comatose that long, not with that degree of autonomic dysfunction. Most long-term coma patients didn't just "wake up," like in movies and TV shows. In reality, *if* they came out of a coma it was almost always a gradual process lasting days or even weeks. There were rare exceptions, of course, but he never thought he'd see one in the flesh. The elevator came to a stop and the doors hissed open.

Three nurses were in the room performing various tasks when Lachmann walked in. They parted to make way for him. The young woman in the bed turned her head toward him slowly, as if it were a great effort. And yet she'd managed to yank out the endotracheal and nasogastric tubes, even with a fully inflated cuff around the trach tube, an impressive feat. She appeared to be alert, but was she responsive?

"Hi, I'm Dr. Lachmann."

Her reply was an inaudible whisper. But she responded, that was the important thing.

He took a silver penlight from his pocket and held her right eyelid open while he shined it in her eye. After repeating it in the left eye he grunted with satisfaction. He opened her chart and in his precise script wrote, *Pupillary size and response normal, both eyes.* The monitor indicated her vitals were all within normal limits, a good sign. "How are you feeling?"

This time the whisper was audible, barely. "Weak."

He wrote, *Responsive to questions.* So far, so good. "What's your name?"

A vertical furrow formed between her eyebrows. "Livvy," she finally whispered.

He wrote the name. "Your last name, Livvy?"

The furrow deepened. "Can't . . . remember."

"Age?"

She shook her head.

"What do you remember, besides your first name?"

Five seconds went by before she whispered, "Nothing."

He wrote, *Partial retrograde.* It wasn't total, because she could remember her first name. "Livvy, it's common for people who've been in a coma to experience confusion and temporary amnesia after awakening. Don't be too concerned about it."

Her tongue moistened dry lips. "So how—how did I end up here?" The whisper changed to a creaky soprano midway though her question.

"An ambulance brought you here. You were found lying unconscious in a downtown parking lot with a head injury caused by a blunt instrument. No purse, no identification of any kind. Police figure you were carjacked in the lot."

"How bad was my . . . head injury?"

"Bad enough. You were in a coma for a month."

"A month." She raised her right arm, the one without the IV, and gingerly touched her scalp.

Lachmann reached over and guided her hand to a spot an inch or so above her right ear. "Here," he said. "Almost completely healed." Even though long-term memories were distributed throughout the cortex, the blow to the temporal lobe region had apparently disrupted the retrieval process. Brain function tests would provide more information about the extent of the impairment, but they would have to wait until tomorrow.

"The amnesia—it's temporary?" No mistaking the concern in her voice.

He took her hand. "In the majority of cases, memory loss due to head trauma has a good chance of being temporary. But let's take things one step at a time. Right now your job is to regain your strength."

She nodded and even managed a fleeting smile.

"Don't be afraid to go to sleep when you're tired. You should sleep normally from now on."

She sighed and seemed to settle deeper into the pillow. In moments her eyelids fluttered and he saw she was struggling to stay awake. He gave her hand a pat and placed it across her stomach, outside the blanket. Her eyes closed and her breathing began to change.

He checked the monitor one last time. Her vitals were remarkably normal. Perfect, in fact. He addressed the nurses: "I want blood and urine workups soon as possible. Bed check every thirty minutes throughout the night. I'll be back in forty-five minutes." Sooner, if the cafeteria was out of coconut cream pie.

At the door he turned and looked back at the patient, who appeared to be sleeping peacefully. Fifteen years in neurology, and he couldn't account for her sudden miraculous return to consciousness. Chalk it up to the resilience of youth. It was as good an explanation as any.

In Brookline, Massachusetts, Nora Cosgrove lay in bed, staring at the ceiling in the subdued light of her bedroom. She turned her head to look at the clock on the nightstand. Quarter past midnight. Finding an empty mailbox earlier in the day had added to her growing anxiety. Over a month since the last letter. Before that, Livvy had written every week without fail. It wasn't like her to suddenly just . . . stop.

Nora's trouble sleeping began back in June, when Livvy informed her that she was flying to Portland to audition for the Oregon Symphony. And that she'd be moving there if she got it. As Livvy's former nanny, Nora was of course concerned about "her" child moving to the other side of the country, even if the child was twenty-five.

Occasional news reports in which girls like Livvy had been beaten or even murdered scared the daylights out of Nora. There were unbalanced, violent people everywhere. Worry that one of them might cross Livvy's path was turning Nora's gray hair white.

For all her handwringing, she couldn't bring herself to call the Portland police and ask them to check on the girl. If Livvy was simply enjoying some breathing room, being contacted by the police would be an unwelcome intrusion.

It was a dilemma.

Nora tossed back the covers, swung her legs off the bed, and sat up. Perhaps some chamomile tea would help her sleep. After a night's rest maybe she could figure out what to do.

2

The next morning two nurses, one with an overbite that eclipsed her other features, removed Livvy's catheter and disconnected her from the monitor and IV. A while later they supported her as she walked to the bathroom for the first time, taking careful steps. Without their help there was no way she could have made it. She was close to collapse when they tucked her back in bed; it took a full three minutes for her heart to stop pounding. Soon after that an aide came in with her breakfast—bran cereal, buttered wheat toast, stewed prunes, orange juice, and lime Jell-O. She was just finishing the Jell-O when a tall man in a white coat walked in. It was the same doctor who'd examined her after she came out of the coma. She had forgotten his name, but it was on his name tag: Dr. Lachmann.

"How are you feeling this morning, Livvy?"

She laid her fork aside. "I can't recall feeling better."

The doctor laughed. "Sarcasm. A good sign, actually." He looked at her chart and then took out his pen and made a brief notation. "Looks like you had a good appetite. Didn't like your cereal?"

"I ate some of it, but it's pretty awful."

"Perhaps, but you haven't eaten solid food for a month. Bran will help get your digestive system back on track. Then you can have bacon, eggs, and hash browns for breakfast."

"Hash browns and eggs sound good. I'll pass on the bacon, though."

"You don't care for bacon?"

"I don't think so. Just the thought of it is nauseating."

"Maybe you're Jewish and observant."

"Wish I could remember."

"Livvy, I know the memory loss is troubling, but do you have any other problems or concerns this morning?"

"Well . . . my throat is really sore and my voice is hoarse. Talking's kind of painful. So's swallowing, especially the bran cereal and toast."

"I'm not surprised. Trach and gastric tubes tend to irritate tissue long-term. Let me have a look." He took out a penlight and inspected the back of her throat. "Inflamed, all right. I'll have one of the nurses bring you some anesthetic spray and lozenges. They should relieve the discomfort."

"Thank you. I'm also concerned about being so weak. I barely made it to the bathroom and back, even with two nurses helping me."

"You're weak because you were bedridden for a month with no physical activity whatsoever. Muscles atrophy rapidly when they're not used. But you're young, so I'll be surprised if you don't regain your strength very quickly. I'm going to order physical therapy for you. In the meantime, get up and walk around. Explore the corridors on this floor, visit with other patients who are up and about, be as active as you can. Okay?"

She nodded. "Okay."

He closed the chart and replaced the pen in the breast pocket of his coat. "I'm very pleased with your progress, Livvy. You're doing great."

"Even though I still can't remember anything except my first name?"

"Try not to worry about that, okay? It hasn't even been a full day yet since you came out of the coma. For now, let's focus on getting you back on your feet, all right?"

"All right."

"Good girl. I'll be back at two o'clock with some tests that will help us evaluate your condition."

"I'll be here."

After Dr. Lachmann left, Livvy yawned and picked up the remote for the wall-mounted television. *Epic Makeovers* was in progress, emceed by a vivacious blonde who seemed to be trying to expose as many of her implausibly white teeth as possible. The makeover subjects were delirious with excitement; there was a lot of squealing, arm waving, and hopping around. Livvy muted it. When the program credits started rolling, she switched it off and glanced at the clock on the wall. It was 9:34. It felt to her like it should be almost noon; her time sense was badly distorted.

Eyes closed, she probed her mind for a memory, any memory, from her life before the coma.

Nothing.

Her earliest recollection was waking up the night before, feeling as though she'd escaped from a lonely, terrifying place. Everything before that was shrouded by an impenetrable fog. Her missing memories were in there somewhere. Her *life* was in there somewhere.

She opened her eyes and looked at the clock. 10:03.

She knew she should get up and try to walk a little to build up her strength, as the doctor had advised. Despite the exhausting trip to the bathroom, she really wanted to get out of bed. The entire length of her body, from the back of her head to her heels, ached from the constant pressure of lying down. She was ready to give it another try.

First, though. she thought she'd take a short nap. Letting go of consciousness was a matter of just shutting her eyes.

From deep within the fog, unseen phantasms called to her.

3

Father Frank Hickey watched the parishioners file out of Portland's St. Rose Cathedral after the Tuesday evening service. He was anxious to get upstairs to his apartment; Turner Classic Movies was showing *Inherit the Wind*, with Spencer Tracy and Frederick March. As he turned to leave he noticed a man standing next to the confessional. The man wore a black coat with a hood that covered his head. Father Hickey pursed his lips. It was troubling, how the Church's customs and rituals were being eroded. It wasn't all that long ago when men wouldn't even consider wearing hats or other headgear inside the church, but now it was a common sight. The hooded man pointed toward the confessional. After the priest nodded, the man stepped into the booth and closed the curtain.

Father Hickey entered the adjoining booth and sat heavily on the padded seat. He slid a panel aside. Through the wicker screen between the two booths he could see the hooded silhouette.

The penitent said, "In the name of the Father and of the Son and of the Holy Spirit, I seek absolution for my sins."

The priest gave the response, from Psalms 32:1-2: "Blessed is he whose transgressions are forgiven, whose sins are covered. Blessed is the man whose sin the Lord does not count against him and in whose spirit is no deceit."

"Bless me, Father, for I have sinned. It's been nineteen years since my last confession."

So, a lost sheep returns to the flock. "Bless you, my son. What is the nature of your sins?"

"I've consorted with . . . wicked women."

Prostitutes, undoubtedly. "How many times?"

"I lost count."

"And you repent of your sins?"

"I do repent."

"*Dominus noster Jesus Christus te absolvatet ego auchtoritate ipsius te absolvo ab omni vinculo excommunicationis et interdicti in quantum possum et tu indiges.*" After making the sign of the cross, Father Hickey continued in English: "I absolve you of your sins in the name of the Father, and the Son, and the Holy Ghost. Amen."

"Amen."

"Your penance is ten Hail Marys."

"Thank you, Father. I have a hypothetical question for you before I go."

"What is your question, my son?"

"God sometimes speaks to us, right?"

"God speaks to every heart that will hear Him."

"And if God commands you to do something that would ordinarily be considered a mortal sin?"

"Can you give me an example?"

"Well, suppose God commanded you to rid the world of certain things that were offensive in His eyes."

"How would this 'ridding' be done?"

"Let's say, by killing them."

The hair on the back of the priest's neck rose. "It is unlikely God would ever ask such a thing."

"In the Bible God asked people to kill for Him, right?"

"My son, I don't see—"

"It's just a hypothetical question, Father. To settle a bet."

Hypothetical or not, the priest had a bad feeling about it. Choosing his words carefully, Father HIckey said, "Speaking hypothetically, then . . . yes, in the bible God told various people to kill. For example, in Genesis He told Abraham to kill his son, Isaac. But as a test of Abraham's love for God, not because his son was evil."

Silence from the other side of the screen.

"In Leviticus," Father Hickey went on, "it is decreed that offenders must be put to death for certain sins, such as cursing one's parents, committing adultery, working on the Sabbath, engaging in homosexual acts—"

"Getting closer," the man said.

"And in Exodus, God said, 'Thou shalt not suffer a witch to live.'"

"Perfect. Exactly what I had in mind. Where in Exodus is that verse?"

Father Hickey took great pride in his ability to recall biblical passages. "Exodus 22, verse 18. But bear in mind that the Old Testament is full of all manner of violent stuff, ritual sacrifices and killings. The New Testament is more relevant to our modern society. Which of course doesn't believe in witches."

"Modern society." Sound of a soft snort. "Modern society doesn't know everything."

"My son, are you *sure* this is hypothetical? You seem quite . . . intense about it."

"Just trying to win a bet, is all. Got a ten-spot riding on it."

"Glad to hear it. Wouldn't want you to go around killing 'witches' in the name of the Lord, you know." The priest tried for a hearty laugh, but it sounded hollow.

"Father, thank you for your help."

"May God's grace be upon you, my son." *And may He keep you out of mischief.*

Father Hickey shut the panel and waited until he heard the metallic snick of the outer door closing before he left the confessional. The cathedral was empty. As he climbed the stairs to his apartment he couldn't shake off a lingering uneasiness.

Outside St. Rose Cathedral, Jimmy Chapman pushed back the hood on his coat. The chilled night air felt good. He lit a cigarette and leaned back against the building. Street lamps gave the fog shrouding 54th Avenue a phosphorescent glow. Runaway leaves scraped against concrete as gusts chased them down the sidewalk.

It had been almost two decades since he'd set foot in a church. When he was a child, his mother, a devout Catholic, made him and his sister attend services with her. It wasn't optional. In the pews at St. Ignatious, struggling to stay awake during the droning sermons, he would pray. Always the same prayer: for a miracle that would cut short the service. The prayer was never answered. His takeaway: Religion was for chumps.

By age thirteen he'd had his fill of church and refused to go. His mother threw up her hands. As a further act of rebellion he stole a Cadillac Eldorado and led police on a high-speed chase before he crashed into a Dunkin' Donuts, critically injuring several customers. The stunt landed him in MacLaren Youth Correctional Facility in Woodburn until he was eighteen.

MacLaren was like a vocational school for budding criminals. After his release the reform-school knowledge he'd acquired didn't go to waste. He embarked on a ten-year robbery spree, starting with home break-ins and burglaries, progressing to armed robberies. But a liquor store job broke bad and he ended up in the state pen in Salem.

Then God reentered his life.

He'd been sweating out the final month of his sentence, keeping his head down and hoping nothing would mess up his upcoming release, when God instilled in him a sense of holy purpose.

And now, on a foggy September night outside St. Mary's, he felt that sense of purpose had been reinforced in the confessional. Not that he'd had any doubts. He flicked the butt into a storm drain and unlocked the black car waiting for him at the curb.

Thou shalt not suffer a witch to live.

Exodus 22:18, the priest had said. Biblical confirmation.

He kissed the gold crucifix he'd bought at a pawn shop near his hotel, and then he started the car and eased away from the curb. In the low beams the fog had a silvery luminescence that gave 54th Avenue a heavenly appearance.

Heaven at night.

4

It was a cold evening on Belmont, and Cassandra was shivering, the icy wind flaying her skin like steel whips. Her thin bolero jacket provided almost no warmth. She wished she could wear a warm coat when she was out there, but of course that wasn't possible. On the stroll she had to look the part. That meant wearing the required uniform: miniskirt, low-cut blouse, push-up bra, and shoes or boots with very high heels. Tommy would slap hell out of her if he caught her wearing anything that wouldn't give the tricks a hard-on. But god, it was cold.

That stretch of Belmont was her turf. She leaned against a parking meter in front of the Avalon Theater. The Avalon was closed now, but the weathered plastic letters on the marquee announced, "TH S ISLAND EART ," the shadowy outlines of the missing letters completing the title. She remembered Saturday afternoons in the balcony, watching sci-fi and horror double features with her brother Danny, munching on Dots, Jujubes, and popcorn. That was a million years ago. These days Danny wouldn't even talk to her.

"To hell with this, I'm freezing my ass off," she said to the parking meter. Tommy or no Tommy, she needed to thaw out for a while. She began stilting down the sidewalk in the direction of the Medallion Club, which was warm inside. And who knows, she might luck out and pick up a trick.

A half-block from the club she saw four provocatively dressed women standing in front, bathed in the pink neon glow. She knew the quartet well; all the working girls on Belmont knew each other. Sabrina, their unofficial leader, spotted Cassandra and called out, "Cassie, get your silicone-pumped ass over here."

Cassandra walked the last ten steps using her "runway strut," invoking hoots of "Work it, girl!" and "Fierce, baby, fierce!" from the group. It was always best to keep a strong front with them or they'd eat her alive. "Hey, girls," she said, "what's the dealio?"

Sabrina inclined her head toward a tall brunette. "Tiffany here is talking about going to Montreal. What d'you think, Cassie?"

The bitches were always fucking with her, throwing shade. Six months earlier she'd gone to Montreal and had the surgery, and now many of the pre-op girls on the track were envious. "Whatever the girl wants is cool with me," she said.

Brianna, a redhead with creamy skin, was next to chime in. "I wouldn't go nowhere but Thailand. Compared to Thai surgeons, the ones in the States and Canada are still in the Dark Ages, baby, and way too expensive."

Sabrina and the black girl named Dierdre chorused, "That's for damned sure," and "You ain't wrong, sister."

Cassandra played it cool. "Oh, I don't know. I'm pretty happy with my result. And I didn't have to fly halfway around the world to get it."

"I've been meaning to ask you," Sabrina said, "what about your regulars, the ones who preferred a little sumpin-sumpin extra, did they bail on you?"

Cassandra shrugged. "A few did, but I'm not concerned. It expanded my clientèle."

"Clientèle?" Dierdre cried. "Did that cute Montreal doctor give you French lessons along with a vajayjay?" She turned to the others and asked them about their "clientèle" in a mocking way. The answering shrieks of laughter could be heard a block away.

Cassandra listened to them carry on and pondered why, when they went to so much trouble to look as female as possible, they made no effort to work on their voices. Did they think they sounded like women? Close your eyes and you'd think you were listening to a gay-boy quartet. All the hormones, surgery, and silicone in the world wouldn't overcome a male-sounding voice. She knew better than to say anything to them about it, though. They'd just accuse her of being shady.

Cassandra was the only one in the group to notice a black car coast to a stop at the curb. The tinted window on the passenger side slid down. Hips swinging, she walked over and leaned down, resting her arms on the window sill.

"What's goin' on, honey?" she asked the driver in her sweetest baby-doll voice. While she waited for an answer, she tried to soak up as much heat from the interior as possible. It felt awesome.

The guy gave her a wide grin. "You tell me, pretty thing."

His shiny black hair was combed straight back, close to his head. Under a black leather jacket he wore an iridescent maroon silk shirt unbuttoned halfway down his chest, exposing a mat of black chest hair and a gold crucifix on a chain. He didn't look much like a vice cop.

Nevertheless, she had to ask. "You a cop, baby?"

The grin grew even wider. "Relax, pretty thing. I got no more use for cops than you do."

She noticed a tattoo on his neck, a mean-looking hooded snake. A shudder ran up her spine. Snakes creeped her out, whether they had hoods or not. "So you lookin' for a date?"

The smiling man drew a question mark in the air with a forefinger.

"Twenty for a blowjob, fifty for a half-and-half."

"Sweet Jesus, does that include a wash and wax for my car? I'm used to paying half that.

She shrugged. "If that was around here it must've been a while back. Blame inflation."

"Not a deal breaker. Let's go."

Cassandra opened the door and wriggled into the bucket seat. Warmth from the heater enveloped her. She marveled at her luck to catch a trick with a warm car when she was so cold. The group of girls on the sidewalk were talking quietly together, casting glances at the car.

As the car pulled away from the curb, Cassandra checked out the driver. There was something familiar about him. "Have I dated you before, sweetie?"

He nodded. "Around three years ago."

She remembered him then; he'd been her trick a few times. His deal was taking her estrogen-shrunken tube of flesh in his mouth while he fondled her breasts. No doubt he'd expected to do it again. She needed to clue him in that she no longer had what she'd had back then. Maybe it wouldn't matter to him, but you never know. It would sure be nice if she could turn the trick. Not to mention, stay in that warm car a bit longer. She crossed her fingers for luck and said, "Listen, I need to tell you something, baby. I had surgery. Back in May."

The silence lasted several seconds. Then he said, "I didn't mind you the other way."

She had a mental image of a fifty-dollar bill, flapping like a pair of wings, flying out the car's window. "Well, now I have what a woman's supposed to have."

But the wide smile returned. "No problem, pretty thing."

The bill came flapping back to her. "Baby, you're gonna have a good time tonight, I promise."

He chuckled. "I'm sure of it."

The car slowed to make a turn. The cyclone fence on each side of the entrance had barbed wire at the top. Even with the light from the sign ("ACCESS MINI-STORAGE - Safe, Secure, Spacious Units") and several pole-mounted mercury vapor lamps, the parking lot was fairly dark. They rolled to a stop and he shut off the car's engine. He got out and walked around and opened her door. She looked up at him. She'd assumed she would do him right there in the car, but apparently he had something else in mind.

"Friend of mine manages this place," he said. "He's moving to Seattle, so I'm taking over his gig. In the meantime, I have a key to his apartment, soon to be mine. Come on, I want to show it to you. I think you'll love the tub."

She got out of the car and again marveled at her good fortune that evening. They didn't call it "The Life" for nothing.

5

Detective Karen Wojanowski arrived back at the 2nd Avenue station house ("the House") at 9:45, after spending an hour and a half investigating a bludgeoning in Pioneer Square. The victim was a hype, well known to his fellow addicts, but of course none of them had any idea who'd taken a baseball-bat length of water pipe and beaten him to a pulp. Junkie deaths by violence or O.D. were common, and no one on the street gave a shit.

She sat down at her desk and tried to concentrate on the paperwork in front of her, but internally a war was being waged—appetite against willpower. And appetite was winning, by a mile. Hard to believe she was hungry again, after devouring a Fast n' Hungry Breakfast Special (*"Omelet, cheddar cheese, ham, and bacon on a toasted English muffin basted with real butter"*) not two hours earlier on the way to the House.

Not that she was grossly overweight, but her figure was a far cry from what it had been even a year ago. It had gotten to the point where she avoided mirrors so she wouldn't have to see the soft muffins overflowing the sides of her waistband, or the floppy undersides of her upper arms, or— keeping it real—her fat ass. Twenty, twenty-five pounds. Thirty, tops. A modest goal, really. That very week a woman on *Biggest Loser* had dropped over a hundred.

And yet, every time the hunger pangs began gnawing at her, her resolve would melt away like ice cream on a slice of hot apple pie. She had become adept at self-deception, at convincing herself that just one more satisfying meal was all she wanted, and after that she'd really, truly ratchet back her eating. And she meant it. She'd surrender then, wolfing down whatever it was she craved, feeling a mixture of pleasure and guilt. The self-loathing came later. Pathetic as those sallow-faced junkies. At least they had methadone; she had nothing. No willpower, certainly.

A tap on her shoulder interrupted the orgy of self-flagellation. She looked up to see Carl Detweiler, her partner for the past four years. He was a good cop, well-liked by most everyone in the Portland Police Bureau. Twenty years on the job and he was counting the days until the first of the year, when he was going to retire.

"Hey, Carl."

"Hate to tear you away from your paperwork, Woj," he said, "but we got a dead one in an alley off Eighty-second."

Appetite forgotten, at least temporarily, Karen took her revolver out of the top desk drawer and holstered it, swearing under her breath. A whole month without a single killing in Portlandia and then two in one day. And her shift wasn't even half over.

"Over here, detectives." The uniformed officer was standing at the entrance to the alley that connected 82nd and 83rd. He had that rookie look: overwhelmed and uncertain, but trying hard to be stoic. Probably his first D.B.

Karen remembered her first, a five-year-old girl beaten to death by her stepfather. A memory she'd erase if she could.

"Hey, you're Harry Ketcham's boy," Detweiler said. "I heard you were on the job. I've known your old man since I was a rookie. He showed me the ropes."

The young officer seemed to relax a bit. "Yeah, huh? He sure misses the job." He indicated behind him with his thumb. "Kind of hard to see in there, what with all these dark clouds smack overhead. Better bring flashlights."

It was good advice. Only midmorning, but it seemed more like dusk. The alley was a dark corridor lined with shadows; the patrol car was midway down. They walked toward it, the young officer in the lead.

"How did you discover the body?" Detweiler asked him.

Ketcham wiped his mouth with his sleeve. "We were checking out some alleys in the area. Lots of meth activity around here, even in the morning. Tweakers don't sleep too much. Anyhow, when we got to this alley, Lewellyn saw something off to the side and shined the spot on it. Then we both shit a brick." He pointed. "Over there. Hope you guys haven't just eaten."

Karen switched on her flashlight. Detweiler did likewise.

The body was at the side of the alley. The nude, very dead girl had been posed like a life-size doll. She was leaning back against the cyclone fence, her clothes folded and stacked with geometric precision beside her. The long blond hair looked like it had been brushed. Her throat had been cut, the incision deep enough to sever her windpipe and both carotids completely. Death would've been quick.

A cross about two inches tall had been carved on her chest, at approximately the same spot a cross on a chain would fall. Her breasts had the pneumatic quality commonly seen with implants. The flashlight's beam proceeded slowly down the torso. When the genitals were illuminated, Karen recoiled.

"Oh, *hell* no," she said, not wanting to believe it.

It looked like a very sharp blade had been inserted in her vagina and then yanked forward toward the pelvic bone, slicing her open like a dissected lab animal. Hopefully, the postmortem would determine that it had been done to her after she was already dead. Jaw clenched, Karen checked for lividity and found none, no surprise there. Exsanguination had given the girl's naturally fair skin a waxy paleness—literally a deathly pallor. No blood around the wounds, no blood under or near the body. That meant someone had cleaned her up after she bled out and then brought her body to the alley.

"She was dumped here, Carl."

"Yeah." Detweiler knelt down and, taking care not to disturb anything, inspected the neat stack of clothing and the pair of stiletto-heeled boots next to it. "Looks like we got a pross killing here, Woj."

Ketcham said, "When I called it in, I advised Dispatch the vic was probably a prostitute. My guess, somebody from Vice'll be joining us soon."

Karen nodded. The rookie was handling himself pretty well, considering. Resuming the examination, she checked a wrist and ankle for freedom of movement. "Some rigor, not much. She hasn't been dead longer than three, four hours. The M.E. can pinpoint the T.O.D. by body temp."

There was a rank, acrid smell coming from somewhere close. Karen shined her flashlight around, trying to discover the source. She found it about ten feet down the alley from the body: a glistening pool of vomit.

"Lewellyn lost it when he saw the body," Ketcham said. "It was the mutilation that did it for him. We'd just pounded down a combination pizza."

She noticed Ketcham's partner hanging back near the squad car, looking sheepish. "Do you have some Visqueen in your trunk?" she asked Ketcham. "I got a feeling it's going to start raining any minute, and C.S.U. will want the body and clothes covered."

"I'm on it." Ketcham started toward the patrol car.

Someone was coming down the alley toward them. It was Ivans, a detective who worked Vice. After he joined them he leaned over to Karen and said, *sotto voce*, "We got to stop meeting like this."

"No shit," Karen said.

With his own flashlight, Ivans illuminated the body and then whistled softly. "I know this one. Busted her a couple times. Tranny hooker, strolls Belmont. Her name's Cassie.

Haven't seen her for a while, though." He directed the beam at the victim's genitals. "Looks like someone felt her previous bottom surgery wasn't radical enough."

"She's transgender?" Karen turned toward the victim. She was soft and delicate. And pretty, or had been.

Ivans nodded. "Bet she fooled a lot of guys. They never had a clue they were shtupping a male."

"Jesus Christ, doesn't *anyone* want the parts they were born with these days?" Detweiler wailed.

Ivans minced toward the older detective, his wrist limp. "I'm having *my* change next week," he said in a falsetto.

"Fuck you, Ivans," Karen said. "How about a little sensitivity here? Nobody deserves what she got. And I say that's a *female* there, no matter what you or anyone else says." Karen knelt beside the dead girl with the thousand-yard stare. "Where's the medical examiner?" she demanded of no one in particular.

"I just heard a car door," Detweiler said. "Maybe that's him."

Lightning lit up the sky to the east, the strobe effect rendering the group as motionless as the dead girl. An ear-splitting report followed three or four seconds later, which placed the strike only a few blocks away. Karen got to her feet and looked up. The blackness glowered overhead, poised to unleash its wrath upon the city. She felt the first raindrops strike her face and run down her cheeks like tears.

6

Livvy sat on a sofa in the lounge area, watching the activity around her, the comings and goings of visitors, patients, nurses, and an occasional doctor. The lounge was as good a place as any to kill some time before her physical exam, scheduled for 3:30. She was supposed to check in with the lab first, at a quarter after. The clock above the information booth across the way indicated 2:37. She felt her hair. Still slightly damp from her shower.

"Good to see you up and about, girl." It was one of the nurses, the one with the prominent overbite, who'd helped her walk to the bathroom the morning after she came out of the coma. At first glance Livvy thought her name tag read "Bunny," which was so wildly appropriate that she was disappointed when a closer look revealed it was actually "Bonny." The nurse gave her a toothy smile and continued on her way.

"I swear, that gal could bite a Big Mac through a Venetian blind." A young woman, dressed like Livvy in hospital-issue pajamas and robe, stood next to the sofa, watching the departing nurse. She had baby-fine hair the color of corn silk that she clipped back, except for chin-length parentheses at the front that framed her face. It was a friendly face, with freckles and blue eyes that sparkled with good humor. She held out her hand. "Leia Dunkleman."

"Livvy." The other girl had a firm handshake. "You said, 'Laya,' right?" Livvy indicated the empty half of the sofa.

The girl nodded her thanks and plopped down and folded her legs under her. "Yeah, spelled L-E-I-A. As in Princess Leia." She sighed. "In their younger days my folks were *Star Wars* fanatics. They also named my brother Luke. They're past all that stuff now, but just to get back at them for roping my brother and me into their obsession, I still call them Anakin and Padmé—only I pronounce it Anerkin and Patty Mae. We should probably count ourselves lucky they weren't *Battlestar Galactica* fans. We could've ended up named Cassiopeia and Starbuck."

Livvy laughed out loud, first time since she woke from the coma. "Nice to meet you. Do you live in Portland?"

"Nope, Texas. My mama and I flew up from Fort Worth last week to visit my grandma and grandpa. They're Mama's folks. Then a couple days ago I got a real funny feeling in my head, like something or other went haywire in my brain. So they did a bunch of tests on me, including an MRI yesterday. They couldn't find anything wrong but they want to keep me here a few more days just in case—" The rapid-fire stream of words stopped. "Sorry. I get carried away sometimes. Just yesterday one of the nurses asked me, 'Say, aren't Texans s'posed to speak with a slow drawl?' But I talk fast, always have."

Livvy envied her. She had her family behind her, support-ing her. No doubt Livvy's family would rush to her side if they knew she needed them. The physical at 3:30 might provide clues about who she was. If they could learn her identity, she could contact her family and—she realized the girl was looking at her expectantly. "I'm sorry, Leia, what did you say?"

"So why are you here, in this place?" Leia indicated the entire hospital with a sweep of her arm.

"Head injury. I was carjacked." Livvy touched the spot, just above her right temple. "And then I was in a coma for a month."

"Omigod, you're the girl who was in the coma?" Leia's voice was higher by half an octave. "I heard the nurses talking about you, about how you came out of it a couple weeks ago, right? Welcome back to the world. It's overrated. You talk like a girl I knew in college from back East. Whereabouts you from?"

Livvy shrugged. "I wish I knew, but I have amnesia. The doctors say it's probably temporary. I'm keeping my fingers crossed."

"Amnesia? That sucks big-time." Leia touched Livvy's knee. "They got some high-powered doctors here. Best in the Northwest, I heard."

"Thanks. I'm trying to be optimistic." Livvy wanted to change the subject. "So what do you do down there in Texas? Do you have a job?"

"Sure do." The girl nodded vigorously and the chin-length strands of fine blond hair flapped like a pair of bird's wings. "I graduated from the University of Texas at Austin last June with a degree in communication studies, even though Daddy had wanted me to study business, so I could handle the bookkeeping for the store. Dunkleman Feed & Seed, third-largest in Fort Worth. Bookkeeping didn't appeal to me much. One thing I can do is communicate, so majoring in communications was a no-brainer for me. After I graduated I wound up working for my daddy anyway."

Livvy glanced at the clock above the information booth; it indicated 3:12. She'd been so engrossed in conversation with Leia, she hadn't been keeping a close eye on the time. "Oops, I'd better go or I'll be late for my exam."

Leia clasped Livvy's hand and pumped it up and down. "Hey, I'm real glad to've met you, Livvy. If you feel like you could use the company, we could hang out some, maybe look for some smokin' hot guys or something."

"I'd like that. See you later, Leia." Livvy stood up and started for the corridor to the left of the lounge. The check-in desk for the lab would be three doors down on the right, according to the directions she'd been given.

7

Lachmann glanced up from the CT scan and saw OMRI Assistant Administrative Director Lawrence Neely making a beeline for him. Lachmann let out his breath through clenched teeth. Neely could be a pain in the ass.

"Hey, man," Neely said. "Got a minute?"

"Sure, Larry. What's up?"

Neely pointed at the image on the screen. "Nobody I know, I hope."

"Some kid who broadsided a Jeep Grand Cherokee that pulled out in front of his motorcycle. Look at this." He pointed to a thin jagged line on the scan. "Hairline fracture in the occipital region about twenty centimeters long. He was wearing one of those half-helmet 'skid lids.' Motorcycles, bicycles, and skateboards generate a lot of business for the neurology department." He turned his chair to face the man. Neely wasn't there to shoot the breeze, he was sure of that. "What's on your mind, Larry?"

"It's your coma patient." Neely took a gold pen from his shirt pocket. With index finger and thumb, he held the pen by the tip and played a ride on an imaginary cymbal. It involved considerable wrist action.

Lachmann suppressed an impulse to excuse himself and leave Neely to his air drumming. Instead, he said, "What about her?"

"Well, as you might expect, your patient's tab is sizable, and the meter's still running. At some point soon, the hospital would like to submit a bill to her insurance company for services rendered. Only one problem: We have no idea which company she has a policy with. The board of directors are getting a bit nervous about that."

"Assuming she *has* insurance."

Neely returned the pen-drumstick to his shirt pocket and resumed his dead-serious administrator persona. "You can bet I'm assuming that. After last quarter's figures—which were less than stellar, if you'll recall—an uncollected two hundred grand or so tends to make the board rather irritable. Judging by the duds your patient was wearing when she was admitted—designer jeans, expensive kidskin boots, suede jacket by Prada—I'm guessing the girl's not indigent. In fact, if she doesn't have the best coverage money can buy, I'll strap on a tin beak and peck at shit with the chickens."

"Guess you'll have to wait until she gets her memory back before you know for sure. I'd keep that tin beak handy, just in case."

"Aaron, she's been here for over five weeks. This is a hospital, not a hotel for amnesiacs."

"Well, I don't know what you expect me to do about the situation, Larry. When she recovers her memories, you'll be the first to know. That's about the only assurance I can give you right now."

"Fine. In the meantime, I've hired a private investigator. If he can find out who she is before her memories return, we'll be ahead of the game."

Lachmann closed the windows, logged out, and stood. "Sounds like a good idea, Larry. You'll keep me posted?"

"Sure thing, man. Well, gotta book. Keep on rockin', Dr. Lachmann."

Lachmann nodded. "Always."

He watched Neely set off down the corridor and reflected on the fact that—unlikely as it seemed—the balding, paunchy, middle-aged man was once the drummer in an Eighties "hair band" named Crystal Pendant, which had only one hit, a power ballad titled "Baby Baby Baby, You Are Drivin' Me Craby," before fading into well-deserved obscurity. In the band photo in his office, Neely looked like an administrator even back then, just more hair and sillier clothes. He'd probably welcomed the chance to trade sex, drugs, and rock n' roll for meetings, projections, and P&Ls.

As he unlocked the door to his office, Lachmann had a fleeting mental image of a flock of bespectacled administrator groupies chasing after Neely, tearing at his white shirt, pulling his tie, scuffing his wingtips.

Lachmann sat down behind the mahogany desk and swiveled his chair around to face the windows. He looked out at the dusk settling over the hospital grounds, thinking about the icy gin and tonic waiting for him at home.

Chapman tossed aside the magazine and lay back, fingers interlaced behind his head. The network of cracks in the yellowed ceiling reminded him of veins and arteries. The Centurian Plaza was a dump, no two ways about it. The room was always cold, hot water was intermittent at best, the bed was lumpy and swaybacked. He'd figured to crash there for only a few weeks after he got out of the joint, but he ended up spending three miserable months in that shithole.

If I had to live here much longer, I'd stick a fucking gun in my mouth.

Fortunately, in ten days he'd be out of there like a striped-ass ape. His bro Benny had hooked him up with the manager's job at the mini-storage; Chapman would slide into the vacated position when Benny took off for Seattle. The job included a studio apartment, located over a couple of the storage units. Chapman had a preview of his future digs last week while Benny was in Seattle getting things squared away for the move. Long enough for Chapman to determine that it couldn't be better suited for his purpose. The sacred task he'd performed there last Wednesday night proved that.

Two down.

Two fewer abominations in the world to transgress the will of God. He had to smile. He was fulfilling his special destiny. He was a soldier of the Lord, ridding the world of evil creatures. It was as if James Lloyd Chapman had been designed for that specific purpose:

"Classic sociopath: narcissistic, opportunistic, higher-than-average intelligence, demonstrates no capacity for empathy or remorse."

That was the terse evaluation by the prison psych (who apparently hadn't realized Chapman could read upside-down). It was on the mark, though. Empathy and remorse were just words to him. As he saw it, that gave him a big advantage over everyone else. He smiled, wondering what the psych would say about the erotic thrill he got from killing the abominations. It was a hell of an incentive—correction, a *heavenly* incentive—to carry out the holy task that had been asked of him.

With a single bark of laughter, he tossed the pillow across the room.

Booyah!

He had the juice. He was a connected guy, the connection as good as it gets. All the years he'd turned his back on the Almighty were forgotten, like they never happened. And it went without saying that all his sins were expunged from the Holy Record.

God moves in a mysterious way His wonders to perform.

8

Thomas J. Griggs trudged down a hospital corridor that seemed endless. Finally, he spotted the door he was looking for:

SARAH SOONG, D.O.
INTERNAL MEDICINE

"Thank God," he said. He leaned a meaty shoulder against the door frame and rested a moment before knocking lightly on the textured glass. Then he opened the door wide enough to stick his head in.

The Asian woman at the desk closed a file folder and set it aside. "Come in, Mr. Griggs."

He shut the door behind him and walked over and shook her hand. "Dr. Soong, a pleasure." Furniture was always an issue for him, and he was relieved to see, in front of the desk, a chair that was sturdy and roomy enough to accommodate a man his size. Even so, he took care settling his bulk into it. It was a snug fit but reasonably comfortable. "I appreciate your taking the time."

"Mr. Neely asked me to help you any way I can. He said you're going to find out who our amnesia patient is." She smiled at him. "A bold statement."

"I'm going to try. I don't have much to go on yet; I'm hoping the results of the exam you conducted will give me a starting point." He unzipped a black canvas bag and took out a laptop computer. A polyphonic chord swelled when he woke it from hibernation. "Okay, we're in business. Hey—it found an open wi-fi. Always seems to be at least one available, no matter where you go these days. Convenient."

The doctor opened a patient chart. "When I spoke with Mr. Neely, he indicated you were particularly interested in whether the patient had any scars, tattoos, piercings, or other identifying marks."

Griggs nodded. "Exactly right."

Dr. Soong looked down at the chart. "The patient is a female who appears to be in her mid-twenties. According to her lab results she's in the peak of health. She has no visible external scars, tattoos, or piercings, with the exception of pierced earlobes, one piercing in each. She has only one small composite filling, in her number fourteen molar. Her breasts have not been augmented. She still has her tonsils, her gall bladder, and her appendix." She paused. "However, I did find something a bit out of the norm for a woman so young."

Griggs stopped typing. She had his full attention.

"When I used ultrasound to look at her appendix and gall bladder, I discovered that she had no ovaries or uterus. She's had a complete hysterectomy. Vaginally, almost certainly, since there weren't any abdominal scars."

"Hysterectomy. That's quite unusual, wouldn't you say?"

"It's a little unusual for someone her age, but not unheard of by any means. There could be any number of reasons why she would need a hysterectomy. She might have had congenitally malformed organs. Or she could have had cervical or uterine sarcoma, ovarian carcinoma, endometrial adenocarcinoma ... Whatever the reason, it explains why subcutaneous hormone pellets were implanted in front of her hip bone, right side, which I discovered when I palpated her abdomen. In the absence of normal hormone production by the ovaries, the pellets deliver estrogen and usually progesterone. It's fast becoming a popular delivery method these days, since implanted pellets can function up to five months. Of course, she can't remember when they were implanted, so she'll need her hormone levels monitored, to determine when they should be replaced."

"I think I already know the answer to my next question. I suppose there would be quite a few young women across the country who've had hysterectomies?"

The doctor seemed to stare into the distance for long seconds before her eyes focused on him. "I'm sorry. What did you ask me?"

"Can you estimate how many young women have had hysterectomies?"

"Thousands, probably."

"I figured as much. Actually, I'd been hoping she had a tattoo. I've located a number of folks by their tattoos." He sighed. "Can you think of anything else that might help me?"

She shook her head. "Sorry." She got up from her chair and walked around to the front of her desk and half-sat on it. The message was clear: The meeting was over.

After he stowed the laptop in the bag, he got a business card from his shirt pocket and held it out to her. "If you think of anything else."

She took it from him and glanced at it.

THOMAS J. GRIGGS
Investigator
(555) 255-FIND

"If I do, I won't hesitate to call you."

Getting to his feet involved considerable effort. "Thank you for your time, Dr. Soong. You've been a great help." At the door he turned back to her. "I think I'm going to follow up on that hysterectomy angle anyway."

After the door closed behind her supersized visitor, Sarah sat for a while, staring at, but not seeing, the patient's chart, still open on the desk in front of her.

A startling possibility had occurred to her when she was talking with Griggs. It would involve some professional risk to check it out, but if her hunch turned out to be right, it would be worth it. She needed to give it some serious thought before placing the bet.

9

After spending the afternoon roaming the hospital with Leia, Livvy was ready for a quick nap before dinner. Just as she opened the door to her room, someone called out her name. The pretty Asian doctor who had given her the physical four days earlier was coming down the corridor at a fast clip, waving her hand in the air. Dr. Soong, that was her name.

"Glad I caught up with you," the doctor said. "With your permission I'd like to do one more quick test." She reached in a side pocket of her coat and took out a small plastic bag that held one cotton swab. "I just need to rub this lightly on the inside of your cheek."

Livvy looked at her blankly. "That's all?"

"It will give us more information about you."

That sounded promising. "Do you think it will help find out who I am?" Hope forced her voice higher in pitch.

"It's entirely possible. You'll need to sign this consent form first." The doctor produced a folded sheet of paper and handed it to her.

Livvy skimmed the legal terminology and then shrugged and took the pen from the doctor. She signed her name—her first name anyway—at the bottom of the form and handed it back to the doctor along with the pen. "Okay," she said and opened her mouth wider than was probably necessary.

The doctor rubbed the swab on the inside of her right cheek several times and then dropped the swab in the plastic bag, sealed it, and slipped it into her coat pocket. "Thank you. Hope you have a very nice evening."

Livvy stood at the doorway watching Dr. Soong until she stepped into the elevator. Was it her imagination or had the doctor been scrutinizing her the entire time, those almond-shaped eyes noting every detail? That was a bit strange. She shrugged and lay back on her bed. Three minutes later she was asleep.

En route to the first-floor lab, Sarah thought about the young woman whose epithelials were on the buccal swab in her coat pocket. Livvy had been only too glad to provide them; the girl would do almost anything to find out who she was. Sarah felt the first twinge of guilt and quickly pushed it away. She knew she was stepping over the line, and she also knew the signed consent form probably wouldn't cover her ass if her actions should come to light. Nevertheless, she felt she had no choice in the matter. She was the only one who knew what was at stake, if her hunch turned out to be right. She opened the door to the lab and walked in.

Elliot Pritchard set down a half-eaten slice of pizza and wiped his mouth with a napkin. "Dr. Sarah Soong, as I live and breathe. To what do I owe the pleasure?" He indicated the open pizza box on his desk. "Can I tempt you with some pepperoni pizza?"

"Thank you, no," Sarah said. According to hospital scuttlebutt, Pritchard was a player. He—allegedly—used his lanky, square-jawed good looks to cut a wide swath through the ladies. Of course, the gossip mill could have it wrong about him. She forced her thoughts to focus on the matter at hand.

"Your loss. It's pretty tasty." Pritchard glanced over his shoulder. "Just a sec." He stood and went over to a work-bench and flipped a switch; a centrifuge stopped spinning.

Back at his desk he picked up the slice of pizza and regarded her as he took a bite.

She sat on one of the lab stools and crossed her legs, aware that Pritchard was looking at them. She felt silly about being so calculating. Intrigue was not her forte. She forged ahead anyway. "So are you going to apply for Koenig's position when he leaves?"

Pritchard nodded. "I'd be crazy not to. Cytogenetic Tech is a big step up from Lab Tech II—more responsibility, better pay, more interesting work. Fact is, I'm way overqualified for what I'm doing now."

"Perhaps I can help. I'd be willing to put in a good word— in return for a favor."

"I'm listening."

"I need something tested quickly, Elliot. On the QT. No paperwork."

"What kind of test did you have in mind?" He took another bite of pizza.

"Karyotyping."

Pritchard stopped chewing for a second or two and then resumed and swallowed. "Sounds kind of mysterious."

She shrugged. "Call it 'extracurricular research.'"

"So you'll take the heat if it goes sideways?" He closed the lid of the pizza box.

"Absolutely. But that's unlikely." If only she were as confident as she sounded.

Pritchard's shrug was almost imperceptible. "Got the sample?"

She took the plastic bag from her pocket and handed it to him across the desk. "When?"

He opened the middle desk drawer and dropped in the bag. "Give me a day."

"I appreciate this, Elliot." She rose to leave. "I have a meeting with McLaughlin on Monday. I'll talk to him then about moving you into Koenig's spot."

Pritchard smiled. "Doc, this could be the beginning of a beautiful friendship." It was a surprisingly good Bogey.

She chuckled in spite of herself. *Casablanca* was one of her favorites. She reached for the door handle. "Thanks again, Elliot."

"No problem," Pritchard said before the door closed behind her.

On the way back to her office her mouth felt as though it were lined with cotton. She stopped at a drinking fountain that produced a metallic groan and a feeble stream of water.

Sarah felt like groaning herself. She was playing a risky poker hand. The business with Pritchard was her bet after the flop. All in. Nothing to do now but hope the turn and river went her way.

Pritchard blew a kiss at the door after it hissed shut. Soong was a beauty, no doubt about it. The cool thing was, she had an intriguing subtlety. His awareness of her had not been immediate; it sort of snuck up on him, and one day he realized he had a crush on her. He preferred that dynamic to one in which a woman was appealing from the jump and then less so as time wore on. There had been far too many of those.

Dr. Soong had reached out to him for a favor. And in return she was going to grease the way for his career advancement.

Worked for him.

10

Neely almost made it out the door on his way to the restroom when the phone on his desk rang. He cursed, shut the door, and picked up the phone a split-second before the second ring. "Neely."

"Griggs here. With a status report."

Neely sat down in his chair, hoping that sitting and crossing his legs tightly would lessen the urge to pee. "Got something, Tom?"

"You be the judge. I found out your patient's from Boston. Or somewhere close to Boston."

"And you came by this knowledge how?"

"I contacted Margo Reid, Associate Professor of Applied Linguistics at Portland State University. Dr. Reid's an expert on regional accents and close to infallible. I've used her before to identify a subject's place of origin. She interviewed Livvy at the hospital this morning. The girl's from the Boston area. No doubt about it."

"Pretty smart," Neely said. "What's next?"

"Start with the most likely. Canvass apartments, hotels, motels, perhaps car rental agencies. See if they had a tenant or customer who matched your patient's description, had a Bostonian accent, and dropped out of sight. It will be a huge undertaking, but one of my assistants has a knack for that kind of thing."

Neely's bladder was sending urgent signals. "Good work, Tom. Keep me posted."

Griggs didn't seem to take the hint. He continued, "I'm going to check with the Boston and Portland police and find out if any of the patient's relatives in the Boston area reported her missing after they couldn't contact her."

"Good thinking. Well, it sounds like you have the situation under control, so—"

"Just one more thing, Larry."

Neely's eyes rolled toward the ceiling. *For crying out loud!* he screamed silently, *Am I talking to Columbo here?* "Tom, I need to get to an important meeting, so please make it fast." The muscles that constricted his urethra began to spasm. Neely covered the mouthpiece and moaned.

"Okay. This last thing is something you might be able to help with. Boston area hospitals could hold the key. Dr. Soong determined that she's had a hysterectomy, unusual for a girl her age. Patient confidentiality is of course a brick wall for me. But perhaps if you were to contact the Boston hospitals in an official OMRI capacity—"

"Yes, we'll need to look at that. Sorry to cut this short, but duty calls. Keep up the good work, Tom, and let me know if you find out anything with those other angles."

"Absolutely, Larry—"

The rest of Griggs' sentence went unheard by Neely, who was halfway out the door and moving toward the men's restroom in a manner any observer would describe as "determined" before Griggs realized he was talking to a dead connection.

Sarah stood at her office window watching several young women toss a Frisbee in the courtyard below. Accuracy was not among their talents; intercepting the wildly thrown disc involved frantic running and lunging. Their shrieks and laughter could be heard through the closed window. She turned away and walked back to her desk.

The manila envelope was still on the desk, where she'd tossed it after finding it on the floor just inside the door. Elliot had delivered the test results in one day, just as he'd promised. However, the envelope had remained on the desk, unopened, for several hours. Long enough. She picked up a letter opener, slid it along the end with the sealed flap, and removed the contents.

Let me be wrong. Let it be a matched pair. It would be easier for all concerned.

Banded patterns of homologous pairs were arranged on the karyotype sheet in rows. Pair number 23 was in the bottom row, far-right.

"Goddamn," she said. "Goddamn, goddamn."

The pair was not 46,XX. It was 46,XY, plain as could be. Too bad. Had the pair been XX, Elliot could have signed the paperwork and then the test results could have been added to Livvy's chart. And if Neely jumped her for ordering the karyotyping, she would've said she was just being diligent and endured the inevitable lecture about keeping lab costs down.

But the results she held in her hands dictated a change in plans. A Latin phrase popped into her head: *Primum non nocere.* It meant, "First, do no harm," widely thought to be part of the Hippocratic Oath. It wasn't, but conscientious doctors followed the precept nevertheless. In this situation it seemed justifiable to recast it: "First, allow no harm to be done."

That was her intention, although those in a position to affect her future at the hospital would undoubtedly disagree with her interpretation of the principle, since it involved ordering a test without official documentation, concealing the results, and generally flouting hospital rules. Nevertheless, she felt she had to take the risk. Considering what was at stake, how could she not?

Lucky, lucky me. A cosmic prankster with a sadistic sense of humor had tossed this in her lap, and now it was her responsibility, like it or not.

She sat at her desk holding the karyotype sheet, but she didn't see it. One of the girls in the courtyard shrieked, but she didn't hear it. Nothing external registered on a conscious level.

As far as she knew, this particular situation had never arisen before. Gender researchers would give up their first-born for a chance to study Livvy. Livvy was proof positive that gender identity was innate, rather than fabricated. It had to be innate, because Livvy was a blank slate, with no memory of having been any other gender, yet her gender identity was clearly and unquestionably female.

Be that as it may, studying Livvy wasn't as important as protecting her. Sarah saw the young woman in her mind's eye: innocent, vulnerable, oblivious. Protecting her meant preventing her situation from being known—by the hospital, by the investigator they hired, and by Livvy herself.

It would give her a chance to have a life others like her only dreamed of. A life that, prior to her amnesia, Livvy herself might have dreamed of. She could be the first of her kind to escape the painful memories of her past. For her, they would not exist.

Sarah was envious.

11

Dennis Stingler figured he was in for an ass chewing when he was summoned to the IT director's office. He was right. William Morley, his boss, was on the warpath. Subject of rant: Stingler's attitude. Big surprise. Stingler had no choice but to sit there and endure Morley the Moron's tiresome spewing.

"Apparently, you don't realize," Morley was saying, "how things work at this hospital. Here's a newsflash: An essential role of the IT department is providing computer support to the other departments. Support that doesn't include informing those other departments' users that they're imbeciles and have no business near a computer. They tend to resent it."

Obviously, that hare-brained bitch in Accounting—Connie something, the one who smelled like cheap perfume and stale cigarette smoke—had bitched to Morley. The feeble-minded twit had somehow managed to spill Diet Coke inside her computer while using the open DVD tray as a drink coaster, no doubt shorting out the motherboard. The pushy nitwit demanded he fix it at once, right then and there. She was a third-tier bean counter and she was ordering him around like she was his superior. He unloaded on her, sure. Who wouldn't?

Maybe, just maybe, he could make the Moron understand. "Bill, let me explain—"

Morley held up his hand. "I don't want to hear it, Dennis. There's nothing you can possibly say that will excuse your behavior. You apparently feel that other people are beneath you. That insufferably arrogant attitude of yours has put your position at this hospital in serious jeopardy."

Stingler clenched his jaw with such force he felt one side pop. He'd never suffered fools gladly and never would, no matter what this asshole said. Morley was a perfect example of the Peter Principle in action: What he knew about software would fit in a thimble, and yet he'd been promoted to director of the IT department, for fuck's sake. The know-nothing clown probably thought big-endian/little-endian referred to Native Americans.

Morley leaned forward over his desk. "Listen to me carefully, Dennis. If I receive one more complaint about your insults and rudeness, you're out of here. I don't give a shit if you *are* a coding whiz, you're not the only one available. Applicants for your job will be lined up around the block." Morley waved his hand dismissively. "That's all. You can go."

Back in his corner cubicle, Stingler stared sightlessly at his terminal's monitor, grinding his molars from side to side. Obviously, he was unappreciated, despite the uncontestable fact that he was the IT department's go-to guy. Without his expertise they'd probably still be debugging the new patient registration software. Single-handedly, he'd transformed it from an error-spewing pile of crap into a functional system nearly ready to go live. Instead of threatening him with dismissal, Morley should be doing everything in his power to make sure he was contented. So he'd been a bit short-tempered with an imbecilic user, big fucking deal. If it weren't for users, programming would be the perfect job.

"Bastards," Stingler said aloud. It was 4:49, by the clock on the wall. Close enough. He logged off his terminal and then stood and put on his jacket, ignoring the quizzical looks on the faces of the other programmers. Most of those guys were incompetent dipshits and the rest were dilettantes. Fuck 'em.

Forty-five minutes later he was unlocking the door to his basement apartment in Tigard. No signs of activity in his parents' house upstairs, which meant they were probably out. He really needed to move out of their basement, get a place where he'd have some privacy for a change. He was almost thirty, for chrissake. If it weren't for the fact that his rent was so reasonable—insanely reasonable, actually—he would've moved long ago. It was a case of simple economics. Same reason he drove the '94 Corolla that used to belong to his parents. It made all kinds of sense to stay right where he was. He could grit his teeth and put up with the lack of privacy, for the time being.

He was just treading water until he made a big score—only a matter of time, with his talent—and then there'd be some changes. It was a familiar fantasy: Live on a houseboat at the marina. Parties on the boat. Hot chicks. Lots and lots of toys, including a sweet ride.

He took off his jacket and tossed it on the back of the well-worn sofa that used to reside upstairs. Then he slouched over to the refrigerator and yanked the handle. A twelve-pack of Mountain Dew was on the bottom shelf; he reached in and extracted a can. A jar of blackberry jam was the only other object in the refrigerator, but that was okay. A dozen microwaveable dinners were stacked in the freezer, emergency rations for when his mother didn't prepare him a meal. And then there were the provisions in the cupboard. Crackers: Ritz, Wheat Thins, and Chicken in a Biskit; cookies: Oreos and Pecan Sandies; and something he considered a staple: Adams chunky-style peanut butter. Brain food, all.

He walked over to his workstation and reached down to tap the space bar on the keyboard. The ancient but still crisp CRT monitor came to life with a crackling hiss, like crushing the cellophane from a pack of cigarettes. After the image stabilized he saw that new email messages had come in since he'd last checked. He downed half the Mountain Dew in several huge gulps and followed up with a mighty belch that echoed off the painted cinder block walls.

"Top that," he said to the Dilbert poster on the wall beside the workstation. He sat down at his desk and reached for the TV remote. A program on G4 was reviewing *Halo 5*. He watched a while, interested in the screen shots and video clips from the game. It wasn't bad, for a first-person shooter. But where was the subtlety? Where was the complexity that would hold a player's interest? First-person shooters were for cretins.

He turned to the computer. Five unread email messages were listed on the screen. The first one, subject "B there or B square," was from the leader of his clan, Structured Chaos, reminding him of an upcoming raid on a rival clan, Army of Light. Stingler tapped out a quick reply, an assurance that they could count on him. The next two messages were spam that went straight to the trash. The fourth message was a notification that someone had replied to his last post in the Gentoo developers' forum. The final unread message's subject was "Results of search: 7 found."

His fists shot into the air. "The Stingman shoots, the Stingman scores."

The email was generated by a server script he'd written a couple of days before. He called his creation "Marauder." Marauder periodically scanned all the messages on the hospital's email server looking for a specified string pattern. If it found any matches it would email a report to its creator. Just a hack to exercise his regular expression chops. Something to relieve the boredom.

At first he couldn't remember the search string he'd chosen for Marauder's test run, only that he'd considered both *breast* and *vagina*. After a few moments' thought he snapped his fingers. *Genital*, that was it. An inspired choice. Seven messages containing the target string had been found. The report listed each message's sender and subject. He scanned through the list; only one message's subject line caught his attention. He opened it and read the message, expecting to see the usual boring crap doctors emailed to other doctors.

```
Message-ID: <459AEC8F.20409@OMRI.edu>
User-Agent: Thunderbird 1.5.0.9
(Toshiba/20061207)
MIME-Version: 1.0
Content-Type: text/plain; charset=ISO-8859-
1; format=flowed
Content-Transfer-Encoding: 7bit
Date: Wed, 10 Sep 2014 03:04:47 -0800
From: Sarah Soong, D.O.
<sarah.soong@OMRI.edu>
To: Kimberly Liu, M.D.
<kliu@tricareassociates.com>
Subject: In over my head
```

Hi,

Hope everything is well with you, and your new practice is picking up. I envy you, living and working in beautiful San Fran. Some people have all the luck. :^)

I need your advice about an unusual situation. It concerns a patient here at the hospital: female, mid-twenties, admitted for cranial trauma, comatose for a month. She came out of it three weeks ago, but with amnesia. Lachmann thinks it might be temporary, but at this point she can't recall anything about herself, except that her first name is Livvy.

The hospital had me give her an exam, during which ultrasound revealed that, although her external genitalia appear normal, she has no ovaries or uterus. It bothered me. While I was talking with with an investigator the hospital hired to find out who she is, it occurred to me that she might be transgender. Well, I had to find

out. I ordered a karyotyping done, but
through unofficial channels, to keep her
identity confidential. The results
confirmed my hunch: Livvy has a male
karyotype, and no AIS marker is present.

Her appearance is phenotypically female,
with narrow shoulders, small waist, wide
pelvic structure, slender hands and feet,
and she has a female vocal range. All of
which indicates she transitioned young. Now
she's an attractive woman in her twenties,
with no memory or knowledge of her life
before the coma. She's a clean slate.

So riddle me this: Am I ethically obligated
to tell her she's transgender? Is she
entitled to know? And the biggie: Given a
choice, would she WANT to know? Maybe she
would prefer to have a fresh start instead.
Here's how I feel about it: If her memory
returns then so be it, but I'll be damned
if I'm going be the one to tell her.

Right now I'm the only one who's aware of
her situation. I haven't mentioned anything
to the hospital. If they find out I ordered
an off-the-books karyotyping and withheld
information about a patient, I'm cooked.
But then, I'm a poker player.

Best,
Sare

"Whoa!" What the hell had Marauder turned up? Stingler
read the message again, top to bottom. It seemed the
inscrutable Dr. Soong had put one over on the hospital.
Shame on her. That information alone could be highly

profitable. But it was insignificant compared to the revelation that one of the hospital patients was a tranny who didn't know she's a tranny. And she was supposedly young and attractive. It sounded like a movie plot.

Stingler interlaced his fingers palms-out and cracked his knuckles, and then, with a flourish worthy of a concert pianist, he positioned his fingers on the keyboard. In a matter of seconds a remote login prompt was waiting for his password. Once inside the hospital's mail server he loaded Maurader into an Emacs editor and modified the script's code to send him copies of *all* mail to and from Dr. Sarah Soong, regardless of content. And tomorrow he'd have a look at the tranny patient. An up-close-and-personal look.

The houseboat at the marina and the sweet ride could be his sooner than he'd thought, if he played it right.

12

Livvy sliced through the water with long, graceful strokes. She had the basement pool all to herself today, Monday. It was rare when she didn't have to share it with other physical therapy patients. The daily workouts were doing wonders for her conditioning. At first she had marveled at how natural swimming felt, how familiar. The reverberation of sounds echoing off concrete surfaces in the huge space, the lines that demarcated the lanes on the bottom of the pool, and especially the chlorine smell—these things stimulated sense-memories of swimming other times in other pools. But the impressions faded before she could bring them into focus. They were objects in the dark, invisible when she looked directly at them.

She'd had enough for the day. She swam to the side, and in an easy motion she grasped the pool's edge and hoisted herself out of the water, turning her torso in mid-air to plant her butt deftly on the concrete. She stood and dripped water all the way to a bench, and then she toweled off, looking forward to shucking the hospital-issue Speedo and stepping into the warm shower that awaited her in her room.

"You make it look easy."

She looked up. A man limped toward her using a cane, his right knee wrapped with an elastic bandage. When he was closer she guessed he was in his late-twenties, possibly early thirties. He was wearing a green T-shirt with a large yellow "O" on the front, tan boxer-style swim trunks, and flip-flops. He looked like an ex-athlete who'd gotten a bit soft.

He sat down on the other end of the bench and propped his cane against the seat's front edge. "I can't swim worth a damn. Never could. You look like you're in your element when you swim, like a dolphin. I, on the other hand, resemble an injured manatee."

She laughed. "That bad, huh?"

He nodded, mock-sadness on his face. "When I get out of the water, people have been known to try to roll me back in."

"But they mean well," she said.

He laughed and then pointed his thumb at his chest. "Jeff Longcypher. And you would be . . . ?"

"I would be Livvy."

"Just Livvy?"

"For now."

"Don't blame you a bit. Can't be too careful, what with all the suspicious-looking characters around here." His smile was lopsided. "Nice to meet you, Livvy." He held out his hand.

After shaking hands she pointed to his clothes. "I take it you're an outpatient?"

"Nope, I'm a full-fledged patient here, at least for a few more days. As for this lovely poolside ensemble, I had a friend go to my place and pick it up for me, along with some other things. The gear the hospital gives you to wear . . . not my style." He gently probed the knee with his fingertips.

"I take it you had surgery on your knee." She grimaced. "I'm sorry, I don't mean to pry."

"No worries." He adjusted the Velcro that secured the elastic wrapping. "I bunged it up playing soccer in college, when I was a mere lad of twenty. Took a really bad hit. The anterior cruciate and lateral collateral ligaments never did heal properly." The crooked smile again. "I know the names of the structures of the knee only too well by now. Anyway, it's been eight years since the injury, and I decided it was time to get it fixed. Which meant endoscopic knee surgery."

He picked up the cane and wielded it as if it were a large endoscopic instrument burrowing into a huge imaginary knee. "The surgery was on Monday, so it's been . . . five days now."

"And you're walking on it already?"

"Doctor's orders. He wanted me on my feet as soon as possible afterward. The doc glossed over that part when he talked to me before the surgery. But according to him it's essential for the rehabilitation process, to maintain strength and limberness. If you're not active after surgery, leg muscles can become weak and adhesions can form, limiting your flexibility and range of motion. Wouldn't want that, so I'm up"—he bounced the rubber-tipped cane vertically off the concrete and caught it in mid-air—"and at 'em." He grinned, and the outside corners of his eyes crinkled. "That's probably more than you wanted to know about my knee."

Livvy studied her companion's features. Thick, sandy-brown hair, worn short. Nose that looked like it had been badly broken, perhaps more than once. Small scar at the apex of his left eyebrow where no hair grew. Pale blue eyes that seemed to regard the world with bemused interest.

Those eyes glanced beyond her, toward the entrance. "Hey, looks like my physical therapist finally made it. Only ten minutes late this time." A man in white pants and short-sleeved shirt was striding toward them, towels draped over one arm, a clipboard in the other. "Aqua therapy for the knee," Jeff said. He didn't sound enthusiastic about it.

"Now I'll get to see if you're as terrible a swimmer as you claim."

He held up his hands with palms outward to ward off the suggestion. "No, no, no," he said, shaking his head. "Please, I've suffered more than enough indignities in this place as it is."

She laughed. "Some other time, perhaps."

"Don't count on it. But maybe I'll see you down here again."

"I swim every day around this time."

Before he could reply, the physical therapist was standing at his elbow. The man sported the early stages of a comb-over that in five years would be an impressive specimen. "Sorry, my last session ran over. Ready?"

Jeff snorted. "You kidding? I live for this." He turned to Livvy and rolled his eyes. "Anyway, it was nice talking with you."

"Same here," she told him, adding, "Good luck with your therapy." She glanced back when she reached the exit. Her new friend was leaning over, unwrapping his bandaged knee. The physical therapist was flipping through forms on his clipboard.

She decided to take the stairs, mostly for the exercise, but also because being enclosed in an elevator car made her uneasy. While she climbed the four flights, she thought about why she hadn't corrected Jeff's misperception that she was being cautious in giving him only her first name. The simple truth was, she hadn't wanted his first impression of her to be "the girl with amnesia." Constantly explaining her situation had become extremely tiresome, as had seeing the sympathetic expressions on the faces of those she told, pity for the poor girl who had her memories taken from her. She didn't want to see that look on Jeff's face. Not then. She opened the door to the third-floor wing.

Jeff said he injured his knee at twenty and waited eight years to have reparative surgery, so he was twenty-eight. The question was, how old was she? And what if she never found out for sure?

13

Karen sat at her desk sipping coffee from the vending machine in the lunchroom and working on her active case reports. Of all her job tasks it was her least favorite; she would rather scrub latrines. When she finished, feeling industrious, she decided to have a look at Vancouver's homicide activity reports. Portland and her sister city across the river routinely shared information, since many crimes overlapped the two metropolitan areas. She was way behind, as usual.

Her practiced eye scanned the reports. There were the usual knifings, shootings, bludgeonings, and a strangling or two. She yawned, wishing she could sneak off to a quiet place and take a nap. Since that wasn't possible, more coffee was definitely required. It wasn't bad coffee, considering it came from a damn vending machine. She was about to go get another cup when some phrases in a two-week-old report jumped out at her: "transgender prostitute," "genital mutilation," "cross carved on chest."

"Holy shit," she said. She reached for the phone on her desk and punched in a number, twirling the handset's coiled cord around her finger while it rang.

"Vancouver Police."

"This is Detective Wojanowski, Portland Police. Can you transfer me to the Homicide desk? Thanks."

Click. "Homicide, Buchanan."

"Detective Wojanowski, Portland Police. I need to talk to whoever's assigned to a case. Transgender prostitute was murdered and carved up."

"Oh. You want Matthews or Burson. It's their case. Just a minute . . ." Away from the mouthpiece: "Hey, Matthews—pick up line four."

Click. "Matthews." His voice had the familiar flatness of tone common to cops.

"Detective Matthews, this is Detective Wojanowski, Portland Homicide."

"What can I do for you, Detective?"

"I understand you caught a case involving the murder of a transgender prostitute?"

"That's right, end of August. What about it?"

"On September fifth the nude body of a transgender prostitute was found in an alley off Eighty-second. Killer slit her throat, carved a cross on her chest, mutilated her genitals. Sound familiar?"

"Holy shit," Matthews said.

"That was my reaction when I read your report. Looks like we've got a serial on our hands."

Matthews sighed into the phone. "I'd hoped it was a one-off. Jesus Christ on a cracker."

"Listen, I'll send over everything I have on mine if you'll return the favor."

"Sure thing. Keep me in the loop if you turn up anything interesting."

After hanging up, Karen sat there drinking the dregs of the lukewarm coffee and thinking sour thoughts. Sometimes she envied her colleagues on traffic detail.

Chapman sat on the bed and opened a Barnes & Noble bag and took out a hard cover book. The store didn't carry the book in stock; they'd had to special order it for him. It was identical to the prison library's copy.

The author of *Abomination* was Richard Ronson, who, according to the bio on the inside flap, was the director of something called The Family Morality Council. *Abomination* warned of a dangerous conspiracy that threatened to destroy the moral fabric of society: The Transgender Agenda. According to Ronson, "transgenders" and their advocates were determined to deconstruct the biological reality of male and female. And their sinister plan was working. "This is an era of political correctness," Ronson wrote, "where diversity rules, and social and psychological aberrations are portrayed as normal. So now we're faced with the growing acceptance of so-called gender reassignment. It should be clear that the transgender threat is far more serious than gay marriage."

The arguments set forth in *Abomination* all had a biblical basis, beginning with Genesis 1:27: *God created man in his own image, in the image of God created He him; male and female created He them.* As designed by God, the two sexes are immutable; maleness and femaleness cannot be changed. By refusing to accept their God-given gender and mutilating their bodies with hormones and surgery, transgenders pervert God's perfect design. "They are abominations," Ronson declared, "and the wrath of God shall be upon them."

Chapman located the passage that had caught his attention when he'd read it in the prison's copy: "Any man who consorts with abominations shall forfeit his manhood, lest he change his ways." That struck home. Before he found the book he'd "consorted" more times than he could count, most recently with Loretta. He closed the book and lay back, thinking about her.

Every penitentiary seemed to have a few transgender inmates, and the joint in Salem was no exception. All pre-op, of course, or they wouldn't be in a men's prison, but that's how he'd preferred them. Soon after his arrival he'd hooked up with Loretta, a petite, doe-eyed Puerto Rican doing a ten-year stretch for vehicular manslaughter. They both worked in the prison laundry, which afforded many opportunities for them to be alone together. Her uninhibited sexuality turned him on like no one ever had before. Loretta made doing time almost tolerable.

It would have been perfect, if not for the Coven. That was what Loretta and her girlfriends Teshawna and Brigitte called themselves. The name was appropriate: The trio took wicked delight in stirring up a cauldron of trouble wherever and whenever they could. Using gossip, innuendo, and their seductive wiles, they manipulated sex-starved inmates and wreaked havoc inside the prison. For the most part, he had ignored their mischief, because the sex was so great.

But a friend of his in B-block, a guy from Albany doing five years for robbing a string of 7-Elevens, got shanked in the exercise yard and died soon afterward in the prison hospital. Through the grapevine Chapman heard the Coven had instigated it. When he confronted Loretta about it she just laughed at him. It enraged him. He slapped her, hard. She leaned forward at the waist, hands on hips, her dark eyes flashing as she cursed him in Spanish. Then, trilling her *R*s and stressing the syllables oddly, she screamed, "You like us only because you are cowardly homosexual hiding in closet." Then she turned and stalked off. He wanted to kill her, slice her slender brown throat. No way was he a faggot, closeted or otherwise. In fact, he hated faggots.

He soon learned he'd seriously underestimated the depth of Loretta's anger and the lengths she would go to express it. After being beaten up twice, the second time badly, he narrowly escaped getting shanked one afternoon in the exercise yard. Luckily for him, his cellmate Anatoly got wind of it and tipped him off before it went down. "Only months remain on your sentence," the Russian told him. "You must have eyes on back of head if you wish to taste freedom. Next time, Anatoly might not be there to save Jeemmy's ass."

His best shot was to keep a low profile for the rest of his stretch. He paid an inmate who worked in administration four cartons of Marlboros (supplied by his sister Lena) to reassign him to the prison library, next to the admin offices. It was safer there. Safer than the prison laundry, for sure. When he ate in the cafeteria, it was with Anatoly; nobody dared mess with him when the big Russian was around. Needless to say, he avoided the exercise yard.

The depression caught him by surprise. Not the depression itself—he'd had bouts of depression all his life—but its severity. In comparison, past episodes were only doldrums. This was despair, bleak and hopeless. His manhood was lost, his entire life was pointless. Ironic, because until the uproar with Loretta he'd been convinced that he had a special destiny, that something amazing was in store for him. Hanging himself with a rope made from strips of bedsheets wasn't what he'd had in mind, but given the reality that he had hit rock bottom, the likelihood it was his destiny was shifting from possibility to flat-out inevitability.

But before he could do anything so drastic, a miracle appeared.

The miracle took the form of a book. A month before he was scheduled to be released on parole, he came across *Abomination* in the prison library. He read it cover to cover that same night, the last half by flashlight after lights out. With Anatoly snoring softly in the bunk above, he had an epiphany: The book was divinely inspired. Finding it had not been an accident—he was meant to find it.

Imbued with the Holy Spirit and floating in a state between waking and sleeping, he had a vision. The vision was of a woman. Or rather, an abomination. Nude. Dead. A cross had been carved on her chest, a pink weal that contrasted with her pale, bloodless skin. The cross symbolized her salvation; that was clear to him. Retribution with salvation, that was how God rolled.

A startling realization penetrated his waking-sleeping consciousness: That was how God wanted *him* to roll. It was his special destiny. *Hallelujah.*

Chapman opened his eyes. The four-month-old memories were almost more vivid than the dismal hotel room. He picked up the book and looked at the photo of the author on the inside flap. Richard Ronson was a pale, thin-faced man with wire-rim glasses and a bow tie.

Ordinary-looking, but the man was a latter-day prophet.

14

Sanjit Rajaragavan stared at the list of processes currently active on the hospital's mail server. High-level processes were performing tasks such as handling inbound mail traffic, delivering mail to local users, and sending outbound mail to remote servers. System-level processes were handling more mundane functions, such as logging, screening incoming connections, and keeping the system clock accurate. Around three dozen processes, all necessary to the operation of the server, and Sanjit was familiar with every single one.

So the alien process caught his eye immediately.

"This cannot be right," Sanjit said. The process, named "mrdr," belonged to a running script. As for the script's purpose, that was the mystery.

A bit of detective work revealed where mrdr resided on the server. Sanjit checked the date and time stamp. The script was at least thirteen days old. How had he overlooked it?

The listing scrolled up the screen. He planted his elbows on the desktop and cradled his chin in his hands while he studied the code. A comment at the top indicated the script's actual name was "Marauder." Sanjit recognized the coding style immediately, as though the programmer had signed it. Marauder's purpose was also obvious—to monitor a certain user's incoming and outgoing email and send copies to the programmer.

As a system administrator, Sanjit had complete access to all users' mailboxes. But reading a user's email without their knowledge—he had never done that. Such a thing would be unthinkable, a terrible invasion of privacy. Still, he did not wish to get the programmer in scalding water. The dilemma would confound Vishnu himself.

He opened an online dictionary to find the precise meaning of *marauder*. Rather than allay his suspicion, the definition only increased it. Was Marauder a raider in search of plunder? It appeared so.

One thing he understood clearly: It would be unwise to run off fractionally cocked.

Sanjit prayed to Ganesh for wisdom.

15

The traffic on Sandy Boulevard was sparse at 4 a.m., only a few early-morning commuters and a Portland General Electric utility truck. Chapman maintained a precise thirty-five miles per hour, carefully observing traffic laws. Being pulled over was the last thing he wanted; too much chance of the car being searched. The blood-smeared plastic tarp in the trunk would be hard to explain.

He yawned. The night's work had drained him. It had also been the most satisfying he'd experienced yet, probably because the girl had reminded him of Loretta. In fact, the first time he saw her, two hours earlier, for an unnerving few moments he'd thought it actually *was* Loretta.

He had parked down the street from the Medallion Club, where he could watch the Friday night closing-time crowd drift out, looking for the right candidate. A rap on the driver-side window startled him. Through the tinted glass the girl standing outside the car looked uncannily like Loretta. The manual crank required six revolutions to roll down the window, and for the thousandth time Chapman wished the vintage Camaro had power windows.

A pretty Latina in a low-cut sweater and very short, tight miniskirt leaned down and rested her forearms on the window sill. "Looking for a date, honey?" She wore her ink-black hair long like Loretta's, with a thick cascade that half covered one eye. Her voice was a throaty contralto, huskier than Loretta's. That, and the fact that she was working Belmont, well-known tranny territory, left no doubt about what she was.

He nodded and motioned for her to get in the car. Hips swaying in a manner that bordered on comical, she stilted around to the other side of the car and opened the passenger door. By that time the chloroform-soaked cloth was in his hand, ready for her. She slid into the bucket seat and pulled the door shut. Before she had a chance to turn her head and look at him, he grabbed her by the back of her neck with his right hand, and with his left hand he covered her mouth and nose tightly with the cloth. She struggled, but he held her in a vice-like grip until her body went slack. By the clock in the dash it took slightly over three minutes, total. Not instantaneous, but effective enough. He started the car and drove off with his unconscious passenger slumped against the door, looking as if she had fallen asleep.

She was still unconscious when he switched off the ignition, but she moaned as he was carrying her up the stairs to the small apartment above the mini-storage units. He fumbled with the key in the lock, reluctant to set her down, and finally managed to get it unlocked. Once inside, he gave her another hit of chloroform, to make sure there would be no struggle while he undressed her on the kitchen floor. Once she was completely naked he slipped nylon pull ties around her wrists and ankles and tightened them until they were snug. Then he lifted her, carried her into the bathroom, and set her down in the large bathtub. He pulled on thin latex gloves and then unfurled a clear plastic tarp and spread it on the bathroom floor. That done, he sat on the edge of the tub and examined his prize.

She was pre-op. No surprise there. For one thing, the bottom surgery wasn't cheap, and boob jobs were a higher priority for most of the girls on the track. For another, many of their johns preferred them with their original equipment. That had been *his* preference. Of course, that was before he understood their true nature: abominations, evil incarnate. They seduced unwary men like him and robbed them of their manhood. But that was in the past. Now he had a holy mission, to deliver retribution and salvation. In the process his manhood would be restored.

A moan from the tub snapped him out of his reverie. The girl coughed and winced, her head no doubt pounding from a chloroform-induced headache. Blinking like a child waking up from an afternoon nap, she tried to get up and then realized her wrists and ankles were bound with the pull ties. That jolted her wide-awake. "What the hell is this?" she said.

He continued his inspection, noting a mole on her neck and what looked like a burn scar on the inside of her left thigh.

Her lips drew back in a rictus that was probably intended to be an inviting smile. "Are you kinky, honey? Is that your trip? Listen, I've done all kinds of scenes. Let me loose and I'll show you the best time you ever had." Her Spanish accent was subtly different from Loretta's.

"What's your name?" Chapman wasn't sure why he asked her; he hadn't asked any of the others for their names. Maybe he did it because she looked so much like Loretta.

"Rosaria," she said, rolling the Rs.

"You from Mexico?"

"Guatemala."

"Should have stayed there, Rosaria."

"Why have you done this to me, mister? *Why?*"

He saw no reason not to tell her the truth. "Because of what you are."

"What I am, you say. What am I?"

"You're an abomination."

Her mouth opened, snapped shut, and opened again. "What are you, some kind of kook?" She pronounced it "cook."

"I am . . . an instrument."

She looked at him as if he were a nutcase, instead of a servant of God. "Let me go. Please."

He shook his head. "Can't do that, sorry."

"Look, if you so much as harm one hair on my head, my boyfriend will hunt you down and make you wish you had never been born."

"Boyfriend? Pimp, you mean." He stood up and opened a cabinet.

"Let me go or I will scream."

He snorted. "Go ahead, scream all you want. Nobody's going to hear you."

"Please. I beg of you." She began to cry.

Her plea presumed that Chapman possessed empathy. Unfortunately for her, he didn't, only a sense of holy purpose. And anticipation of what was to come. "Rejoice," he said, "for I bring you redemption."

He ceremoniously unsheathed the knife. It gleamed in the bluish light from the fluorescent panel overhead.

The entire process of transforming her and cleaning up afterward took only forty-five minutes. As for remorse, it was a cousin to empathy and equally lacking in meaning.

With her body in the trunk, securely wrapped in the clear plastic tarp, he drove to the location he'd selected two days earlier, an alley behind a run-down strip mall on Southeast Powell. A secondhand clothing shop, a used book store, a shop that refurbished small appliances, an "As Seen On TV" store—they looked like they were on the verge of shutting their doors. He parked in the alley and unloaded his cargo, Then he began arranging the scene.

With pain-staking precision, he posed Rosaria sitting with her back against a dingy clapboard wall that belonged to one of the shops. He placed her clothing in a neat stack beside her. Then he photographed her with the camera in his cell phone, making sure the cross he'd carved in her chest to signify her salvation could be seen clearly. In the glare of the flash, her bloodless body looked pale gray.

And now, twenty minutes later, he was headed for a 24-hour Safeway on Sandy to dispose of incriminating leftover items. The store appeared on the right. He turned in and parked. When he was reasonably sure he wasn't observed he opened the trunk and quickly removed the folded tarp and a baggie that contained the pull ties and latex gloves. The store had two entrances, each with a trash can beside it. He stuffed the tarp in one, the baggie in the other.

That done, he sauntered into the store and bought a pack of Marlboros.

16

Stingler nudged the mouse to rouse his computer from sleep mode and whistled tunelessly until the Linux KDE desktop materialized. Then he froze, his mouth open. Several folders and icons had been moved from their usual positions. And that meant someone had used his computer while he was out. He'd gone to Best Buy in Beaverton to buy a USB flash drive. Away an hour, tops.

He swiveled his chair around. The basement apartment was definitely cleaner than it was when he left. His mother had done her once-a-week cleaning while he was gone. *Fuck.* He yanked open the door that led upstairs with such force the doorknob almost came off in his hand and yelled, "MOM!"

His mother appeared at the top of the stairs. "What is it, Dennis?"

"Would you come down here a minute, please?" It was an effort to remain calm.

"All right, dear. I have something for you." She came down the stairs holding a covered platter. "I baked an angel food cake today. I know how you love angel food cake." She marched into the kitchenette and set the platter on the counter. She lifted the cover. The glaze on the cake had a pinkish sheen.

"Mom," he said in an offhand manner, "was anybody in here with you while you were cleaning today?"

"Yes, your uncle stopped by for a little while."

Stingler's nails dug into his palms. "What did he want? He never shows up unless he wants something."

"Dennis, please be more understanding. Jimmy's trying very hard to turn his life around. He applied for a job managing some sort of storage rental place and he listed the both of us as references. I told him you wouldn't mind."

"No, not at all. I love vouching for the criminal element."

"Dennis, please. He's still family."

"Yeah. Manson Family."

"Jimmy's my brother and I can't help feeling sorry for him. We had such a good visit. We talked about our dear mother and how much we both miss her. It was so unfair that they wouldn't let him out to attend her funeral."

Stingler struggled to keep his voice even. "Did he happen to use my computer while he was here?"

His mother nodded. "He said he wanted to take a quick peek at it. I didn't see any harm in it."

"How long did he screw around with it?"

"Not long. My friend Madeleine phoned just as he sat down in front of it. I was upstairs ten, maybe fifteen minutes. When I came back down, Jimmy was sitting on your sofa reading a magazine."

Stingler wanted to scream and tear his hair out. Instead, he said, "Mom, listen. I don't want him near my computer. I keep personal, private stuff on it." *Not to mention, valuable stuff.*

"I'm sure Jimmy respected your privacy, Dennis."

"Yeah, right. He has such sterling character." Stingler pointed to his computer. "Off-limits, no exceptions. Please respect my wishes."

"All right, dear. I won't let anyone near your precious computer from now on, okay?" She stood on tiptoe to give him a peck on the cheek. "Enjoy your cake."

"Sonofabitch bastard," Stingler said though clenched teeth after the door closed behind her.

Multnomah County Central Library on Southwest 10th was crowded that evening, and all the computers were in use. But Chapman was a patient man. Being confined to an eight-by-twelve cell for three years had taught him patience, if nothing else. While he waited he watched the other library patrons.

People on the outside amused him to no end. So trusting, so unsuspecting, so vulnerable. Prey, oblivious to the presence of a predator in their midst. If he chose, he could spirit any one of them off to a place where screaming wouldn't matter. A taste of terror and hopelessness would cure them of their trusting natures real quick. The knowledge he was capable of such deeds, and without a trace of remorse, made him feel powerful.

Stop.

Reset.

That kind of action would definitely be outside the bounds of his covenant with God. It was important that he focus on the task before him. His hunting must always be on God's behalf, limited to a certain special prey, and there must be no exceptions.

Twenty-three minutes had gone by, according to the wall clock, when a redheaded woman at a computer stood up and put on her coat. Chapman hurried toward the workstation, but a young guy wearing an Army surplus field jacket beat him to it by mere seconds. The punk dropped his backpack heavily on the floor and reached to slide the chair away from the desk. It didn't move; Chapman had his hand firmly on the back of the chair, holding it in place. The guy looked up in surprise. He was nineteen, maybe twenty. Another chinless wonder, like his sister's dickweed kid.

Chapman started out polite. "Sport, I'd consider it a personal favor if you'd let me have this computer."

"Hey, mister, I got here first," the kid said, his expression and tone sullen.

Chapman bared his teeth in a broad smile. "Maybe you didn't hear me, sport. I said I would look on it as a personal favor."

The kid opened his mouth to say something and shut it again, his eyes fixed on the cobra tattoo on Chapman's neck. His change in attitude, from sullen to submissive, was quick. He picked up the backpack. "Okay, whatever."

"I appreciate it, sport."

Chapman sat down and reached for the mouse. He first checked to see if the computer had a program he could use to connect with a remote host. No such luck. A visit to Download.com solved that problem. Five minutes later the program (*Putty*, an SSH client) was installed and ready to go. When the login screen appeared, he entered an IP address, user name, and password. He couldn't resist a small flourish when he pressed *Enter*.

Then he was in, controlling his nephew's computer remotely, just as if he were sitting in front of it. Too bad he couldn't gloat to Anatoly. The Russian, who bragged that he could hack any computer, had patiently shared his specialized knowledge with his cellmate. It made the time pass more quickly for them both. Anatoly would be proud of his former pupil.

He took a flash drive from his pocket and plugged it into a USB port. On the remote host he navigated to the directory he'd found earlier, changed all the file permissions to world-readable, and, using FileZilla, an FTP program, downloaded the contents to the tiny drive. Before logging out he restored the directory's original file permissions and edited the wtmp file to erase all traces of his uninvited visit, just like Anatoly had taught him.

He unplugged the flash drive and slipped it into his pocket. The information on it was gold. Hell, platinum. Dennis had heisted the whole package—email messages, medical records, photo, and current address. No telling what he planned to do with it, but now it was also Uncle Jimmy's. Finder's keepers.

Divine providence, that's what it was. God meant for him to find the information, to help him carry out his purpose. Because an abomination was an abomination, regardless of her backstory.

Still, this one was special. The photo of her was proof of that. Even in the hospital gown, hair messy, no makeup, she was . . . special. She reminded him of a girl who'd lived across the street from him on Alder. She'd had no time for him, a stab to his 13-year-old heart.

The new quarry would have plenty of time for him. He'd make sure of that. First, though, he would have to find her. Not that he minded. The hunt was almost the best part.

Almost.

17

Sanjit looked up from his monitor to see Dennis Stingler standing at the entrance to his cubicle. Stingler aimed his index finger at Sanjit like a pistol; a yellow Post-It note was hanging from the finger-gun's barrel.

"Found this on my monitor, Sanjit." Stingler's tone was that of a superior speaking to an underling. "I'd appreciate it if you wouldn't stick anything to my screen. I like looking at a clean display, and I take pains to ensure it's pristine at all times. The adhesive on these"—he snapped the Post-It with the middle finger of his other hand—"leaves a smudgy residue that's hard to remove."

Sanjit bowed his head. "A thousand apologies, Dennis. In my humble defense, I wanted to be certain you saw it. I will be sure to adhere any notes to the top surface of your desk from now on." He looked up from under his eyebrows and saw the satisfaction on Stingler's face at having yet another opportunity to rebuke him.

Stingler squinted at the yellow note. "You wrote, 'Dennis, I need to talk with you at your earliest convenience. Sanjit.'" It was said with a musical lilt—Stingler seemed to think mocking the way Sanjit spoke was very humorous—and then in his usual nasal voice Stingler said, "Well, it's not exactly convenient, given my workload, but here I am anyway. What do you need, Sanjit?"

Sanjit opened the desk's top drawer and took out the program listing he'd printed out earlier and handed it to the other man. Stingler scanned the listing and looked at him with one eyebrow raised. "So?"

"You wrote this script, this Marauder." It was not a question.

Stingler directed a cold stare at him for several long seconds. "Sanjit, do you see my name on the script anywhere? How do you know that Richie or Gage—shit, even Marvin—didn't write it?"

"Surely you are pushing my leg. It is obvious this is your code."

A flush appeared on Stingler's cheeks, and he loomed imperiously over Sanjit, arms crossed. "How long have you worked here?"

"It has been my honor to work here eleven months."

"Not even one full year. I've been here for almost six years. I have seniority." His tone changed abruptly, becoming confidential. "Listen, Sanjit, I work on lots of projects you know nothing about. Special requests from upstairs." He pointed toward the acoustically tiled ceiling. That was very odd, because the administration's offices were located on the same floor as the IT department's.

"You are telling me this script, this Marauder, was written at the request of a superior?"

"Sanjit, I've said enough already. This stuff is highly classified, very hush-hush." He folded the program listing twice and slipped it in his shirt pocket. "It does not concern you in any way. You need to forget you saw it. That is, if you expect to celebrate the anniversary of being hired at this hospital."

Sanjit could only look at the other man. Stingler reminded him of the large rats that foraged for food in the streets of his village. The resemblance was unmistakable.

"Do you understand what I'm saying, Sanjit?"

"I understand." He understood quite well. The veiled threat was quite clear.

Stingler stalked off, headed back to his cubicle.

Sanjit sat at his desk thinking about the explanation Stingler had given him, that the Marauder script was part of a secret project commissioned by a hospital administrator. Sanjit's mother had not given birth to him yesterday. The explanation did not make sense. It was obviously an attempt by Stingler to divert him from the trail.

An experienced chess player since his youth, Sanjit knew his next move must be contemplated very carefully. He sensed that his opponent—for that was what he considered Stingler now—would savagely attack anyone who challenged him. Sanjit did not underestimate him.

But clearly he had underestimated Sanjit.

18

Sarah stared out the window while her laptop booted up. It seemed to be taking longer than usual. The Toshiba was nearly four years old, ancient in computer years, but she had no intention of replacing it anytime soon. It was more than adequate for email and surfing the Web, which was all she cared about. After the desktop finally appeared, she opened the mail program. One unread message:

```
Date: Mon, 15 Sep 2014 05:47:47 -0800
From: Kimberly Liu, M.D.
<kliu@tricareassociates.com>
To: Sarah Soong, D.O.
<sarah.soong@OMRI.edu>
Subject: Re: In over my head


Sare,


Sorry about the tardy reply. Too much work
and too little time. I'm sure you can
relate.


I've been wondering how things are going
for you up there in the City of Roses. I
```

miss Portland, and I miss you. Good luck in
the Winter Poker Challenge in Reno. Wish I
could be there in your cheering section.

As for your dilemma, it's clear to me your
decision is based on an assumption: You
assume this girl, given a choice, would
prefer to remain unaware of her situation.
Perhaps you're right, but you assume this
because that's what you would want in the
same circumstance. Trouble is, she doesn't
have a choice in the matter. I think that's
what makes me uneasy about it.

In support of your position, Livvy probably
has enough to deal with right now without
being blindsided by the news she's
transgender.

I realize you feel you need to protect her,
but it could blow up in your face, so
please be careful.

Keep me posted, 'kay?

Best,
Kim

Sarah closed the mail program and stood up and yawned.
It had been a long, arduous day, and the aching tension in
her neck and shoulders was more acute than usual. She
reached around and massaged the area as best she could. It
felt like the muscles were knotted under the skin, right
where they connected to the base of her skull. Fortunately,
an effective relaxant was close at hand. She went to the
kitchen, got a chilled bottle of Sauvignon Blanc out of the
refrigerator, and filled the glass to the brim.

She sat in the recliner-rocker and looked out over the sprawl of city lights. The view through the condo's living room window was the main reason she'd bought the place. She rocked herself gently and sipped the dry white wine.

It wasn't that she'd expected Kim to have any answers for her. In this situation there were no answers, only more questions. But it was comforting to be able to share the problem with someone else. It helped her feel less alone.

Her eyes burned with fatigue. She closed them, just for a moment. When she opened them again she was groggily surprised to see by the clock on the mantel that almost three hours had passed. She stood up and walked unsteadily to the bedroom. Fumbling with buttons, zippers, and clasps, she managed to finish undressing before collapsing into the bed, instantly asleep again.

19

Chapman switched on the 19-inch flat-screen TV he'd found on sale at Fred Meyer, and damned if the built-in antenna didn't pull in a clear Portland broadcast channel. At 4:00 a.m. the over-the-air programming selection was sparse. He paused at a channel that featured a theatrical-looking older couple. The man had a silver pompadour and a mouthful of Chiclet-sized capped teeth, and the woman wore a glitzy dress and heavy makeup, her face tight as a snare drum. Television evangelists. Chapman turned up the volume.

The man was speaking: "*... and the godless liberal media would have us believe the victims are just innocent citizens. That, friends, is a lie straight from the pit of Hell. These are deviants we're talking about, purveyors of perversion. Instead of arresting the killer, they ought to give him a medal.*"

"*Amen,*" the woman said, her voice saccharine-sweet. "*He's doing our community a favor. He's a hero.*"

"*Friends, the lovely Della Luna is absolutely right. These she-male freaks are a blight on our fair city and a threat to decent society. They are minions of Satan, evil incarnate. And now they are reaping what they have sown.*"

"*Hallelujah!*" the woman said.

"*Well, that does it for this week, friends. Be sure to tune in next week, when we'll show you how science is a tool of Satan. Until then, I'm Pastor Benny Singleton.*"

"And I'm Della Luna. We'll leave you with this thought: God knows the falling of a sparrow and the depth of a pocket, so dig deep and give glory to Him at the address shown on the screen. May God bless you with prosperity."

Chuckling, Chapman switched off the TV.

He had fans.

At noon the next day Chapman pulled into the drive-through lane at the McDonald's on 82nd. When his turn came he ordered a Quarter Pounder with cheese, mustard and pickle only, large fries, and a Coke. A pimply faced kid at the pick-up window took his money and handed him his order. Chapman asked him if the restaurant's wi-fi would reach the parking lot.

"Sure," the kid said. "Sometimes on my break I sit in my car and play *Warcraft*."

"What's the wi-fi password?"

"Um, ronaldmac. All one word, lower-case ."

He eased the black car into a parking space and shut off the ignition. After gulping down the burger and fries and degreasing his fingers with a napkin, he opened the new laptop's lid. It was a $198 Walmart special and had a diminutive 10.1-inch display, but it was a powerful little bastard. He peeled the protective film from the screen and pressed the power button. After it booted he configured the wi-fi, entered the password, and—hallelujah!—he was online, sitting in a car in Mc-fucking-Donald's parking lot.

With Google's assistance he located what he was looking for in a matter of seconds. *TextProxy* was free and required no registration. The software would enable him to send a text message from the laptop to a cell phone. An untraceable message. It would look like it was from any bogus phone number Chapman chose. He just happened to have one in mind: the phone number for Avalon Escort Service, before they got busted. No one could accuse him of not having a sense of humor.

A different wi-fi location for each message, of course, so his IP address would constantly change. No possible way to trace a message back to him, even if they subpoenaed the proxy server's connection log. Total anonymity.

He closed the laptop's lid. The fun was about to begin.

The hooker dressed while Chapman watched from the bed. She had told him she was twenty-two, but her eyes were old. It seemed to be an occupational trait. She reached around to zip up her short, tight black dress and then stepped into a pair of black pumps with absurdly high heels. After applying lipstick she snapped the clutch shut and quickly smoothed her shoulder-length dark hair with her fingers. She had very long nails, talons that made her small, slender hands look like a pteradactyl's claws. During the previous half-hour those claws had been very busy, futilely trying to elicit a response from him.

She looked at him and gave him a thousand-watt smile that had not a trace of warmth. "See you, sugar." Then she was out the door, and he was glad.

It had been the third miserable failure with a woman who wasn't an abomination. The women he selected were all young and attractive, of course. One of them modeled in addition to working for the escort service. None of their professional tricks and techniques had worked. Their attempts to reassure him were from the same script: "Don't beat yourself up, honey. Lots of guys have temporary problems. Get yourself some Viagra."

But he was only thirty-two, for God's sake, not sixty-four. At his age he shouldn't need any chemical help. He inhaled deeply through his nostrils and exhaled though his mouth in a loud sigh that echoed off the hotel room's dingy walls.

No use denying it—ordinary females still didn't turn him on, no matter how attractive they were. Abominations still dominated his sexual fantasies. Doing God's bidding was supposed to take care of that problem, but so far it hadn't.

However, it was still early in the process, too early to be bummed. He'd done only three so far—the brunette in Vancouver, the blonde, and the Latina from Guatemala.

The next one would be black. For the sake of diversity.

20

It was a warm day for late September in Oregon. Livvy and Jeff sat on a bench in the hospital's courtyard admiring the autumn colors in the trees around them. Livvy pointed to an ant on the concrete walk in front of the bench. The ant was dragging a bread crumb twice its size to the other side of the walk. It was slow going.

While they watched the ant's progress she told him about her amnesia. He was quiet after she finished, and then he said, "I can't imagine how frustrating that must be. But looking on the bright side, the doctor said your memories could come back any time and not to worry about it. So what do you say we go grab a couple bowls of ice cream? I'm buying."

"Okay, sure," she said. "Thanks for not making a big deal about it."

Jeff got to his feet and, with a flourish, held out his hand to her. "Shall we?"

Standing, she was closer to looking him in the eye than usual, due to the three extra inches of height her boots added. Livvy was dressed in the only non-hospital clothes she had, the same outfit she'd been wearing the night she was admitted. Her companion wore faded jeans, a blue sweat shirt, and black hi-top Converse All-Stars that looked well broken-in ("my Chucks," he called them).

They walked hand in hand to the hospital's side entrance.

For once there was no line in the cafeteria. They carried their ice cream to a table in the corner and sat down.

"Well," she said, carving out a spoonful of ice cream, "your memory is in perfect working order, right? Tell me about Jeff Longcypher."

"Do you want the unabridged version or just the high points?"

"Start with the high points and you can fill in the details if needed."

"Okay. You asked." He took a deep breath, clearly over-doing it for effect. "Born and raised in Portland. Went to college at the University of Oregon in Eugene, majored in business. After I graduated I went to law school—U of O again. Then I was a public defender for a couple of years, in Eugene. At my father's insistence I joined Longcypher, Cannady, and Moore, his Portland law firm."

"So you're a lawyer?"

"No. I'm still a member of the Oregon Bar, but I'm not practicing law anymore. I quit the firm after a year and a half. My father was—and is—unhappy about my decision." An unreadable expression flickered across his face.

"So what is it you do now?"

"These days I'm a Republican congressman." The deadpan expression lasted five seconds, and then the lopsided grin appeared. "Not buying it? Okay, the straight skinny." He took another deep breath.

"My mom's older brother built an airstrip at Colby, small town up the Columbia Gorge. Uncle Pete taught me to fly. Got my pilot's license on my eighteenth birthday.

"Uncle Pete and I were pretty close. Around the time I was deciding lawyering wasn't my thing, he up and died. Pancreatic cancer. He left everything to me—his log cabin, airstrip and hangers, four airplanes, and all the tools and equipment.

"So I moved up to Colby and became an FBO—fixed base operator. Aircraft and hanger rental, tie-down facilities, flight instruction, and from time to time a little charter work.

I'm not getting rich, but it's a living. I enjoy what I do and that trumps money." He put his spoon down and sat back and smiled. "Enough?"

"More than I expected. I envy you, having all that history and being able to remember it."

"Some things I'd just as soon forget, believe me. Having a clean slate might have a big upside." He wadded his napkin into a ball and tossed it into his empty bowl with a hook shot. "Three points."

"It might. But it would be nice to have a choice in the matter. Could we talk about something else?"

"Okay, new topic: Maybe you'd like to go flying with me sometime? I'm going to be coming down in the Cherokee a couple times a week for physical therapy. You could see how much fun it is to go sniffing around the clouds."

Before Livvy could answer she heard Leia's distinctive voice. "There y'all are. Mama and I couldn't find you." Leia and her mother stood next to the table juggling shopping bags with familiar logos: Nordstrom, J. Crew, Macy's, Old Navy, Express, and Victoria's Secret.

"Well, well. Princess Leia has returned," Jeff said, getting to his feet. "You told me I was going to meet your mother, Leia. Apparently you decided to introduce me to your twin sister instead."

The woman's laugh was throaty and uninhibited, a contralto version of Leia's. "Charlotte Dunkleman, mother of record. And you, sir, are a silver-tongued devil." She had a leisurely Texas drawl, a contrast to Leia's rapid-fire delivery.

Jeff shook her hand. "Jeff Longcypher. Seriously, your resemblance to your daughter is uncanny."

"Pleased to know you."

Leia turned to Livvy. "Mama and I went shopping at Lloyd Center. We picked up a few things we figured you could use." She held up the bags she was carrying.

"I hope you didn't go overboard," Livvy said. The thought of being a recipient of their generosity when she was in no position to reciprocate made her uncomfortable.

Charlotte dismissed her concern with a wave of her hand. "Young lady, let us have our fun. If you two are finished with your ice cream, maybe we can hie ourselves to Livvy's room and admire her new clothes."

Jeff begged off, due to a physical therapy session in fifteen minutes. "Very nice to have met you, Mrs. Dunkleman." He nodded goodbye to the group and started toward the cafeteria's exit.

They watched him walk away. Leia's mother was the first to speak. "Gal, if I was a bit younger and single, you'd have a fight on your hands over that one. I'd try to lasso him for myself, cane and all."

"He's crazy cute," Leia said. "I can't even get mad at him for calling me Princess Leia. It's my own fault for telling him that stupid story."

"C'mon, girls, let's get out of here," Charlotte said. "Livvy, lead the way."

21

Thomas Griggs, P.I. had a hobby that consumed much of his free time: He collected photographs of breasts. When it came to the female breast he regarded himself a connoisseur. His collection was extensive, the result of years of diligent effort, a labor of love. The photos themselves, all in digital format, were not stored on his computer's hard drive; they resided in the cloud, on a remote server. Besides being more secure, they were accessible from wherever he happened to be, as long as a browser was available.

This evening he was logged in from home. A knock at his bedroom door made him jump. As the door opened, a familiar voice called out his name.

He swore under his breath and minimized the browser window. The prized collection shrank, becoming a nondescript icon at the bottom of the screen. His mother always seemed to pick the worst possible time to interrupt him and this evening was no exception—just as he was about to upload his latest acquisition, a B-cup pair that were undeniably close to perfection.

"What do you need, Mom?" He couldn't keep the irritation out of his voice. "I'm kind of busy at the moment."

"What else is new? You're always busy," Noreen Griggs said as she shut the door behind her. "You know what the doctor told you about stress and overwork. Why don't you make more time for yourself?" She was a compact woman with doughy features and hair tinted an improbable shade of auburn.

"Okay, Mom, what's up?"

She walked over to an overstuffed green brocade chair and sat down. "I've been working my way down the list of apartments you gave me. I'm only halfway through them, but I just now had a call-back that sounds very promising." She paused, obviously looking for a reaction from him.

He drummed his thick fingers on the mousepad.

She continued, "A Mr. Delbert McClone, who manages Birchwood Manor Apartments—they're on the west side— told me that one of their tenants, a young woman name of Olivia Covington, abandoned her apartment and all her belongings. It's been nearly two months since anyone around there has seen her. He said he waited until the legal waiting period was up, and then he put her stuff in storage so the apartment could be cleaned and rerented. One more thing . . . McClone is pretty sure his missing tenant is from somewhere back East." She sat back with an expectant expression on her face.

"That does sound promising." In fact, it sounded more than promising; something told him his mother had hit the jackpot.

"Am I not the best investigative assistant you could ask for? The truth, now."

His mother could be irritating as hell, but she was a big help when it came to canvassing for information on the phone. "Good work, Mom. Seriously."

She beamed and held out a Post-It note to him. "Here's the address and phone number of Birchwood Manor."

He took the note from her and reached for his jacket. "It's early enough, I'm going over there to talk to the manager in person and have a look at the girl's belongings."

"Should I continue calling apartments on the list?"

"No, hold off until I talk to McClone."

Delbert McClone turned out to be an odd-looking little fellow with close-set eyes and a nose that would be in better proportion on a larger face. He regarded Griggs suspiciously. "You say you're from the hospital where she's at?"

"That's right. I'm here on Miss Covington's behalf." Which was more-or-less true, assuming the patient and McClone's former tenant were same person.

"Lost her memory, did she? Hell of a thing. Getting carjacked and hit on the head like that. Did they find the punk who did it?"

"Not so far, and it's unlikely they ever will," Griggs said.

"Too bad. The missus kept saying something must've happened to that girl. Nice, quiet gal like that wasn't the type to just up and take off with no warning." He produced a handkerchief from the back pocket of his trousers and blew into it with a resonant honk. "Storage area's around back. Follow me."

The unlikely pair walked down a covered breezeway that connected two buildings, until McClone stopped in front of a door. "Her stuff's in here." He fumbled with keys on a ring until he located one and inserted it in the lock. "She didn't have all that much, compared to some."

McClone switched on the light. The storage room was about eight by ten and nearly empty, except for some things piled in the back corner: three suitcases, a portable wardrobe, and three medium-sized cardboard boxes with lids, the type used by moving companies. An oddly shaped, canvas-covered object about four feet tall leaned against the wall, nearly hidden by the wardrobe. On closer inspection it appeared to be an instrument case.

McClone apparently noticed his interest and spoke up. "That's some sort of bass fiddle. But it's sure a lot smaller than any of the ones I seen."

Griggs unzipped the case halfway and inspected the instrument inside. He saw a reddish-brown spruce top and thick strings made of gut. "Cello," he said. "Here's the bow in a side pocket."

"Come to think on it, I mighta overheard her playing it once or twice when I passed by her apartment. At the time I figured it was a hi-fi or something." He pointed to the row of suitcases. "That little one there, all her papers and that kind of stuff are inside it."

Griggs picked up the smallest suitcase and looked around for something to set it on so he wouldn't have to get down on his knees. He turned a large suitcase on end as a makeshift table and snapped open the latches on the smaller one. He sifted through the contents. Receipts for various purchases, including rosin for the bow, a bridge adjustment and tuning peg repair on the cello. Sheet music, all classical pieces. Letters from a Nora Cosgrove, Brookline, MA, bundled together with a rubber band. Several official-looking envelopes from Atlantic Trust in Boston. And buried at the bottom, underneath everything, a passport. "Ah," he said and snatched it up.

The photo on the inside, despite its small size and poor quality, confirmed that Olivia Leigh Covington was OMRI's amnesia patient. And that she had lived in Newton, Massachusetts when the passport was issued. Furthermore, the date of birth revealed the melancholy fact that she had turned twenty-five while comatose.

Griggs flipped through the pages, noting stamps from England, France, and Italy. The most recent stamps were dated seven years ago; she flew to Thailand for a three-week visit. The girl was well-traveled. He grunted with satisfaction and tossed the passport back in the suitcase.

Larry Neely and his superiors were going to be extremely pleased.

22

The Piper Cherokee cruised along at 115 knots 5,000 feet above the Columbia River. The vast river stretched into the distance, its surface reflecting the cloudless late September sky. From the air the Columbia Gorge was always breathtaking, but especially in autumn. Evergreens were of course prevalent, but other types of trees on the Oregon and Washington sides of the river were displaying their fall foliage, a riot of greens, yellows, oranges, and fiery reds.

Through the left side window, Jeff could see the scenic Columbia River Highway, which followed the river on the Oregon side between The Dalles and Troutdale. Only two lanes, but he preferred the venerable highway to I-84, the Interstate, which he avoided whenever he could. But then, he almost always flew to Portland and back. Along certain stretches of the Gorge the Cascades loomed above the airplane by at least a thousand feet, but the mountain range diminished considerably as it extended westward, and now the tops of the hills were well below the single-engine craft. The excellent visibility on this day enabled him to see the sprawl of Portland ahead in the distance.

Other than a slight tailwind, the air was relatively calm at altitude. The airplane was perfectly in trim and making good time; he'd departed from the little strip in Colby only twenty minutes earlier. With any luck, he would have the Cherokee tied down on the tarmac in Troutdale in another twenty minutes, and then a half-hour drive in a borrowed truck would put him at OMRI around 2:30. Livvy had said her meeting with the hospital administrator was scheduled for 3:00. He wanted to get there well before that.

The thought of seeing Livvy made his pulse quicken. She was unlike any girl he'd ever met. No coyness or subterfuge to her, no guile or artifice. She was completely unspoiled, a rare quality. Rarer still was her sense of humor: It was every bit as dry as his, and that was something he'd never before encountered in a woman. Rarest of all was her intelligence. Most other women he'd known looked like dogs listening to an ultrasonic whistle whenever the conversation turned the least bit esoteric. Not Livvy. She could keep up, no problem. In fact, keeping up with *her* was sometimes a challenge.

The hamlet of Corbett crawled into view off to the left. He listened to the ATIS broadcast for Troutdale, and then he retuned the radio and keyed the mic. "Troutdale, Cherokee Four Seven Whiskey ten miles out at five thousand, inbound on your niner zero radial for landing. Have information Foxtrot."

A laconic male voice answered, *"Four Seven Whiskey, Troutdale tower. Descend and maintain three thousand. Active runway zero seven. Light traffic this afternoon, and you're cleared for pattern entry. Give a shout one mile out."*

"Roger, will do."

He decreased power, applied a bit of carb heat, and began his descent to the requested altitude. When he estimated he was within a mile of the airport he checked in again with the tower and descended to pattern altitude before entering the downwind leg. As he turned base he saw a Cessna 310 taking off below. On final, after bleeding off speed and deploying full flaps, he pulled power and flared. The Cherokee floated in ground effect and then settled to the runway with a gentle bump. He taxied to the tie-down area and switched off the magnetos and master switch. Then he gathered up his brown leather jacket and climbed out of the cockpit.

A man in blue coveralls walked toward him, wiping his hands with a shop rag. "I thought that was you, Longcypher. I told the fire truck to stand by."

"Thanks, Ethan. I'll return the favor next time you land at my strip."

"Sure, but your so-called fire truck is just an extinguisher strapped to a kid's Radio Flyer wagon."

"I wouldn't be so choosy if my airplane was held together with duct tape and bailing wire."

The two men shook hands, the ritual greeting completed. In fact, Ethan flew a beautifully restored 1947 Luscombe and had done every last bit of the work himself. Ethan was one of only two A&Ps Jeff trusted to work on his aircraft.

"Catch." Ethan tossed a set of keys.

"I appreciate it, my friend. Should have it back to you by six." He started toward Ethan's red pickup, eager to get going in case traffic was heavy on the way to the hospital.

23

Traffic turned out to be light, so the eighteen-mile drive took only twenty-four minutes. The clock in the dash indicated 2:33 when Jeff pulled into OMRI's parking lot. Ten minutes later he was sharing an elevator with a gaggle of young female aides, all intently texting on their phones, oblivious to his presence. Oblivious to each other as well. He stepped out of the elevator on the third floor just in time to see Livvy emerge from her room and start for the stairwell with a determined stride.

"Hold up there, Speedy," he called out.

She stopped in her tracks, a smile on her face. "I didn't think you were going to get here in time."

"Neither sleet nor hail . . ." He pointed at the outfit she was wearing. "Nice duds. Trendy, but in a good way."

"Thanks. Leia and her mother have good taste."

"I thought your meeting wasn't until three."

"I didn't want to be late. I guess I'm a little anxious."

"Are you dead set on taking the stairs down?" He tapped his cane on the floor as a reminder of his still-healing knee. "If so, I'm going to have to meet you on the ground floor."

"I'll ride the elevator with you." She wagged a finger in his face. "But you owe me."

"Put it on my tab." He jabbed the down-arrow button with the cane's tip.

In the elevator during the descent, Livvy's eyes darted around. She had a thing about close, confined places, he'd learned. When the car reached the ground floor and the doors opened, her relief was palpable.

"The hospital administration offices are that way," she said, pointing.

They set off in that direction. Halfway across the lobby, Livvy grabbed his elbow and brought him to a dead stop. In an urgent whisper she said, "Remember me telling you about the weirdo who came to my room and acted so strange? See that person in the information booth? That's him. That's the guy."

As if he'd heard her from fifty feet away, the booth's sole occupant looked up and stared at them fixedly for several seconds before turning his attention back to what he'd been doing.

From force of habit formed by sizing up an endless stream of defendants, witnesses, and prospective jurors, Jeff studied the man's appearance. Late twenties or early thirties, tall, skinny, poor posture, pasty complexion, receding chin. The neck opening of his T-shirt provided much more room than his pencil neck required. His short brown hair was combed forward and then straight up in front, the tips frosted, a style that had been popular with trendy young men five years ago. Or maybe longer.

"That guy creeps me out," Livvy said.

Jeff put a protective arm around her and glowered at the fellow, who was sneaking sidelong glances at them from time to time. "Just some dork gawking at a pretty girl. Probably never had a girlfriend in his life. Forget that loser, let's get you to your meeting on time."

It was 2:53 when they walked into the administration office. Three people were sitting in the waiting area reading magazines. Livvy gave her name at the reception desk, expecting to be told to have a seat. Instead, the receptionist picked up her phone, spoke into it briefly, and returned it to the cradle. "Mr. Neely will be right out."

Livvy turned to Jeff.

"Don't worry about me," he said. "I might go putter around the lobby for a minute. I'll be here when you come out." He gave her hand a reassuring squeeze.

One of the double doors behind the reception desk opened. The administrator was a tall, balding man in his forties, white shirt and tie, dark slacks, and long, narrow brown wingtips. He saw Livvy and headed directly for her with long strides, hand outstretched and a friendly smile on his face. "Thanks for coming." He shook her hand and gestured toward his office. "Shall we?"

Livvy glanced nervously at Jeff and he gave her a thumbs-up. Neely held the door open for her.

Dennis Stingler tapped out a military cadence on the Formica desktop with his fingernails while he waited for the software update to finish installing. The damned progress bar looked frozen. He hated doing this kind of crap. Updating software was the sort of thing he usually delegated to one of the junior technicians. Rank doth have its privileges—most of the time. Today his seniority didn't do him much good; all his techs were tied up with other tasks. He looked again at the progress bar. It was moving, if glacially.

"Hi there." The male voice was hearty, jovial. A large silhouette eclipsed the sunlight streaming through the lobby's floor-to-ceiling windows.

He squinted, trying to see who it was. The clouds decided to accommodate him by blocking the sun. His visitor was the big guy he saw walking with—what was her name?—Livvy. But she wasn't with him now.

Stingler bowed his head to conceal his smirk. Livvy didn't know it yet, but she had a starring role in his plan for financial independence. He'd paid a visit to her hospital room to scope her out, on the pretext he was looking for someone else. When he saw her he almost fell over. Even knowing what he knew, he'd hit that. But he had other plans for her.

Stingler looked up. His unwelcome visitor was smiling at him. The guy's eyes, though, they weren't smiling. What did this pain in the ass want? An officious edge to his voice, Stingler asked him, "Can I help you with something?"

"Nope," the guy said. Then he hooked his cane on the edge of the booth's counter and stood there, stance wide, arms crossed, stare unwavering, drilling into Stingler.

WTF?

Whatever the hell the gimp was up to, Stingler didn't want any part of it. He turned away to face the computer terminal. Maybe if he looked busy, the big jerk would get the message and split. The update's progress bar was at 98%. *Come on, you piece of crap. . . .*

But the asshole didn't make a move. Instead, he asked, "What're you up to back there?"

Why? You writing a fucking book? Stingler wanted to say that, but instead he said, "Updating some software." He arched one eyebrow to communicate his disdain.

"Sorry, just being friendly." The big lunk didn't look a bit sorry or friendly, even though his dopey smile was wider.

Things had somehow turned real creepy real fast. Stingler was looking at the progress bar when the software update process reached 100%. *Thank God.* "Well, take it easy," he said and scooped up an unlabeled disc and the empty coffee cup embossed with "Stingman." When he was thirty feet from the booth he glanced back over his shoulder.

The guy was still standing there, still staring, still smiling.

"Imbecile," Stingler muttered and walked a little faster.

Jeff watched the "Stingman"—he of the receding chin, short upper lip, and incisors that slanted back, a combination of features that gave him a mouth like a rodent—until he was out of sight. Then Jeff picked up his cane and began the trek back to the administration office's waiting room. Maybe he could find something worth reading in their magazine rack.

24

Neely indicated a chair in front of his desk. "Have a seat, Livvy. I believe you've already met Tom." He gestured toward a huge man who took up most of a couch.

"Yes. Hello again, Mr. Griggs." A couple of weeks earlier the big man had come to her hospital room, accompanied by a woman who asked her to read a list of words and phrases aloud. Griggs introduced the woman as a speech professor at a local college and said Livvy's pronunciation would help determine where she was from. Livvy read every word on the list, glad to do it.

She glanced around the office. A pair of tall plants stood like sentries at each side of the window behind Neely's desk. Tapestries of various sizes with geometric patterns in browns, oranges, reds, and yellows hung on walls. Woven baskets with similar designs and colors were displayed on shelves and tables. A framed poster and the front head of a bass drum were mounted on one wall; both had the same cryptic logo, written in an elaborate script, which she finally deciphered as "Crystal Pendant." The name meant nothing to her.

"Can I get you something to drink?" Neely asked her. "Some water or a Coke?"

"No, I'm fine, thanks." Fine, except for the trepidation she felt. She was afraid they were going to inform her that their efforts to learn her identity had been unsuccessful, which of course would mean she'd have to go on as a person without a past.

But Neely said, "Mr. Griggs and I have some good news for you."

Her breath caught. "Does that mean you've—did you find out who I am?"

"Yes," Neely said, and looked at her with a broad smile on his face.

Livvy opened her mouth to speak but nothing came out. When she finally found her voice, she said only, "Thank you."

"Mr. Griggs," Neely said, "you have the floor."

The big man looked down at his notes and cleared his throat. "Let's begin with your name. You are Olivia Leigh Covington. You are twenty-five years of age. You had a birthday on September third." He looked up at her. "Happy belated birthday, Miss Covington."

Miss Covington. Olivia Leigh Covington. Before she had time to taste it, to roll it around her tongue, Griggs continued.

"You're originally from Newton, Massachusetts, a suburb of Boston. You arrived in Portland last June and rented an apartment. You also bought a new car, a Ford Fusion station wagon, at Gresham Ford. You purchased it outright. Among the documents in your belongings were the bill of sale, vehicle title, and DMV temporary registration form; the permanent registration was no doubt in the car. The vehicle itself is nowhere to be found. As you know, the police think you were carjacked in the downtown parking lot where you were found unconscious. More than likely, your car ended up at a chop shop, where it was disassembled and sold for parts. Your insurance company will undoubtedly reimburse you for its value."

At that moment, reimbursement for the car was the last thing she cared about.

"There's quite a bit more," Neely said. "I hope we're not giving you too much information all at once. Let us know if you're overwhelmed."

She shook her head. "No, I want to hear all of it." And there was one thing she wanted to hear about most of all. "My family . . . what about my family?"

Neely glanced at Griggs before he answered. "Livvy, your mother and father were both killed in an automobile accident in Boston five years ago when an oncoming vehicle swerved into their lane. I'm very sorry." He went on. "You had a sister three years older than you who died when you were four, of leukemia. An aunt, your father's sister, died last year. Colon cancer."

Livvy bit her lip. She'd counted on being reunited with her family most of all. But she was on her own, as it turned out. That was the reality, and she'd have to come to terms with it. Right now, though, she wanted to hear everything they could tell her. She took a deep breath. "Go on, please."

Neely glanced down at his notes. "Your father's name was Preston Covington. He founded Covington Fund, a mutual fund with an impressive performance record. He and your mother, Katherine, were active in Boston society, and gave a number of generous endowments. They also established the Covington Foundation and the Covington Center for the Performing Arts. Beyond basic information, little is known about your family's private life. Wealth can buy a great deal of insulation if privacy is the goal.

"When your parents passed away, their estate was left to you in a living trust, administered by Atlantic Trust in Boston. I spoke on the phone to Mr. Harold Cavenaugh of that institution this morning and briefed him on your situation. He was quite concerned. He indicated your trust is . . . substantial. In addition, your property in Newton was sold before you came out here. According to the records it sold for nineteen-point-two million and had no encumbrances. In short, Livvy, money is most definitely not one of your worries."

Big deal. She would gladly trade the money for a family, people who loved her. Still, the money would provide security, a lot of it, and that was some comfort.

Griggs took over. "Music has played an important role in your life. You attended Columbia University—which was also your father's alma mater—graduating cum laude with degrees in music and comparative literature. You then went on to earn a master's in music, also from Columbia." He paused and added, "Incidentally, it seems you were a mainstay of the women's swim team while you were an undergraduate."

Which explained why she felt completely at home in the water.

Griggs continued, "After Columbia you occasionally performed on cello with the Boston Symphony, as a 'sub,' filling in for the regular musicians. By the way, your cello is with your belongings, which your former landlord is holding for you in storage. On a hunch, I phoned the Oregon Symphony office and found out that one of the reasons you came out to Oregon was to audition for the second cello chair as a regular, which you got. After you missed three rehearsals, the symphony director tried to contact you, unaware you'd had an unfortunate accident, and when he couldn't reach you after numerous tries, he gave the chair to someone else."

"I guess that about covers the high points," Neely said. "Do you have any questions?"

"I'll need some time to for all this to sink in, but right now ..." Right now the inside of her mouth felt like cotton. "I'll have that glass of water, please."

Neely filled a glass from a pitcher on his desk. "You know," he said as he handed her the glass, "there's no reason why you can't be discharged as soon as you're ready."

"How about tomorrow morning? That will give me enough time to make arrangements for a place to stay."

"Are you sure? It's short notice, so if we can help you find accommodations we'll be only too glad—"

"I don't think that's going to be a problem." Livvy set the empty glass on Neely's desk. "I'm going to stay temporarily with friends. I met them here at the hospital, actually. Very nice people."

Charlotte had been insistent when Livvy expressed concern about where she'd live after she was discharged. "Listen here, missy," Charlotte had said, hands on hips, "my mama and daddy have plenty of room, so there's no reason why you can't stay with us until you get lined out. We won't take no for an answer." Livvy made a mental note to call Charlotte right away and take her up on her offer.

"Okay, then," Neely said. "I'll start the ball rolling. And unless you have some questions, I guess that's about it."

She was glad the meeting was over. She couldn't wait to share her news with Jeff. "Mr. Neely, Mr. Griggs, thank you for everything."

"We're here to help," Neely said as he opened the door for her. "I'll let you know when your discharge has been processed. In the meantime, you can make arrangements with your friends."

Impulsively, she hugged Neely, who reciprocated stiffly, and then she went to Griggs and gave him a hug as well. "Thank you again," she said before she left.

After the door closed behind her, Neely returned to his chair and leaned back with this fingers steepled in front of him. He looked at Griggs, who was in the process of getting to his feet. "There you have it, Tom. She's happy to get her life back and the hospital's happy it didn't get stiffed. Everybody wins."

"Larry, that is one lucky girl," Griggs said before he opened the door. "She's got youth, beauty, and wealth." Halfway through the doorway he turned back. "Too bad about the amnesia."

Neely watched the door swing shut and then reached for a pencil and began playing a sixteenth-note ride on the metal shade of his desk lamp and a backbeat on the blotter. The crowd roared their approval.

25

Detweiler replaced the phone in its cradle just as Karen returned to her desk with a cup of coffee. "Don't get too comfortable, Woj," he said. "A body turned up at Laurelhurst Park. Tranny hooker, carved up like the others. A couple kids found her. Let's saddle up." He took a revolver from a desk drawer and slipped it in his shoulder rig. Then he got to his feet and put on a plaid sport coat that clashed violently with his paisley tie.

"Damn," Karen said and holstered her snub .38 (which hadn't ever been fired in the line of duty, thank heaven). "Not even a week since the last one. He's a busy boy." It was a safe assumption the perp was male; female serials were almost nonexistent.

They made a fast trip across town, the unmarked cruiser's red and blue lights flashing all the way, and parked behind a patrol car on Southeast Oak. Karen got a roll of yellow crime scene tape from the trunk, and they started down the short path leading to Firwood Lake, in the park's east end. Halfway there they were met by a uniformed officer named Braunstein, who she'd seen around the House. He accompanied them the rest of the way. When they reached the lake she wasn't surprised to see the usual handful of curious onlookers milling about, kept at bay by Braunstein's partner, a black officer named Fouts. The faces of people at murder scenes always seemed to wear the same excited, ghoulish expression.

"Who discovered the body?" Karen asked Fouts.

"They did." Fouts inclined his head toward two boys standing under a nearby conifer tree, their eyes big. "I told them to wait over there."

"We'll want to talk to them after I examine the victim. In the meantime, suppose you and Fouts chase away these gawkers and cordon off the area." She handed the roll of yellow tape to Braunstein and started toward the body. "Also," she called over her shoulder, "get some plastic to drape over the body after we're finished looking it over. I don't want her left exposed."

The victim was young, black, and probably had been very attractive. Exsanguination gave her dark skin a grayish pallor. Her sightless eyes stared at eternity. Like the others, she'd been posed, this time leaning back against a sycamore tree, a neatly folded stack of clothing next to her. Karen noted the the slit throat, the cross carved on her chest, and the carnage between her legs.

Detweiler grunted. "Pre-op."

"You got it. Looks like the killer gave her some amateur surgery, though."

An uncircumcised severed brown penis was lying on the ground between the victim's spread thighs. The crudely improvised vagina testified to her killer's mind-numbing savagery. No blood was evident, which meant the killer had performed his handiwork elsewhere, consistent with the other killings.

Karen walked over to the two boys. "Hi, guys. I understand you were the ones who found the body." She opened her notepad. "Who am I talking to here?"

The older, taller one said, "I'm Jason Bryant. This is my brother, Tyler. We live near the park. Over that way." He pointed south.

"Ages and address?"

"I'm eleven, Tyler's ten. Thirty-seven fifty-seven Alder."

She wrote down the information. "Now, tell me how you found the body."

"Well, me and Tyler came here to feed the ducks. We brought some bread." He held up a half-full bread sack.

"What time was this?"

"Right after breakfast," he said. "Mom told us we could goof around the park until it was time for lunch."

"We thought the black woman was just sitting there resting at first," his brother continued. "But when we got closer we saw that she didn't have any clothes on. Then we saw that somebody had . . . hurt her. I called nine-one-one on my phone." He took an inexpensive cell phone from his front pants pocket and showed it to her.

"You did exactly the right thing."

"Geez," Jason said. "Who would do something like that to a person?"

"That's what we're going to find out."

Tyler said, "We never seen a naked dead person before. It's creepy."

"Very creepy." Karen put her notebook and pen away. "But you two were a big help and we appreciate it very much. You're free to go now."

"Good," they said in unison. They wasted no time getting away from the horror.

The C.S.U. team arrived to process the scene. The medical examiner wouldn't be far behind. Karen ambled down to the lake and kneeled at the edge. A half-dozen ducks and a pair of white geese swam toward her, expecting to be fed.

"Sorry, kids," she told them. "I don't have anything for you."

Unfortunately, she didn't have anything for the poor mutilated creature back there either.

26

The pickup's GPS issued directions with scathing sarcasm and a pronounced lisp. Shortly after Jeff punched in the address for the Birchwood Manor apartments, the reedy male voice said, "*Turn left at the nektht interthecthun, athuming you know left from right.*"

Livvy looked at Jeff. He shrugged and turned left.

"*Congratulationth, Brainiac. Now change to the right lane and protheed for two mileth.*"

"Sheesh," Jeff said. "What a caustic bastard."

Livvy laughed. "I thought I was hearing things. Why would anyone want a GPS that insults them?"

"Beats me." He reached into his jacket pocket and pulled out a phone. "I'll ask Ethan. I need to hit him up for another favor anyway." He held down a button with his thumb until the beep sounded. "Call Ethan . . . work," he said, enunciating carefully. After he received the robotic acknowledgment he placed the phone on the center console.

Five rings from the tiny speaker before a voice answered, "Yeah?"

"It's Jeff, Ethan. What are the chances of crashing at your place tonight? I want to stay in town one more day."

"Sure thing. Allison will be delighted to see you. In that case, don't worry about getting the truck back by six. Allie can come get me or I'll catch a ride with one of the guys."

"Appreciate it, pal. By the way, about your truck's GPS—"

"Wait, let me guess. You met Lance, am I right? My son Seth's a computer guru, a 'hacker,' he calls himself. Last month he borrowed the truck for a few days. When I got it back the GPS had two new personalities, Lance and Marge. Marge has a whiskey tenor and swears like a stevedore if you don't follow her directions. Seth said the next time he borrows the truck he's going to add one more personality, Wolfgang. If you make a wrong turn, Wolfgang screams, 'Dummkopf! Let me zee your papers!'"

"Your boy has way, *way* too much free time on his hands."

"That's what I told him. Anyhow, keep the truck as long as you need it."

"Thanks again, Ethan. See you later on tonight."

"Copy that."

After he put the phone back in his pocket, Jeff looked at Livvy and pointed to the GPS unit. "Lance."

"So I heard."

As if on cue, Lance said, *"You jutht mithed the turn, Einthtein. If you ekthpect to arrive at your dethtinathun thumtime today, turn left in one-quarter mile."*

"Keep it up, smartass," Jeff said, shaking his fist at the device. "We'll see how high you can bounce off the pavement."

Lance entertained them until they pulled into the parking lot of the Birchwood Manor. Their intention was to collect Livvy's belongings as quickly as possible so they could get to Leia's grandparents' place in the Southwest Hills at a reasonable hour. However, deflecting McClone's questions and attempts to engage them in a long-winded conversation proved to be a challenge. The little man with the huge proboscis was relentless. Nevertheless, they managed to get back on the road a half-hour later with her stuff stowed in the bed of the pickup, the cello seatbelted securely in the extended cab's back seat.

Livvy reached up and adjusted the visor to block the late afternoon sun, low on the horizon. Although the possessions from the storage room were vaguely familiar to her, they didn't jog her memory as she'd hoped they would. Still no solid connections with her life before, only the same indistinct impressions, shadows dancing in the fog. She sighed audibly.

"You're looking awfully morose over there, kiddo."

"Am I? Sorry, just thinking."

Jeff reached over and took her hand. "I think maybe you could use a diversion. After you get settled in, would you be up for doing something tomorrow evening?"

"Sure. That would be nice."

"I have some business that will take up the morning and most of the afternoon, but I'd love to see you after that. We'll celebrate your newfound freedom with a gourmet dinner, and after that we can go listen to some music."

She squeezed his hand. "It will be my first date, sort of."

He returned the squeeze. "I'll do my best to make it a memorable one."

She readjusted the sun visor. The road noise and vibration were making her drowsy. She rested her cheek on the seat back and fell asleep.

She dreamed. In the dream she was a young child, four or five. It was her birthday, and her party guests were downstairs, waiting for her. Before going down to join them, she looked at herself in a mirror. She was wearing a yellow party dress. Satisfied with her appearance, she left her room and started down the staircase. When she was halfway down, a group of children at the bottom spotted her and began pointing at her and laughing. Other kids appeared and joined in the derisive laughter. She was confused and embarrassed. Why they were making fun of her, she had no idea. A familiar-looking man and woman stood at the bottom of the staircase, their arms folded. They looked angry. She fled back up the stairs to her room, where she hid in the closet and cried. The dream ended abruptly and she came awake with a start.

"You okay?" Jeff asked, concern on his face. "You look like you've been crying."

Her cheeks were wet; she wiped them with the backs of her hands. "I had the weirdest dream. I was really young and it was my birthday, and for some reason the kids were all laughing at me. I was devastated."

He patted her knee. "Poor baby. But it was only a dream."

"I wonder what it means."

"Nothing, probably," he said. "Lots of crazy stuff happens in dreams. I once dreamed I was eating some incredibly dry pancakes, and when I woke up, my blanket was missing." He gave her knee a playful squeeze. "Hey, we'll be at Leia's grandparents' place pretty soon. That should take your mind off that sucky dream."

Maybe he was right and the dream was meaningless. Then why did she still feel like crying?

27

It was after five when Lance said, "*Dethtinathun on right, in one-eighth mile. Try not to mith it.*" Jeff slowed the pickup and signaled a right turn. The mailbox at the corner of the driveway had "CONOVER" painted on the side in neat lettering. Gravel crunched under the pickup's tires as they proceeded up the drive, through acreage heavily wooded with pine trees and thick brush. Whatever else, the rural location had plenty of privacy.

Livvy had expected to see a rustic two-story farmhouse at the end of the driveway. One with a front porch, perhaps, and a clothesline and apple trees in the back yard. Instead, she saw a contemporary structure built into the hillside, constructed of stone and glass. An amalgam of oblique angles, geometric shapes, and cantilevered terraces, it was as far from a traditional farmhouse as you could get. And yet, the unusual structure had an organic feel, as if it were growing out of the hillside. Integration with nearby rock outcroppings and plantings contributed to the impression that it belonged in the rural setting.

"Frank Lloyd Wright lives," Jeff said.

The driveway's graveled surface changed to asphalt that led to a sizable parking area in front of a four-car garage. Jeff pulled up next to a white Suburban and shut off the engine. They got out and started up the path to the house above. It ended at a courtyard paved in granite. A shallow ramp led to a pair of large double doors overlooking the courtyard.

They were walking toward the entrance when a massive silver and black German shepherd appeared from around the corner of the house. Hackles raised, teeth bared, eyes fixed on them, the dog advanced slowly, a predator stalking prey. Jeff stepped between her and the animal.

"Henry, stand down!" The huge dog halted and looked back, toward the speaker. A white-bearded man in a wheelchair was at the top of the ramp, framed by the open doorway behind him. "These folks are friends," he said. "Make them feel welcome."

The shepherd approached them and sniffed each in turn, and then he gave a perfunctory wag of his tail and trotted off in the direction he'd come from.

"Impressive animal," Jeff called out.

"He's a good boy." The man nudged a joystick and the wheelchair started down the ramp, the whine of its motor clearly audible. He maneuvered the powered chair across the courtyard and brought it to a stop in front of them. Then he got to his feet. Standing, he was an imposing figure, a bit taller than Jeff, but rail-thin. His white hair was thick, his full beard neatly trimmed. Probably in response to their surprised expressions, he said, "Bad knees. Arthritis. Riding is faster and less painful." He pointed to Jeff's cane. "What's your excuse, son?"

"Knee surgery for an old sports injury."

"Ah." The man turned to Livvy and winked. "You can outrun him if you need to." His blue eyes twinkled with intelligence and humor. He extended his hand. "Floyd Conover. And you're Livvy?"

"Yes," she said, shaking his large hand, "and this is my friend, Jeff Longcypher."

The tall man shook Jeff's hand. "Pleased to meet you both. The gals are busy readying a guest room for Livvy. They thought they'd have it done before you got here. Looks like they miscalculated."

"No problem," Livvy said, "Mr. Conover, thank you for letting me stay here a few days. I appreciate it so much."

"Call me Floyd. And you're welcome. My daughter and granddaughter think a lot of you, and that buys you a pile of gold chips around here." He sat down in the powered chair. "Follow me. I'll give you a grand tour of our modest little abode."

Livvy and Jeff followed behind the chair as it climbed the ramp, whining as if in protest. Once inside, standing in the vestibule, it was hard to believe they were indoors. Natural light streamed in through huge skylights in the vaulted ceiling at least forty feet above them. There were plants of every size and description.

"Very nice," Jeff said. "And the southern exposure gives you plenty of light."

"The roof has an array of sixty-four solar panels," Floyd said. "There's passive solar as well, for heating water. And we have a nearby creek that powers a generator."

"Do you produce enough power to get you completely off the grid?"

Before Floyd could answer him, a call came from above. They looked up and saw Leia leaning over the guardrail of the topmost level, about thirty feet above them. "I'll be right down," she said and then turned her head and shouted over her shoulder, "Grandma! Patty Mae! Livvy and Jeff are here!"

Leia and her mother appeared a couple of minutes later, accompanied by a woman who looked like an older version of Charlotte (who looked like an older version of Leia). Hugs were exchanged, and then Leia introduced them to her grandmother, Elinor Conover. "Call me Ellie," she told them.

"Well, what do you think of it?" Charlotte made a sweeping gesture.

Livvy and Jeff spoke at the same time, both stumbling over superlatives.

"Daddy designed it. It's his pride and joy."

Jeff looked at Floyd. "*You* designed this place?"

Floyd smiled and nodded. "And a few others."

Jeff smacked his forehead with his palm. "Wait a minute, I know who you are now. I saw your picture on the cover of *Time*." He turned to Livvy. "Leia's grandfather has designed more famous buildings than anyone else alive. He designed the Teseract in Hong Kong, one of the tallest skyscrapers in the world. An honor to meet you, sir."

Floyd seemed embarrassed by the adulation. "Thanks, son. What do you say we continue the tour?"

The house was deceptively large—slightly over six thousand square feet, Floyd told them. It had: a great room dominated by a stone fireplace fifteen feet high; a library with a saltwater aquarium that extended the length of an entire wall, floor to ceiling, stocked with exotic fish and other sea creatures; a kitchen that would be the pride of a five-star restaurant; a formal dining room with an enormous cut-crystal chandelier suspended over an intricately inlaid table twenty feet long; a music conservatory with an ebony Steinway grand piano; an expansive game room with a full bar and billiard tables; a Jacuzzi, sauna, and exercise room; and lastly, a glassed-in terrarium full of exotic plants and trees.

"So much for the first level," Floyd said as they arrived back in the foyer. "There are two upper levels. Let's go have a look at 'em." His powered chair leaped forward in response to the joystick. He carefully steered it into the elevator beside a curved stairway and beckoned them to follow him. Clearly, he was enjoying showing off his creation.

The two upper levels housed Floyd's office, which contained a large drafting table and various architectural tools and materials (but no computer; he detested the things, he told them), as well as five bedrooms, each with its own distinctive decor, a fireplace, and French doors that opened to a private terrace. The bathrooms were equipped with bidets. The last bedroom they inspected was on the top level.

"And this will be Livvy's room," Ellie said. "We hope you'll be comfortable here, dear."

Livvy stared, open-mouthed. "It's beautiful."

The room had a fireplace made of white marble. All the cloth items in the room—canopy over the four-poster bed, bedcover, dust ruffle, pillows, lampshades, and two chairs in front of the fireplace—were covered in lustrous copper and green silk fabric. The terrace overlooked an undulating sea of treetops beyond the parking area.

"Definitely a step up from your hospital room," Jeff said. He looked at his watch. "I need to get going before long, so we should bring your stuff up from the truck."

"I'll help," Leia said.

Between the three of them they managed to get her belongings up to the room in only two trips. After the last boxes were dropped on the bedroom floor, Leia left them alone. Livvy opened the French doors and beckoned for Jeff to join her on the terrace.

"Look," Livvy said, pointing to the horizon. A flotilla of clouds had moved in from the west, resulting in a sunset resplendent with glowing pinks and lavenders. Jeff put his arm around her shoulder and they watched it in silence.

"Private terrace, warm autumn evening, splendid sunset," Jeff said. "Shame to let all that go to waste, don't you agree?"

"What do you mean?"

"I mean this is the perfect setting for a first kiss."

She looked up at him to see if he was joking. He leaned down. She closed her eyes, expecting the press of his mouth on hers. Instead, his lips brushed hers lightly several times. The kiss that followed was unexpectedly soft and gentle. After they parted she sensed that something had changed between them. The way he looked at her confirmed it.

She liked his face. Not that it didn't have flaws: a nose he'd broken several times, a tooth that slightly overlapped the one next to it, a fleck of gray in the iris of one pale blue eye, a scar in his left eyebrow where no hair grew. Assorted imperfections that made it a more interesting face.

"Well," he said, "I guess I'd better get out of here so you can get settled in." He put on his jacket. "I'll be back here tomorrow evening at seven sharp to pick you up."

"I'll be ready."

"C'mon, walk me out."

They started down the staircase. At the bottom they found everyone standing in the vestibule listening to Floyd. They caught the tail end of his story: ". . . so the grasshopper says to the bartender, 'You mean you have a drink named *Steve*?'" The group didn't notice them until the laughter subsided.

"There they are," Floyd said. "Everything unloaded?"

Jeff nodded. "And now I've got to shove off. It was very nice meeting you and your wife."

Floyd shook Jeff's hand. "You're welcome here anytime, son."

Livvy accompanied Jeff outside. Once the door closed behind them, he reached for her. She didn't resist. Their second kiss was tantalizingly brief.

Jeff shook his head, pretending to be dizzy. "See you tomorrow, kiddo."

As he walked away he whistled a merry tune and twirled his cane like a baton, hardly limping at all. Just before he stepped onto the path to the parking lot, he turned and waved to her.

She returned the wave and opened the door to rejoin the group inside.

28

In Brookline, Massachusetts Nora Cosgrove poured herself a steaming cup of Earl Grey and sat down in the dinette nook. She blew gently on the surface of the tea and took a cautious sip, and then she opened her book club's selection for that week. After she read the first page for the third or fourth time without the faintest impression of what she'd read, she closed the book and sighed. It was no use; her mind was elsewhere. She hadn't been able to focus on anything since the phone call earlier that day. The caller was Mr. Cavenaugh from Atlantic Trust. In his soft, confidential voice, he informed her that Livvy was fine and that Nora should expect a call from her around seven that evening. Nora had been on tenterhooks ever since.

She glanced again at the smiling Kit-Kat clock on her kitchen wall, its black plastic tail swinging like a pendulum, counting off the passing seconds. It was 6:33—still twenty-seven agonizing minutes to go. She closed her eyes and took several slow, deep breaths. She needed to calm down. The sweet child was alive and well, that was the important thing. Nora's frequent, fervent prayers had been answered. *Dear Lord, thank you, thank you, thank you.*

At 6:49 she decided she had time to get another cup of tea. While she was pouring it, the phone's sudden shrill ring startled her, and she splashed a saucer-sized dollop of the steaming liquid on the counter top. Cleaning it up could wait. It was much more important to get rid of the caller so that the line would be free for Livvy's call. She snatched the wall-mounted phone's handset and said, "Hello? Hello?"

"Hello, Nora?" It was Livvy, ten minutes early.

"Honey, you have no idea how relieved I am to hear your voice."

"Mr. Cavenaugh said you've been worried, so I wanted to phone you as soon as possible. With all the confusion, this is the first chance I've gotten. I don't think I've had a spare minute since I was discharged from the hospital earlier this morning."

"I understand, dear. The important thing is, you're all right."

"I'm fine. Physically, at least." Livvy recounted her ordeal in matter-of-fact fashion, as if she were describing an incident that happened to someone else. It was a confirmation of the fears that had haunted Nora since Livvy first announced her intention to go to Oregon. "So that's all of it, Nora. And if—no, *when*—I get my memories back, everything will be back the way it was before."

"So what do you remember?"

"At this point, not much. I get flashes of things, vague impressions, but nothing I can latch onto. So far."

Nora swallowed. "Do you remember me?"

"Well . . . your voice is familiar, and I can sort of visualize a face that might be yours, but I can't be sure. I wish I could see a photo of you. Maybe it would be the trigger that restores my memory. Dr. Lachmann said it might might happen that way."

Nora sighed. If she weren't such a techniphobe, she would have a cellular phone with a built-in camera, like nearly everyone else in the world, and she could send Livvy a photograph she would receive instantly. Nora decided then and there to get one. In the meantime, there was always the U.S. Postal Service. "I'll mail you one, honey. Do you still have the same mailing address?"

"No, I don't have that apartment anymore. A girl I met at the hospital invited me to stay with her and her mother at her grandparents' home outside of Portland until I can make other arrangements. They treat me like family. I don't have their address with me right now, but I'll send you a postcard."

"I'll mail you the photograph as soon as I receive it. I'm just so relieved you're safe and among friends, dear. I can't tell you how frantic I've been." Almost frantic enough to book a flight to Oregon.

"Last night I read all the letters you sent me. I was hoping they would help me make some connections. But I just had faint impressions of things. They were like ghosts hovering on the periphery. Nothing I could latch onto."

"That must be so upsetting." Nora hesitated before asking the question. "Do you remember . . . Oliver?"

Livvy repeated the name.

"You and he were close once." It was the truth, in a literal sense.

"I'd like to hear about him sometime, but I'd better go now or I'll be late to a barbecue hosted by the Conovers, the people I'm staying with. Listen, I'll call you again soon. I have a million questions to ask you. Wait—I need to ask you something right now. Was I a vegetarian?"

"Pescetarian. You ate fish, but no other kind of meat."

"That explains a lot. Thanks, Nora. Talk to you soon."

"Take care, now. Love you."

Thus ended the first conversation she'd had with Livvy in over two months. After she hung up the phone she hummed "Amazing Grace" and wiped up the spill on the counter top. She made a trip to the "micturition chamber," as her father used to call it, and then settled into her favorite chair, the soft one with the ottoman that elevated her feet just right. The knowledge that Livvy was alive and well would enable her to sleep peacefully again, free of the nightmarish scenarios that had haunted her for the past month.

The vivid dream jolted Nora awake. A vestige of the dream lingered for several seconds as a spectral figure at the foot of her bed. It was a boy, small and fragile-looking, his dark eyes windows to an infinite sadness within.

Oliver, as he'd looked twenty years ago.

He was five years old, a precocious five, when he whispered his secret yearning to her. He tried to tell his mommy, he said, but she acted like she didn't hear him. He was scared to tell his daddy, and that was understandable; Preston Covington was an imposing figure, even to Nora. So it was only natural that Oliver would turn to his nanny, who had taken care of him since he was born.

"God must've made a mistake," Oliver told her. "When I say my prayers at night I ask God to fix me, but when I wake up in the morning I'm still the same."

She promised him she would talk to his mother and father—not that she looked forward to the conversation, but a promise was a promise. As it happened, an opportunity presented itself that very evening.

Mr. C's reaction was five seconds of silence, and then he guffawed. "Right. Oliver's only five. Next month he'll decide he's a fireman. When I was his age I told everyone I was a billionaire. I was thirty years premature."

"Sir, forgive me for saying so," Nora said, "but this is different."

"Are you trying to tell us Oliver actually thinks he's a girl?"

"That's what he said. I believe him."

Mr. C folded his arms and turned to his wife. "Are you listening to this, Katherine? Can you believe your ears?"

Mrs. C didn't share her husband's incredulity. "Oliver tried to tell me yesterday," she said. "I was busy at the time, working on a budget proposal. Honestly, I thought he was parroting something he'd heard on television. He's always doing that."

Mr. C made a sound that was half-grunt, half-growl. "I say it's just a childish phase." No mistaking the finality in his tone.

Later, she cornered Mrs. C. "I know Oliver," Nora told her. "I've been his nanny all his life. He's serious. And he sounds desperate."

Mrs. C was quiet for a moment before she said, "I realize I haven't given much time to Oliver lately. I've been so busy setting up the foundation. You were always there, so I wasn't too concerned. In some ways, he's closer to you than to me. But we want what's best for our son. I'm going to suggest to Preston that we bring in a professional, a psychologist, and get an expert opinion."

"Mrs. Covington, I think that would be very wise."

"Preston will probably have some resistance to the idea, but I can make him see it's the best way to deal with the situation."

"If you don't mind me saying so, I think whoever you choose should have extensive experience in gender matters."

"I agree."

"I just had a thought," Nora said. "My youngest brother is a psychology professor at Harvard. I'm sure he can recommend someone. It could save you a lot of time." She knew saving time was almost a religion with Mrs. C.

"You wouldn't mind asking him?"

"Consider it done. And if I can help you with anything else, anything at all, please let me know."

"Well, since you mention it," Mrs. C said, "I have two meetings tomorrow and three the next day. Plus, this Saturday is the charity auction. You know I trust your judgment, Nora. Could I delegate this to you? Would you mind?"

Exactly what Nora was hoping to hear. "Don't worry, Mrs. Covington. I will take care of everything."

Oliver was thrilled when Nora talked to him about it. "The doctor . . . he's going to fix me?"

"The doctor will help you," she said, choosing her words carefully. "But first he'll want to get to know you. It might take a while."

"That's okay," Oliver said, and then his face lit up. "Do you think God chose this way to answer my prayers?"

"I think it's possible." She meant it. A devout Methodist, Nora firmly believed that God's wishes were sometimes manifested through others.

Within a week, Dr. Brent Cosgrove, professor and brother, found her a Boston psychologist who did, in fact, have extensive experience working with children with gender issues. And his credentials were impressive, which would carry a great deal of weight with the Covingtons.

She met with Dr. Aylworth two days later. While the psychologist cleaned his horn-rimmed glasses with a cloth, Nora told him about Oliver and about the Covingtons. He was particularly interested in Mr. C's reaction to Oliver's declaration. By the time Nora was finished talking, the glasses were undoubtedly very clean, and Dr. Aylworth's interest was evident. He wanted to meet Oliver. The meeting took place later two days later. While Oliver talked with the psychologist in his office, Nora sat in the outer room and read a *Reader's Digest*. She was reading "Humor In Uniform" when Dr. Aylworth escorted Oliver out of his office, a fatherly hand on his shoulders.

"See you next Tuesday, Oliver," the psychologist said.

"Okay." Oliver was smiling, his first smile in months.

Two months later, with Nora present, Dr. Aylworth presented his findings to the Covingtons. He held out a half-inch thick, bound report. "It contains the results of diagnostic tests, therapy session transcripts, consultations with other psychologists, treatment recommendations—everything relevant."

Mrs. C took it from him.

"I'll summarize it for you," Dr. Aylworth said. "Oliver is transgender. The results were conclusive."

"How conclusive?" The tone of Mr. C's question was equal parts skepticism and hostility.

"On a scale of one to ten, Oliver is a ten. A classic case. Two colleagues concur."

That put a scowl on Mr. C's face. "You said something about treatment recommendations. So he can be treated?"

"Yes, but not in the sense of 'curing' him." Dr. Aylworth had formed air quotes around the word with his fingers. "Gender dysphoria cannot be cured, only accommodated. In this case that would mean allowing Oliver to transition."

Muscles worked at the corners of Mr. C's jaw. "And if he's not allowed to . . . transition?"

"That's a good question. I want to share something Oliver told me. He's been very depressed about 'being in the wrong body,' as he described it. Depression is quite common in transgender children. Oliver said he crawled out an upstairs window and climbed up the roof to the peak, where he stood close to the edge with his eyes closed. He stood there for a long time, he said, but then he 'chickened out' and climbed back in the window. He didn't jump. That time."

"Dear God," Mrs. C said, her face pale.

Mr. C was stone-faced.

Nora swallowed. The house had four floors, plus an attic. The roof's peak had to be nearly fifty feet high. A fall from that height onto the concrete drive would surely be fatal.

"It boils down to this," the psychologist said, 'would you rather have a live daughter or a dead son?"

That fall, a bright-eyed girl named Olivia Leigh Covington entered first grade at Newton Academy. She was accepted without question as just an ordinary six-year-old girl.

Livvy's happiness would have been complete, but for an unexpected development: Her parents were not as accepting as her schoolmates. Although they stoically followed the psychologist's recommendation that she be allowed to transition, they were unhappy and resentful about it. Especially Mr. C, who had been counting on having a son who would step into his shoes someday. Not a daughter. A son. So the Covingtons immersed themselves in foundations, philanthropy, and mutual fund management. All of which effectively shunted the unwanted daughter aside.

Livvy wouldn't talk with Nora about the rejection, but the pain showed in her eyes. She began spending more and more time alone in her room, and Nora began having a recurring nightmare: Livvy, teetering on the peak of the roof with her eyes closed. A call to Dr. Aylworth proved fruitless; he was in Los Angeles, his service said, attending a psychology conference, and after that he was going to Japan for two weeks. The situation seemed hopeless.

And then Nora noticed an abrupt change in Livvy. The pain in her eyes was gone. In its place, determination.

At school Livvy astounded her teachers with her scholastic ability, in particular her reading development. She had read extensively by the time she entered first grade, including the entire leather-bound set of *Grimm's Fairy Tales* in the first-floor library. In short, she was well beyond "Run, Spot, run!" The school proposed that she skip several grades, but Nora met with the headmistress and nixed the idea, at Livvy's insistence. "Skipping grades would make me stand out," Livvy said. "I don't want to stand out." So she remained in grades commensurate with her age, blending in with the other girls.

Fast forward . . .

When Livvy was twelve she decided to take up the cello. Dwarfed by the instrument at first, she approached it with total commitment. "This girl is a prodigy," her music teacher declared. "She plays with passion and understanding for one so young." She had been playing only a year. Livvy could always count on seeing Nora in the audience during recitals and performances, applauding along with all the proud parents.

Fast forward . . .

When Livvy turned eighteen Nora accompanied her to Thailand to have gender reassignment surgery, which, after twelve years of being fully accepted as female, seemed like an afterthought. The soft-spoken Thai surgeon presumed that Nora was Livvy's mother. Livvy didn't correct the misunderstanding, which warmed Nora's heart. In the recovery room, still groggy from the anesthesia, Livvy said, "Now I can go swimming." She tried to wink, as if it were a joke, but there was no mistaking the joy in her slurred words.

Fast forward . . .

While attending Columbia, Livvy joined the university's swim team. Nora watched her compete many times, hoarsely cheering her on from the bleachers. In her sophomore year Livvy's first-place finishes in the 100-meter and 200-meter freestyle events clinched a NCAA division championship for Columbia.

Nora didn't need a psychologist to explain why Livvy was driven to excel. It was heartbreakingly clear that she was trying to prove to her parents she was worthy of their acceptance, worthy of their love. But the Covingtons were killed in an auto accident when Livvy was still in college, and her long-held hopes died with them.

A pain-filled past, resulting in memories better left forgotten. Amnesia, despite its downside, would be an escape from those old hurts.

29

OMRI Information Technology Director William Morley was operating with a massive sleep deficit, after staying up until 3 a.m. four nights running, immersed in *Second Chance*. The virtual reality environment was quickly becoming a major part of his life, and he was spending more and more time there. The simple truth was, his real life paled by comparison. In *Second Chance* his name was Morgan Phoenix, and his avatar was everything he was not—tall, muscular, handsome, tanned, expensively dressed—but when you can specify your avatar's physical characteristics, why not? And, unlike real life, in *Second Chance* he had a girlfriend, a blond, stacked sex-pot named Angie Starchild. He and Angie had never met in real life, but that was perfectly okay. Their online relationship was more than enough for him.

Last night had been the grand opening of Panopticon, a new virtual nightclub. The event had featured two famous virtual bands, The Allegations and Ipecac, so he was glad he'd sprung for the new Altec Lansing speakers with the sub-woofer capable of rattling fillings. Throngs of avatars were packed into the virtual space, Morgan and Angie among them. They made an eye-catching couple. He'd worn a silver-gray Armani knock-off (which had cost him a stack of Louden dollars, the virtual currency of *Second Chance*, named for its creator), and Angie had chosen a skin-tight leather dominatrix outfit, which, on her avatar's incredible body, garnered her a lot of attention from other men. But she was his, all his. After they left Panopticon they hopped in his DeLorean and drove to his place. Then, in the bedroom of his penthouse apartment with the floor-to-ceiling windows overlooking the digital metropolis, they'd had the hottest virtual sex he'd ever experienced, lasting into the early morning hours.

So even though he was running on fumes today, it had been worth it. If he could find an unoccupied hospital room, he could catch a quick nap. In the middle of a jaw-creaking yawn, his phone buzzed. He swore and picked it up. "What is it, Britney?"

"Mr. Raja—Raja-something is here to see you. He says it's important."

Morley grimaced. He really needed that nap. "Okay, send him in, I guess."

The door opened and Sanjit entered, his manner hesitant as a dog in places where dogs get kicked a lot. He closed the door behind him and stood until Morley indicated the chair in front of the desk. After he was seated Sanjit's eyes remained courteously downcast. "I am grateful that you would see me without an appointment."

Morley acknowledged his politeness with a nod. "What's on your mind, Sanjit?"

Sanjit looked up. "Mr. Morley, I feel I must call a matter to your attention." His soft brown eyes pleaded for indulgence. "A co-worker has spoken to me of secret projects on which he has been working—"

"Secret projects?"

"Yes. In particular, one that involves intercepting email."

Morley held up his hand. "Hold on now. Intercepting email? Whose email?"

Sanjit took a deep breath. "The incoming and outgoing email of one of the doctors. My co-worker claims he was asked to intercept it."

"By whom?"

"By the hospital administration, that is what he told me. I have brought this to show you." Sanjit handed a printout to Morley. "It is the script he created to do this thing."

Morley scanned the lines of code. It was obvious whose handiwork it was. Sanjit explained how he'd discovered the script and what its author had said when Sanjit confronted him about it. Morley listened open-mouthed, incredulous at what he was hearing. It was the absolute truth, he had no doubt about that. Sanjit's tongue would probably snap off if he even exaggerated, let alone lied.

The fatigue Morley had been feeling left him completely, vanquished by adrenaline. He thanked Sanjit for calling the matter to his attention and assured him he would look into it. After he showed Sanjit out, Morley returned his desk in two long strides and snatched up the phone. He stabbed at the keypad and ground his teeth while he listened to the rings.

Under the watchful eye of a security guard, Stingler tossed his personal belongings into a cardboard box, making no attempt to pack it sensibly. Of all the chickenshit stuff the hospital had pulled on him, this took the prize.

"Mr. Stingler, your position at this hospital is untenable," Morley had told him. "You're terminated."

He was fucking *terminated*.

Sanjit ratted him out, the little prick. Stingler felt foolish for not seeing it coming, would've bet money the guy was cowed. Because when Sanjit had confronted him again about Marauder, Stingler had done his level best to frighten the stubborn little bastard so bad he'd drop the matter for good.

It should have worked.

Job security was Sanjit's main concern, Stingler knew. His face only inches from the smaller man's, Stingler told him, "You've continued to meddle in confidential matters after you were warned to mind your own business. Disobeying a supervisor is grounds for dismissal. Let it go, or you'll be flipping burgers at Jack in the Box, making minimum wage."

Sanjit had been as impassive as one of those ridiculous Hindu statues he kept on his desk. And for ten days all was quiet, which Stingler interpreted as Sanjit's total surrender.

Wrong.

But there was no point in rehashing past events. Sanjit and Morley the Moron could go fuck themselves.

Stingler picked up the box and glared in the direction of Sanjit's empty cubicle and sneered. The little coward didn't have the guts to face him. But if he thought he'd seen the last of Stingler, he was full of shit. The Stingman always got even, you could count on that.

The guard escorted him out of the building and then watched silently while Stingler tossed the box in the Corolla's trunk, rattling the contents. He was still watching as Stingler pulled out of the hospital staff parking lot for the last time. The little car's tires barked when he power-shifted to second gear.

Article from the online edition of *The Oregonian*, Technology section:

REDMOND, WA—Microsoft and computer security professionals are concerned about a virulent new virus that so far has infected millions of computers worldwide, a digital epidemic that seems to be growing exponentially. The virus, known as "Winders" because it changes all occurrences of "Windows" to the folksy-sounding "Winders," infects only computers that run Microsoft's Windows 7 and 8 operating systems. As yet, no infections of other versions of Windows have been reported. Experts say the virus' sole purpose is to replace the trademarked logo, in both text and graphics, throughout the operating system's internals.

Microsoft spokesman Rudy Bolman said it's no laughing matter. "Viruses like this cost consumers millions of dollars in lost productivity and investment in virus eradication software. Make no mistake, this is nothing less than cyber-terrorism."

Windows users don't seem to be taking the matter seriously, however. An overwhelming majority feel like Kelly Panter of Garden City, CA, who said, "I think it's hilarious. Every time I see 'Winders' on my screen I can't help laughing."

But mirth will be in short supply at Microsoft until Winders is reined in. Bruce Mitchell, a vice president at anti-virus software maker Symantec, said: "Symantec is working hard to develop a virus definition that will eradicate Winders. We should have something real soon now." Spokespersons for McAfee and AVG Technologies, both leading makers of virus protection software, could not be reached for comment.

According to celebrity hacker Ursel Petrosian, author of the troublesome Big Ass virus that plagued PCs in 2013, Winders is a "clever hack." Petrosian explained, "It's pure genius. As viruses go, it's relatively benign; it doesn't mess with applications or data files. And except for the changed logos, Winders removes all traces of itself after completing its task. How do you get rid of something that's already gone? Microsoft ought to hire its creator." Microsoft's Bolman says that's unlikely. "Hopefully, whoever's responsible for this virus will be prosecuted and sent to jail."

In the meantime, Winders continues to imbue PCs with a homespun, backwoods flavor, tickling the funny bones of users around the world.

Stingler closed the browser window.

Inspiring, that was the word for it. Petrosian was right; whoever created Winders was a friggin' genius. Stingler loved stuff like that, hacks that incorporated wit and humor. Maybe he'd get a chance to meet Winders' author someday. They probably had a lot in common.

If he wanted to, he could devise a virus that would screw up OMRI's databases so bad that Morley the Moron and his team wouldn't have a prayer of unfucking things. Morley would probably come crawling, hat in hand, and beg him for help. Stingler could demand reinstatement in his old job with full seniority and benefits. And a hefty raise.

The more he toyed with the idea, the better it sounded. It would even the score but good. Maybe he should actually do it. Why the hell not? After all, one clever hack deserved another. He let out a whoop of excitement, opened the Emacs editor, and bent to the task.

He'd call his creation "Staph." And only the Stingman would have the cure.

30

The venerable Talbot Building was located in the epicenter of Portland's downtown, surrounded by banks, brokerage houses, and other financial institutions. Jeff swore when he saw the underground parking garage was full. Finding a spot to park downtown was always a thrash. But today he caught a break: A car pulled away from one of the metered spaces directly in front of the Talbot. Unbelievable. He slid the pickup into the vacated space with no hesitation. Then he fed quarters into the meter until it showed two hours. More than enough time. If his luck held he'd be back with thirty minutes to spare.

The entrance was an old-fashioned revolving door made of brass and thick glass. It took a steady, determined push to get the ponderous door moving. Apparently, the weak were not welcome within.

Wasted space in a building is often a measure of wealth and status, and the Talbot's high-ceilinged lobby was spacious indeed. The decor—green marble floor, dark wood paneling, and polished brass trim—cultivated the impression that important activities took place within the Talbot's walls.

In the elevator he held the brass handrail and admired the old car's ornate appointments, especially the elaborately carved crown molding. The doors clanked open and he stepped out onto the sixth floor. He strolled down the hall, taking his time, until he stood before a set of oak doors with "LONGCYPHER, CANNADY & MOORE" engraved on a brass plaque.

The receptionist was a Kate Upton clone, with flawless makeup and carefully tousled blond hair. She smiled at him, her perfect teeth preternaturally white. They had probably cost her enough to enable her dentist—or was it "dental aesthetician"?—to buy a new BMW. "We haven't seen you in here for a while," she said, picking up the phone. "I'll let your father know you're here."

Two minutes later his father appeared, buttoning his overcoat. Douglas Longcypher was almost as tall as his son, and they shared the same pale blue eyes. He looked at his watch. "You're late."

It begins. "Sorry. The rain slowed traffic on the freeway."

After a noncommittal grunt his father said, "My club's only three blocks away, so we'll walk." He looked at Jeff's cane. "Will that be a problem?"

Jeff shook his head. "I'm game if you are."

They didn't talk much on the way. Thankfully, the rain had stopped for a while.

After they were seated at a table, Jeff looked around the private club's interior. It was exactly as he remembered it, from the few times he'd been there with his father: dark paneling, deep wine-colored carpet, leather chairs, billiard tables, air thick with cigar smoke. No women were present, of course, not in that bastion of masculinity. The members and their guests, Jeff being the one exception, were older white men in expensive suits who looked like they were used to having people jump when they spoke. The few black and Hispanic men he saw were servers.

His father puffed on his cigar, regarding him silently. Finally, he asked, "So how's your flying business doing?" He managed to make "flying business" sound like "pornography business."

"It has its ups and downs," Jeff said, not caring that it sounded flip.

His father snorted. "I ran into Beth last week. She asked me what you were up to these days."

"And what did you tell Portland's perennial débutante?"

"I told her the truth—that you were still wasting your time flying around the sky, chasing some adolescent dream, instead of fulfilling your potential as a talented lawyer with a bright future."

"Christ, let's not have that discussion again."

"Jeffrey, for God's sake, you were on a fast track to full partnership at the firm. Someday you would have been managing partner. The world was your oyster. And Beth would have been behind you all the way."

"Yes, no doubt." Beth would have been squarely behind him, so long as he fit into the future she had mapped out: mansion in an exclusive area, expensive cars, designer clothes, jewelry, lavish parties, country club membership— all the accouterments of a society princess. But voicing the cynical assessment would only make his father ask what was wrong with those things, and that summed up the essential difference between them.

His father blew smoke toward the ceiling. "Beth's a lovely girl, Jeffrey."

"Yes, she's a vision." Which was true. She was beautiful, if you considered only her exterior.

Their waiter appeared and set their lunch orders in front of them: soup and a salad for Jeff and a steak and baked potato for his father.

After the waiter left, his father asked, "Are you seeing any other young ladies these days?"

Jeff nodded. "One."

"What does she do?"

Jeff mentally kicked himself for mentioning anything. "She's a cellist. Symphonic."

His father cut into his steak with surgical precision; bloody juice oozed from the extra-rare piece of meat. "Is it serious?"

Jeff hesitated, partly due to reluctance to discuss his love life with his father, but mostly because he realized that, yes, it was serious. That was a revelation. But he shrugged and changed the subject. "How's Mom?"

"She's well. I told her you'd phoned me this morning and that we were going to have lunch. She told me to ask you to call her. Message delivered."

"I intend to give her a call after lunch, as a matter of fact." He and his mother were close. Much to her husband's frustration, she'd supported Jeff's decision to resign from the law firm. "Whatever it takes to make you happy, you should do," she told him.

They made small talk for the rest of the lunch—Jeff's knee surgery, his father's new Mercedes S600, and the state of the economy. During the two-block walk back to the Talbot, they encountered several homeless people who hit them up for money. Jeff handed each of them a dollar. Predictably, his father commented that he was only "enabling" them; Jeff countered that panhandling was a tough gig and they earned the money they were given. His father only shook his head. Jeff smiled.

Back at the Talbot, Jeff had an oh-shit moment when he saw the meter had expired. Parking tickets were a pain in the ass. But fortune had smiled upon him: under the wiper, nada. Before stepping into the revolving door, his father put a hand on his shoulder. "Jeffrey, think about what I said, okay?" Jeff just stared at him, wondering if there was anything he could possibly say that would convince his father that he wouldn't be returning to the firm. Not in this lifetime, at least.

Jeff climbed in the pickup and sat there a moment, breathing deeply until his abdominal muscles began to relax. He massaged the back of his neck. Nothing ratcheted up the tension like being subjected to the "you're wasting your life, come back to the firm" pitch again. The irony was, he'd quit the firm precisely because he felt he was wasting his life there. Fat chance dear old Dad would ever understand that.

He took out his phone and punched in a number. When his mother answered, he asked her if she was prepared for a visit from her only son. She insisted he drive over right away. He started the truck and pulled away from the curb. He had a couple of hours to kill before picking up Livvy in the Southwest Hills, just enough time for a pleasant visit with his mother.

Who did understand.

31

It was a few minutes before six when Jeff parked next to Floyd Conover's white Suburban. The rain had stopped a couple of hours before; the sky to the west was clear and a high-pressure area had brought warmer temperatures, both harbingers of a perfect evening to come. With any luck, it would hold through tomorrow for the flight back to Colby.

At he stepped from the walkway to the courtyard, Henry appeared out of nowhere to challenge him, ears and hackles at full alert. The dog began wagging his tail when he was four feet away. Jeff leaned over patted his head.

Leia's grandmother answered the door, and her face lit up when she saw him. "Jeff! Come in, come in. How nice to see you again." She was wearing an apron decorated with a pair of cartoon forks dueling with lightsabers. "May the Forks Be With You" was the caption.

"Thank you, Mrs. Conover. Nice to see you too."

"Ellie, if you please. Unless you want me addressing you as Mr. Longcypher."

"Okay, Ellie."

"Livvy's almost ready and she looks just lovely." She checked her watch and smiled at him apologetically. "Would you excuse me, Jeff? I need to get something out of the oven." She hurried off, leaving him to wait at the foot of the stairs.

He heard Livvy call out and turned around to see her coming down the staircase. She was wearing a dress. It was the first time he'd seen her in one. Teal in color with subtle geometric patterns, it was a halter affair that revealed her shoulders. And lovely shoulders they were. Jeff was glad to see a cardigan sweater draped over one arm; although the day had been relatively warm for October, the evening would probably get a bit chilly. Livvy's shiny dark hair was pulled back smoothly on her well-shaped head and gathered into a high ponytail long enough to brush the thin halter strap in back. The style emphasized her high cheekbones. Makeup, which she hardly ever wore, made her eyes seem even larger than usual. When she reached the bottom of the stairs she pirouetted for him and the dress's full skirt swirled around her legs.

He nodded with approval. "Very nice."

"Thank you. I bought the dress and shoes today." In heels she came closer to looking him in the eye than most women did. "I'll let Ellie know we're leaving. Back in a minute."

He watched her walk away from him, moving well on those perfect legs, the ponytail swinging from side to side, contrasting with the paleness of her finely sculpted shoulders.

"*Very* nice," he repeated to Henry. The dog chose that moment to begin panting. "Exactly," Jeff said.

Jeff had made dinner reservations at Merovingian's overlooking the Columbia River. From their window table they could see a forest of masts that belonged to boats moored at the marina below. A young woman with a buzz cut introduced herself as their server and filled their water glasses. The menus she gave them offered a vast selection of seafood dishes. When they were ready to give her their orders, Livvy chose baked salmon with a lemon glaze, a salad, and a dry white wine. That sounded good, so Jeff told the server to make it two. She left and returned a few minutes later with their wine.

He picked up his glass and proposed a toast. "To swimming," he said, and clinked his glass against Livvy's. With his first sip he made a big deal of swirling the wine around in his mouth before swallowing, and then he held the glass of clear liquid up to the light, as if studying it. "Hmmm . . . assertive without being impertinent."

Livvy laughed, shaking her head. "Speaking of swimming, on the drive over you started to tell me what caught your attention the very first time you saw me. Was it my form in the water?"

"Nope, although your form is worthy of attention, in or out of the water."

"Give me a hint."

"Okay, it's a physical feature."

"You call that a hint? Well, let's see . . ." Her guesses ranged from the obvious to the obscure, all receiving a negative shake of his head. "Okay, I give up," she said. "Tell me."

He set his glass of wine on the table. "Your earlobes."

"Excuse me?"

"You have earlobes."

She stared at him without comprehension. "So do you. So does everybody."

"Not so. See our server over there? Look at her ears."

She turned her head to look at the young woman filling water glasses at a nearby table. "I still don't see what you're getting at."

"Notice the bottom of her ear—it goes straight down and attaches directly to the corner of her jaw. There's no lobe there, none at all."

"And your point is?"

"I think you can be trusted with what I'm about to tell you." He glanced around the restaurant and his voice assumed a confidential tone: "Two distinct humanoid species currently co-exist on this planet, those with earlobes and those without."

"What about those who are in-between?"

"Shhh . . . keep your voice down." He glanced around the restaurant again. "Lobeless extraterrestrials have covertly infiltrated Earth's population for millennia, interbreeding with Earthlings to create a hybrid race of half-lobed drones bent on world conquest."

"Sounds like a screenplay for a sci-fi movie," she said. "A low-budget one."

"Mock me if you must, but don't shut your eyes to the aliens' sinister plot. Know them by their lobelessness."

Livvy raised an eyebrow. "Jeff, you're a peculiar person."

He feigned being miffed. "All men of vision face ridicule. I shall not be deterred."

Their food arrived, and Livvy wasted no time on preliminaries, attacking hers with single-minded intensity, not talking, just making "umm" noises from time to time. After swallowing the last bite she sat back and appeared to stifle a gentle belch. "I was famished," she said.

He drank the last of his wine. "I didn't notice."

"I have one more question about your . . . theory. Do people without earlobes have other physical differences?"

"Sure they do, but the other differences are concealed by their clothes. I won't go into detail, but earlobes are not their only deficiency. We'll just leave it at that."

"Jeff, this evening has been . . . enlightening." She tilted her head to one side. "*Very* enlightening."

"Thanks. But getting back to you, besides your perfect, fully human earlobes, you do have another appealing quality."

"I'm holding my breath."

"You get all my jokes."

"It's a curse, not a blessing."

"You're a tough audience." He signaled for the check. "What do you say we get out of here before we're abducted by our server and her alien pals? I don't know how you feel about it, but I hate the idea of being probed."

"I take it back. You're not peculiar, you're totally insane."

"Nobody's perfect."

The blue neon sign was visible from two blocks away: STRAIGHT, NO CHASER. Below it, a marquee announced, "Live Jazz Thur-Sat, No Cover." They parked in front of the old brick building, under a street lamp. Jeff walked around and opened her door, which gave him another view of those legs. Most guys seemed to be breast men. He was a shoulder, arm, and leg man. Different strokes.

At the club's entrance he stopped and turned to her. "Wait a minute. This is a great setup for a joke. Listen to this: A gimp and an amnesiac go into a bar—"

Livvy rolled her eyes.

He held the door open for her. "Well, I do try."

They stood just inside the door for a moment, waiting for their eyes to adjust to the subdued lighting. Jeff pointed to an empty table for two against the wall and led her to it. They sat down just as the quartet was returning to the stage from a break and taking up their respective instruments—grand piano, alto saxophone, upright bass, and drums. The pianist counted off, and the band launched into a Monk tune, "I Need You." They followed up with a selection of jazz and Latin numbers, including "Stolen Moments," a samba called "Mas Que Nada," and an original up-tempo swing composed by the pianist.

Jeff glanced at his companion. Livvy's head was moving in time to the music as she listened intently. Her eyes were on the acoustic bass. That made sense, given that she played cello, a scaled-down bass. The fingers of her left hand moved on the fretboard of an imagined stringed instrument.

The sax player announced a tune as his "favorite Coltrane ballad" and slowly counted it off. The haunting melody was familiar; Jeff was trying to recall the name of the song when Livvy touched his arm. "'Naima,' right?"

Impressed, he nodded. Livvy was full of surprises. After the song ended he leaned over to her. "Is it possible you played some jazz in addition to classical music?"

After a moment of silent reflection, Livvy shrugged. "I guess it's possible. Wish I could remember."

The band took a break. The lanky, bearded sax player stopped by their table and talked with them, hardly taking his eyes off Livvy the entire time. She seemed disconcerted by the unexpected attention. Jeff winked at her. He really couldn't blame the guy; Livvy looked pretty spectacular. Her beauty made Beth's seem as artificial as a mannequin's.

"I thought something was wrong with me, the way he kept looking at me," Livvy said after the horn player left.

Jeff had to laugh. "That wasn't why he was looking at you, naive one. Has it escaped your notice that he's been gawking at you since we walked in?"

"Actually, I couldn't see his eyes very well until he sat down with us. He has small eyes."

"Take my word for it, those beebleberries he calls eyes were checking you out but good. My theory? He's an earlobe connoisseur and he's captivated by yours. As well he should be."

"Yeah," she said in a monotone. "Right."

"Or maybe it was your diamond earrings that caught his eye. What are they, a half-caret each?"

Livvy nodded. "They're Ellie's. She insisted I wear them tonight. She told me she thinks of me as a granddaughter, same as Leia. How sweet is that?"

"You won't find any sweeter."

The players returned to the bandstand and kicked off the third set with "Four," followed by a blistering rendition of "Cherokee" that ended to enthusiastic applause.

After that came "Bluesette," "Scrapple from the Apple," "Desifinado," and "You Don't Know What Love Is," after which Livvy leaned over and said, "I've enjoyed listening to the music, Jeff. In fact, I've enjoyed the whole evening."

"Me, too. And it's not over yet."

"Almost, though. Beebleberry Eyes just announced the last tune."

"You're pretty, but cruel."

"It's payback for the staring."

"He wasn't staring, he was leering. Big difference."

In the pickup, headed back toward the Southwest Hills, Livvy seemed elated. "I can't explain it, but everything they played was so familiar to me. I guess the amnesia didn't affect my connection with music."

Jeff nodded. "Stands to reason. Years of musical training have made it ingrained, like all the time I spent in an airplane cockpit did for me. Flying is automatic; I don't even have to think about it. It's probably the same with you and music."

"I've been worried that I'd lost it, afraid the amnesia had taken it from me along with everything else, but now . . . I'm hopeful I can still play."

He reached over and took her hand. "I'm sure you can play beautifully."

She leaned against him and laid her head on his shoulder. "So when are you going to take me flying?"

"How about tomorrow?"

"Sorry, can't tomorrow. Leia and Charlotte are going to help me get a cell phone and maybe look for a car."

"Saturday, then?"

"Saturday would be perfect."

"Great. We'll fly up to my strip in Colby for the afternoon. I'll show you my rustic little log cabin."

"I'm looking forward to it."

The Conovers' mailbox loomed in the headlights and he turned into the driveway. They saw no sign of activity when they reached the parking area. After shutting off the engine Jeff looked at his watch. Half past one.

Twenty feet from the entrance to the house Livvy said, "We have a chaperone."

"Hiya, Henry." Jeff kneeled down and scratched behind the dog's ears and received a sandpapery lick on his forearm.

In front of the door, Jeff turned to Livvy and in a smooth, well-modulated voice said, "Their eyes locked. They took a half-step toward each other, and she came neatly into his arms. Her mouth softened and her eyelids took on a sultry heaviness."

Livvy gave him an opaque stare.

Undaunted, he resumed the narrative: "He could feel her rapid heartbeat against his chest. In the kiss that followed, the tips of their tongues met in a ritual of invitation and acceptance. When they finally separated, her eyes were unfocused for a second or two."

"Is that from your sci-fi screenplay?"

He nodded. "It's a genre-bending sci-fi romance. A fully lobed Earthman falls in love with an earlobe-challenged alien girl."

"Innovative."

"In the interest of research, shouldn't we study how the characters would react to having the tips of their tongues meet in a ritual of invitation and acceptance?"

"Well, if it's for research . . ." She took a half-step toward him and came neatly into his arms.

He wasn't prepared for how sensuous the kiss would be. Neither was Livvy, if her rapid heartbeat was any indication. When they finally separated, her eyes were unfocused for a second or two.

He smiled at her. "Saturday."

"Saturday," she repeated.

He leaned over and kissed each diamond-studded earlobe in turn. "Goodnight."

In his last glimpse of her before the door closed, she was touching one of her earlobes. He did a quick calculation. Saturday was only thirty-five hours away, give or take.

32

S anjit stood and stretched. He was not surprised to see the other cubicles in the IT department were empty. Hardly anyone else worked late on Fridays, not if they could help it. He did not understand their work ethic. Sanjit worked late every chance he got. It was overtime, after all, and he appreciated the extra money. It enabled him to send more to his mother.

He was organizing a few documents before leaving for the night when his eyes fell on the printout of Marauder's code. Once again he felt a pang of guilt that bringing it to Mr. Morley's attention had resulted in Dennis being fired. True, Dennis had done a very bad thing, but Sanjit had not fore-seen that he would lose his job over it. He had assumed that, at worst, Dennis would be reprimanded.

The staff parking lot was full. Sanjit had trouble locating the white three-year-old Ford Focus he had bought from Thomason Ford in Beaverton. His friend Deepak was a salesman there and had arranged a "super-special deal" on the Focus. Still, the money it had cost him would be a fortune in India. He spotted a white top six rows over on the right and threaded his way between vehicles until he was beside his most excellent automobile.

He sensed rather than saw the figure that emerged swiftly from the shadows behind the car, but before he could cry out in alarm, he felt an unspeakable pain, pain such as he had never known, deep within his chest. A low voice spoke softly, intimately into his ear: "It's not nice to snitch."

He collapsed to the asphalt and time seemed to expand—microseconds became seconds, seconds became minutes. He had time enough to contemplate the terrible knowledge that the moment of his death was at hand.

He who is born begins to die. He who dies begins to live.

But the words of Swami Shivanand provided no comfort.

Regret that he would never be married or father children washed over him. He prayed to saguna Brahman that his soul be safely transmigrated. Sanjit's final thoughts were of his beloved mother, who would now be alone and destitute without her only son's assistance.

Like a panther downing a chital deer in the jungle, the blackness took him.

The responding unit's red and blue lights were visible from a block away. Karen parked her unmarked car on the street and walked to the scene. She was alone; Detweiler was back at the House, wrangling with Accounting about his PERS, his retirement account. Near the scene patrolmen Evans and Simmelink were talking with two nurses. Trying to get their phone numbers, probably.

Simmelink noticed her approaching. "Hey, Detective," he called out.

She acknowledged him with a nod and took out her notebook. "What's the skinny?"

He gave her the rundown: "A nurse who left after her shift discovered the body, almost tripped over it. She felt for a pulse, found none, and ran for security." Simmelink looked down at his notes. "The vic is Sanjit Rajaragavan, twenty-seven, originally from Baharampur, India, over here on a work visa, been here eleven months. He was a programmer in the hospital's IT department. Looks like he was ambushed as he was unlocking his car. We found his keys beside him.

One odd thing, he still had his wallet, eighty-six dollars still in it. Something must've spooked the perp before he could finish the job." He glanced over at his partner, still talking to the nurses. "We're canvassing, but looks like nobody else was in the parking lot at the time. The M.E. got here before you did."

"Thanks." She walked over to the body lying beside the Ford Focus. The medical examiner turned out to be Jon Wu. Karen had worked with him before; he was good at his job. "Hey, Jon."

He looked up. "Hey, Karen."

"What's the word?"

"Seems our vic got himself stabbed to death, by someone who knew what he was doing. The entrance wound was just under the sternum; the thrust was at an upward angle with a blade at least six-inches long, puncturing the pericardium and right ventricle, I'm guessing. Death was fairly quick, probably a matter of seconds, from hemorrhagic shock, possibly cardiac tamponade. T.O.D. around eleven. I'll know more after the postmortem."

"Okay, thanks, Jon."

The headlights from Evans' and Simmelink's squad car illuminated the area behind the victim's car. Karen immediately noticed three cigarette butts on the asphalt. Marlboros. They'd been stepped on. The Marlboro Man had spent some time there, patiently lying in wait.

She signaled for Evans to come over. "Keep everyone away from the car and the cars around it. I don't want any evidence contaminated." The C.S.U. team would photograph and bag the butts and check the cars for latent prints.

Before taking off, she decided to have one last look at the victim. Sanjit something, Simmelink had said. Poor devil. The expression on his face was a mixture of disbelief and sadness. She bent down and looked closer. Sanjit's cheeks were wet with tears.

She straightened up and started for the car, feeling depressed. It came with the job.

Chapman had trouble pouring the shot of bourbon, his hands were shaking so violently. After tossing it back he poured another. By the third or fourth shot—he'd lost count—he began to settle down a little.

How could it have happened? He asked himself the question over and over.

Killing the Indian punk had seemed like a good idea at the time. The little snitch needed killing for getting his nephew fired, and he was glad to do his sister's kid the solid, unasked. Nobody could say he wasn't loyal to family. The way he figured it, as long as he was getting rid of abominations—four, so far—why not also do a favor for a relative?

But he hadn't been prepared for what happened when he slid the thin blade into the man's heart: He came. Intensely. It sickened him afterward. True, each time he'd snuffed one of the abominations the act had been accompanied by a teeth-grinding orgasm. He'd considered it a reward for carrying out the task and anticipated it eagerly. But the snitch was male, an ordinary man. To get sexual pleasure from killing a *man* made him feel unclean. Made him feel like a fucking faggot.

He sat staring at the empty shot glass. The bourbon was smoothing the rough edges, but it hadn't touched the sick feeling in the pit of his stomach. It remained, because he had bigger problems than involuntary orgasms. He'd realized while driving home that he had screwed up, big-time. He'd planned to collect his cigarette butts before he left the parking lot. But he wasn't thinking clearly and spaced it. A careless mistake like that could land his ass on death row. Like all felons in the state of Oregon, his DNA was on file in CODIS, the national DNA database. Sure as shit, the cops would match it with the DNA on the butts. And he couldn't swear he hadn't touched one of the cars, he'd been so rattled.

He hammered the dinette table top with his fist, causing the shot glass and half-empty bottle of bourbon to dance around on the Formica. He felt like puking. Instead, he poured another shot and downed it. He was royally fucked.

Or maybe not . . .

He bowed his head and prayed for deliverance. He promised it wouldn't happen again, straying from the path. His activities would be confined to the holy work that lay ahead, the fulfillment of his sacred mission. Before long he received a reply. It wasn't a voice, exactly, but he heard it loud and clear:

Be not afraid, for I am with thee.

The fear and the panic drained out of him. The best thing he could do was chill, look at things coolly and logically. Somewhere he'd heard that a DNA match through CODIS could take a month or more. A lot could happen in a month. By that time he'd have delivered retribution and salvation to four more abominations, figuring one a week.

But first he needed to take care of another little matter. Some of his shit was still in his room at the Centurian Plaza. He'd been putting off getting it, because those other . . . obligations had kept him busy. When it came right down to it, the only thing in the room he cared about was his watch. Not that it was worth much, but his mother had given it to him and it had sentimental value. Everything else was replaceable. Going back there to get it would be dicey, but it was worth the risk.

The situation was straight out of *Pulp Fiction.* But unlike Butch Coolidge, Chapman had the protection of the Divine.

33

Jeff was pleased. His passenger seemed filled with childlike delight. En route up the Gorge from Troutdale to Colby, the view from the air clearly enchanted Livvy.

"Everything is so beautiful from up here," she said. "Such a feeling of freedom."

"You get a different perspective from five thousand feet."

"Jeff, look down there." She pointed out the Piper Cherokee's side window at the Columbia River below. "What are those? They look like miniature sailboats." From that altitude the objects of her attention looked like tiny triangles skimming over the water.

"Windsurfing, also known as sailboarding. They're basically surfboards with sails. The water's cold as hell, so their riders wear wetsuits. The Columbia Gorge is the windsurfing capital of the world."

"They seem to be going fast. They're leaving wakes."

"The winds get pretty fierce down there. If you ask me, those guys are nuts."

"They'd probably think the same about us, cavorting around the sky in this contraption."

"Point taken."

Jeff began the descent a few miles from the airport, visible directly ahead. He pointed through the windshield. "That's where we'll be landing in about five minutes."

"It looks really tiny from up here." She sounded concerned.

"The runway is twenty-nine hundred feet long; more than adequate." He didn't mention that the fifty-foot pine trees at both ends made the runway's almost three-thousand-foot length a requirement.

He switched the radio to 122.7 and reached for the mic. "Colby unicom, this is Cherokee Four Seven Whiskey, three miles out due west at one thousand, inbound. How's it looking, Pauly?"

The reply took a long ten seconds. *"Sorry, Jeff. I was out in the hangar working on the 150. One magneto was tits-up, just like you thought, so I installed the replacement. Anyway, the wind is— let me have a look-see—zero eight zero at one five. Looks like you're golden for a straight-in."*

"Thanks, Pauly. See you in a few."

By the time he added carb heat and flaps, the runway looming ahead looked considerably longer and wider than before, which seemed to reassure Livvy. He tried to grease it on to impress his passenger, but as luck would have it, a sudden downdraft caused the Cherokee to drop to the runway with a teeth-jarring bump that made him groan with embarrassment. Fortunately, Livvy was craning her neck to look around and didn't seem to notice.

They taxied up to the tie-down area and Jeff switched off the magnetos and master switch. As always, the sudden silence was eerie. He reached above Livvy's head and rotated the latch that opened the airplane's single door. Then, in that peculiar, impersonal tone favored by flight attendants everywhere, he said, "Thank you for flying Longcypher Airways, ladies and gentlemen. Please make sure that all cigarettes are extinguished and no belongings are left behind. You may deplane using the exit to your right."

"You forgot to say, 'Bub-bye.'"

She climbed out of the cockpit, stepping gingerly on the abrasive strip on the part of the wing next to the fuselage, and hopped nimbly down to the concrete. Jeff climbed out and closed and latched the cockpit door.

The sign on the door of the office said, "Flight Operations Center," which was hyperbole, considering the size of the airport, but it sounded pleasingly official. The stocky man inside the office was leaning back in his chair with his big boots propped on the desk when Jeff and Livvy walked in. Several things about the man's appearance—the bushy beard, the long ponytail down his back, the tie-dyed T-shirt visible at the neck opening of his coveralls—attested that he was a stubborn Love Generation holdout. Nevertheless, he was also an experienced A&E and Jeff's right-hand man at the airport. He lived in the small apartment over the office with his dog.

"Livvy, I'd like you to meet Pauly Dupree, formerly a roadie for the Grateful Dead—I'm not kidding—and currently the man who helps me keep my airplanes flying."

"Hey, Livvy," Pauly said, getting to his feet. "Any friend of Jeff's."

"Nice to meet you," she told him as she shook his permanently grease-stained paw.

A small white dog with a brown spot over one eye and one brown ear came around the desk, growling and baring his teeth at Livvy.

"Jerry!" Pauly shouted at the dog. "She's a friend." To Livvy, he said, "Jerry Garcia's a little antisocial around strangers. Let him sniff you. That's it. He won't bother you now."

"He's a Jack Russell terrier, right?" Livvy bent down to scratch his rump at the base of his tail. The dog stood transfixed in a wide-legged stance, a faraway look in his eyes.

"Right. He's my wingman."

"We flew up from Portland for the afternoon," Jeff said. "I'm going to show Livvy around the airport and then feed her a late lunch before we fly back."

"Groovy. Think I'll go upstairs and relax a while."

Pauly's relaxation almost always involved herbal assistance. It was of no concern to Jeff. Pauly had another unicom radio up there and could handle the occasional call, no matter how "relaxed" he was.

Jeff escorted Livvy through the metal-clad hangar next to the office and pointed out his other airplanes: a Cessna 150, used for rentals and flying lessons, and a twin-engined Piper Apache, used mostly for the infrequent charter. At the far end of the hangar he paused in front of a padlocked door.

"Now I'm going to show you my baby." He unlocked the padlock and gave the hangar door a shove; it slid sideways on its tracks until the opening was wide enough for them to enter. He flicked the light switch. A sleek white craft with gold accents seemed to crouch there, gleaming under the overhead lights.

"This," he said, "is a Lancair Evolution. Retractable gear, composite construction, very high-tech. It was a kit, manufactured in Redmond, Oregon. Uncle Pete managed to get it about seventy-five percent complete before he got sick; Pauly and I have been working on it for several years off and on, and now it's close to being finished. I just had it painted, and Pauly's installing the avionics. Then it'll be ready for its maiden flight."

"Okay, I'm impressed." Livvy said. "It's really beautiful. So shiny and sleek."

"That's what *she* said. Sorry, couldn't help myself. As for this airplane, it should perform like a light jet. It's turbocharged, and the cabin is pressurized. It can cruise at three hundred knots at twenty-eight thousand feet." He caressed the engine cowling. "She's my baby."

"The way you're fondling her makes that abundantly clear. Honestly, though, your love interest looks a little flighty."

The silly pun got a laugh out of him and reinforced his feeling that Livvy was a keeper. Which was not to presume she wanted to be kept. He said, "Next on the tour is my rustic little log cabin, hand-hewn by Uncle Pete. That is where we shall fortify ourselves with tasty victuals. Hungry?"

"God, yes. My stomach is growling."

He put his arm around her waist and they walked up the path that led to his cabin.

"Here we are," Jeff said as they emerged from the path. "Home sweet home."

Livvy stopped walking. Jeff's references to his "hand-hewn, rustic little log cabin" had conjured up an image of a primitive one-room cabin in the woods, but this structure was big and certainly not primitive. It was constructed of logs, true, but large windows gave it contemporary look, as did the skylights in its green metal roof.

"Your uncle built that?"

"Log by log. C'mon."

A covered porch ran the full width of the cabin's front. Suspended from the porch's roof with sturdy chains was a wooden bench swing wide enough for two people.

"Hey!" Livvy shouted. "Hey now . . ." She ran up the half-log steps, sat down, and began swinging.

Timing the swings, Jeff got in beside her. "This was my idea. I like to sit out here in the evening, nurse a beer and listen to the night. I don't usually swing much."

"Good thing you're not a jazz musician." She indicated the dense surrounding forest with a sweeping motion. "Your uncle must have wanted privacy."

"He appreciated what a rare and precious commodity it is. After living here, so do I." He hopped off the swing. "C'mon, I'll show you the inside."

After he unlocked the front door, Jeff pushed it open and waved her inside ahead of him. Her first impression was of a lot of wood—knotty pine walls and ceiling, plain pine floor, cedar trim. Thick area rugs and comfortable-looking brown leather furniture softened the interior considerably. Double doors made of wood and glass opened to a cedar deck with a majestic view of the Columbia River, visible also from the large living room window. Jeff pointed at the loft overlooking the living room. "The mawster's bedchamber. Veddy posh."

"That's possibly the worst British accent ever."

"Pretty harsh, kiddo. I was using a dialect from a remote region in northern England. I'm having a problem with the fricatives."

"Well, it was frickin' lame. No offense."

Jeff laughed. "None taken."

In addition to the living room, the ground floor had two bedrooms, one for guests and the other utilized as an office. Like the walls and ceiling, the kitchen cupboards were knotty pine. It was a lot of knotty pine, but she liked its warmth. An assortment of copper pans and utensils hung from hooks above a center island. The appliances—refrigerator, stove, dish washer—were stainless steel.

"It's great," she said. "Perfect."

"That's the way I feel about it too."

"Don't tell Floyd, but I prefer your house to his. It's cozier."

"Maybe so, but when my knee was really hurting I would have traded one of the airplanes for an elevator like his." He touched her elbow. "Would you excuse me a minute? I'm just going to trot down and get the mail. Make yourself at home."

After he left she noticed the cane in the umbrella rack by the door. There was a bounce to his step lately, so she wouldn't be surprised if the cane remained in the rack. She explored the room, looking at the paintings of old biplanes on the walls, some large-leaved plants, a pair of conga drums on a stand in one corner, a yellowed Martin acoustic guitar, an oak bookcase full of old books, and shelves filled with vinyl albums, mostly jazz. She was about to inspect the books when a giant cat with black-tipped gray fur entered the room through a partly open door to the deck.

"Hello," she said. "And who might you be?"

The huge cat produced a growl that sounded to Livvy like "Ralph." It strolled up to her and carefully sniffed her ankle. That done, the feline inspected her face with a laser stare for a moment, and then it began stropping her leg insistently, alternating sides. Livvy bent over and gently scratched the top of his head and received the cat's closed-eyed, purring approval.

Jeff returned, a stack of unopened mail in his hand. "I see you've met Ralph."

"Ralph," the cat echoed.

"He strolled in like he owned the place and introduced himself. How old is he?"

"About three. He was just a kitten when he showed up on my doorstep. He announced his name when I opened the door. Turned out to be a big sonofagun, didn't he?"

"He's beautiful."

Jeff kneeled and stroked the cat, and its fur undulated in response. "Loves human contact." He gave the animal a final firm pat on its flank and stood up. The cat pounced on a red ball near the bookcase and brought it to Jeff, dropping it at his feet. "He fetches. Watch this." Jeff picked up the ball and tossed it across the room. Ralph bounded after it and trapped it with his front paws. After dropping the ball at Jeff's feet again the cat backed away, looking expectant.

"Come on," Livvy said. "That's a dog in a cat costume."

"Hear that, Ralph? The jig's up." Jeff indulged the cat with another toss and then bent down and scratched him between the ears. "That's all for now, big guy." Jeff straightened up and nodded in the direction of the kitchen. "What do you say we rustle up that lunch I promised you?"

"Now you're talking."

After he washed his hands at the kitchen sink, Jeff opened the refrigerator and began taking things out and handing them to Livvy. "Let's see, we have breast of turkey. We have three kinds of cheese—provolone, pepper jack, and sharp cheddar. We have fresh sprouts, avocado, tomatoes, and onions. We have crisp kosher dills. We have mayonnaise and Dijon mustard. We have coarse sourdough bread. For beverages we have wine and beer. And for dessert we have"—he held it up for her inspection—"cheesecake."

"Yummy. Except I'll pass on the turkey. A veggie san will do just fine."

"Sorry, I forgot. One veggie special, coming right up."

"Allow me to assist, doctor."

In short order they constructed two splendid, but laughably thick, sandwiches.

"Beer or wine?"

"Beer, please."

They decided to eat on the deck, at a table with a top made from a cross section of a tree that had been four feet in diameter. Eating the thick sandwiches proved to be a challenge, but they tasted every bit as good as they looked, they agreed, and the beer was a perfect complement.

While they ate, Livvy told him all about the new Subaru Forester she'd purchased the day before, with Leia's and Charlotte's help. It was gorgeous, a striking metallic gray-green. Unfortunately, she'd had to leave it at the dealership while her bank in Boston made arrangements for payment and insurance coverage.

The bank was also handling other matters for her, getting all her credit cards and documentation replaced, with the exception of her Oregon driver's license. She would need to appear in person at the DMV to get a replacement license. Mr. Cavenaugh had seemed anxious to assist her in any way possible, even offering to send someone from Boston, which she declined. He made her promise to contact him if she had any problems whatsoever.

It had been necessary to call him that very afternoon, when Verizon refused to let her buy a phone without a credit card. She asked the store manager to phone Cavenaugh. As the manager talked to the banker, his attitude seemed to morph from aloof unconcern to fawning supplication. After he hung up, the manager went back to the stockroom and reappeared smiling broadly, holding a box that contained her new phone. Besides giving the Conovers and the Dunklemans her new cell number, she gave it to the hospital, in case they needed to get hold of her for something.

"Anyway, that's what I did yesterday," she said, wiping the last few crumbs from the corner of her mouth with her napkin.

He pointed to her empty plate. "Get enough to eat?"

"God, yes. I'm going to hold off for a while on that cheese-cake."

He started to say something but a loud thunderclap, followed by a lengthy rumble, silenced him. They looked to the west, the direction the thunder had come from, and saw a tower of dark clouds.

"Will you look at that. It's the 'small, contained front' that wasn't supposed to get here until early tomorrow morning, according to ATIS."

"Can you fly in that kind of weather?"

"I can, but I'd rather not, given a choice."

"So I guess we won't be flying back this evening like we planned."

"I can drive you back in my truck, though."

"Or I could stay in your guest room tonight, and we can fly back tomorrow, after the storm passes through. If you wouldn't mind having a guest, that is."

"Would you rather do that?"

"I think I would. I was really looking forward to the flight back."

"You got it, kiddo. *Mi casa es su casa.*"

"*Gracias, señor.*"

"*Usted es recepción, señorita.*"

34

Karen listened outside the basement apartment before knocking. She could hear the television through the door, which meant someone was probably inside. She rapped on the door, and a few moments later an eye regarded her through a one-inch crack.

"Mr. Stingler?"

"Yes?" His voice had a nasal quality.

"Detective Wojanowski, Portland Police." She flashed her badge and ID. "Do you have a few minutes? I'd like to ask you a few questions."

"What about?"

"May I come in?"

"Sure, I guess." He opened the door wider to allow her to enter.

Inside, the apartment was dark; thick curtains covered the high, small windows.

"Mind if I sit down?" She had a choice between a well-used sofa or a chrome-legged dinette chair covered in vinyl with a design like a faded pizza supreme. She picked the sofa. After she sat down she sized up his lair. Posters on the wall, elaborate computer setup, several game consoles next to a large-screen television, and stacks of *Gamer* magazines. The guy was a geek's geek. "To answer your question, Mr. Stingler, I'm hoping you can help us."

Stingler turned a dinette chair backward and straddled it, resting his crossed arms on its back. "Help you how?"

"Hopefully, in our investigation of the murder of a former colleague of yours, Sanjit Rajaragavan."

"I heard about it on the news. Tragic."

Karen looked him over. His face reminded her of a hamster her daughter once had. "Can you think of anyone who might have had a grudge against Mr. Rajaragavan, someone he was having problems with?"

"Besides me, you mean? Look, I'm not an idiot, Detective. You're here, so you must've talked to Morley or somebody from the hospital. You probably already know I got fired after Sanjit ran to Morley and tattled on me. I was plenty angry at him, sure, but I didn't snuff the guy."

"Then you won't have a problem accounting for your whereabouts Friday night around ten-thirty." She shrugged. "Sorry. Have to ask."

Stingler's smile was smug. "I was here, gaming online. *Realm of Warlords.* My clan raided a rival clan Friday night. They hit us a couple of weeks ago so we hit them back."

"Sounds kind of violent."

"It's just a game," he said, irritation in his tone. "The violence is only virtual."

"Your fellow gamers can attest that you participated in this raid?"

"About two dozen of them. If you want, I can give you their online names."

"Were there any witnesses to the fact that you were here at the time, using that specific computer?" She pointed to the machine across the room.

"My mom brought me a piece of pie between nine-thirty and ten. After that I was here alone, gaming until three a.m. or so. The *Realm* server logs players' IP addresses and time-stamps all logins and logouts. That should prove I was here."

"Isn't it possible to program a bot to take a player's place in a game, so it looks to the other players like a human is playing?" She'd read about gamers using bots in a *Huffington*

Post article. She could almost see the wheels turning as he tried to figure out how much she knew about computers and gaming.

"Sure, it's theoretically possible," he said. "But I did my own playing."

She switched gears. "You were fired over something you did. Tell me about it."

He shrugged. "I wrote a server script that scanned users' email, looking for certain words. Morley couldn't understand that it had a legitimate purpose."

"Which was?"

"Tracking down missing email. It was just a utility, a tool programmed to look for specific words in email. It could have been very useful to the IT department, but Morley was too incompetent to see that. Trust me, most upper-echelon IT administrators are totally clueless."

"So you think you didn't deserve to be fired?"

"You better believe it, Detective. And when my attorney is finished with those weasels, they'll regret it." Stingler made a sound that might have been a chuckle.

"What was the name of your utility?"

His smile faded. "I called it 'Marauder.'"

"Marauder. As in roaming around in search of spoils? Kind of an odd name for a utility, wouldn't you say?" She gave him the X-ray Stare.

"I had to name it something." He glared at her for several seconds before lowering his eyes.

"What were the words you programmed Marauder to look for?"

Stingler hesitated. "Well, this is sort of embarrassing, but for the test run I used 'genital' as the target string."

"So Marauder went looking for any mention of genital in hospital employees' email?"

"Just as a test, like I said. But Sanjit discovered it and made a beeline to Morley. And then that moron fired me without giving me a chance to explain." His head hung down. "That's about it."

"Why that one particular doctor's mail, a Dr.—" She looked at her notes. "Dr. Soong?"

Stingler hesitated again. A patina of moisture glistened on his forehead. "My script happened to find the target string in Soong's email first. After that, I had it scan only her email, so I could fine-tune the code.

"Do you have copies of the email Marauder intercepted?"

"Nope, deleted them. There wasn't anything special about them. No reason to keep them."

He'd said it casually and convincingly, and Karen didn't believe a word of it. Regardless, there wasn't probable cause to get a warrant to seize his computer, and anyway she didn't like Stingler for the homicide. He was a cyberspace Peeping Tom who spied on his fellow employees' mail, but she didn't make him for a killer.

She stood. "Okay, Mr. Stingler, I think that'll do it. For now."

He walked with her to the door and opened it. "Look, I'm real sorry for Sanjit. Nobody deserves that. But honest, I didn't even learn about it until I heard it on the news."

She paused in the open doorway. "One more thing—do you smoke cigarettes?"

He shook his head. "No way. Never have, never will."

"Very wise. Thank you for your time, Mr. Stingler." *You ferret-faced geek.*

"Glad to help."

After the door closed behind the detective, Stingler mentally replayed the conversation. At first it had seemed like she considered him a suspect. Probably a standard interview technique—try to rattle him and see how he reacted. He held his own pretty well, all in all. People tended to underestimate him, and that was in his favor. The detective apparently wasn't aware of the contents of Soong's email, also in his favor. No way in hell was he going to give up something that valuable. It was money in the bank, if he played it right.

But it *was* strange about Sanjit. Stingler felt guilty about the fantasies of offing the little bastard himself. But someone else did the deed. Probably a crackhead after money for drugs. Whoever did it, Sanjit was history. Stingler smiled. Sanjit was always talking about "karma." *There's your karma, dude. Enjoy.*

He picked up the remote and switched on the TV. On-screen a pair of wheeled robots, one with a circular saw attachment and the other with a large mallet, were furiously trying to hammer and saw each other into piles of metallic junk.

"Cool," he said and sat down to watch the battle.

35

The first rays of morning light streamed through the loft's skylight as she lay beside him. He was on his left side facing her, eyes tightly closed, a Breathe Right strip across his nose. He couldn't breathe at night without one, he'd told her. As she lay there, the previous night's events played on a continuous loop inside her head.

It had not been a foregone conclusion that they would end up in bed together, despite the undercurrent of sexual tension between them. She realized early in the evening that something was amiss. Jeff's manner changed abruptly, from casual affection to formal courtesy. He carefully maintained his distance, physically and otherwise. Not that he wasn't cordial, even affable, but his conversation and attempts at humor seemed stiff and forced. Either he was moody as hell or some as-yet-unknown factor was in play. Whichever it was, she was baffled.

The reality was, she hadn't known him very long at all, only a little over a month. It seemed longer. Until that evening he'd been close to perfect—intelligent, funny, and self-effacing. But maybe he was *too* perfect. Maybe now she was seeing another side of him, a darker side. She studied him as he stood at the sink washing their lunch dishes. ("As the guest, you just relax while I do the honors," he told her when she started to wash them.)

After seeing a "Network busy" message on her phone an aggravating four times, she finally managed to get through to Leia to let her know she wouldn't be back that night, due to the storm. True to form, Leia remarked on her good fortune to have the weather be so cooperative with her love life. Livvy glanced over at Jeff, who was drying his hands with a kitchen towel. "Not necessarily."

Leia jumped on that. "What's the matter? Trouble in paradise already?"

"I'll be home tomorrow," Livvy said. (Subtext: "—and I'll fill you in then.")

Leia, dependably quick on the uptake, dropped it. "Grandma's looking forward to playing a duet with you. She mentioned it to me again this morning."

Ellie was serious about music. The 100-year-old Steinway grand in the Conover's conservatory was a testament to her commitment. When Livvy suggested they play a piano-cello duet sometime, Ellie couldn't hide her excitement.

"Well, tomorrow night might be a possib—" The phone in Livvy's hand vibrated and chimed simultaneously, startling her. "Just a sec," she told Leia. The on-screen alert informed her she had a new text message, from 555-505-0447. She read the message:

```
i no something about u that u dont no
```

Livvy raised the phone to her ear. "I just got my first text message. It's pretty strange." She read the message to Leia and described the abbreviated spelling.

"It could be cell phone spam," Leia said. "It's becoming a real nuisance. You know—computers dial cell numbers one after the other and eventually they hit yours."

"What if they really do have some information about me? Maybe they expect me to call them back."

"Yeah, but what if it's some creep?"

Livvy chewed on her lower lip a moment. "Good point. I'll just ignore it."

"That's probably best."

"Anyway, see you tomorrow, weather permitting. Tell Ellie to get her fingers warmed up."

"Okie-doke, girlfriend. See you then. Hope your evening improves."

"Thanks. 'Bye." After tapping the "End Call" button, Livvy read the cryptic text message again before blanking the screen. Too bad the very first one on her new phone had to be something strange. She joined Jeff in the living room, anticipating more oddly formal behavior from him.

They sipped wine, nibbled on cheesecake, and listened to music. During a Latin number he went over to the conga drums in the corner and began playing along. He was an enthusiastic, but terrible, conga player.

"Ask me if I care," he said. "It's cathartic." At least he'd dropped the weirdness for a few minutes.

A bit later the blaze in the fireplace began to make the room uncomfortably warm, so they opened the doors to the deck. The rain had temporarily let up and the night coolness felt marvelously refreshing. They walked around to the front porch and sat on the swing for a while, watching the fog creep stealthily toward them.

"In flying, this is what's called 'below minimums,'" he told her.

And still there was the odd dynamic between them.

Around eleven, after she stifled a second yawn, Jeff disappeared for a few minutes and came back carrying a folded towel and washcloth, a new toothbrush still in its wrapper, a traveler-sized tube of toothpaste, and a faded blue T-shirt she assumed came from his seemingly inexhaustible supply of well-worn casual clothes.

"Thought you might need something to sleep in," he said. "C'mon, I'll show you to your accommodations."

At the doorway to the guest room, he gave her a brief kiss on the lips, told her goodnight, and left her standing there, bewildered. In a minute she heard him climb the stairs to the loft. She shrugged and undressed and then slipped the oversized T-shirt on over her head. It was long enough to cover her hips, and it had the kind of softness that comes from many launderings. After she brushed her teeth in the guest room's small bathroom she turned back the bedcovers and slipped between the cool sheets. She started to switch off the bedside lamp and then wondered whether she could get by without a glass of water on the bedside stand in case she got thirsty during the night.

"No way," she said, pushing back the covers.

She padded out to the dark kitchen in her bare feet and took a drinking glass from the cupboard. She was filling it at the sink when she felt a cold draft. One of the glass-paned doors to the deck was slightly ajar. Beyond it, a pale, ghostly figure was standing on the deck. She crept forward to get a better look. The apparition turned out to be Jeff, shirtless in the brisk night air, doing what looked like deep breathing exercises. She remained frozen, watching him. Illuminated by moonlight, his upper body, while not flabby, seemed a bit soft—

She realized suddenly that he was looking through the glass directly at her.

He pulled his shirt on over his head and then pushed the door open and stepped into the room, one eyebrow raised in inquiry.

"I felt a draft," she said. *Lame.*

He looked at her without speaking, his mouth a thin, straight line. Finally he said, "You have no idea how difficult the past few hours have been for me. And now—well, look at you. That's just great."

Her reflection in the dark glass of one of the doors reminded her that she was wearing only an oversized T-shirt and panties. Nevertheless, she wasn't self-conscious, so much as perplexed. "Excuse me?"

"You don't have the slightest idea what I'm talking about, do you?"

"Well . . . all evening I had the impression you didn't want me here. Is that what you mean?"

"Oh, dear Jesus . . ." His expression was pained. "No. I was trying to be considerate. After all, you're spending the night in my house due to circumstances beyond your control. I wanted to make absolutely sure you wouldn't feel like you were under any obligation to . . ."

She stared at him for long seconds. "Wait a minute. You mean that's why you were distant all night? Out of consideration for me?" She shook her head wonderingly. "Well, it threw me a curve. I felt like I was intruding in your native habitat."

He groaned. "I'm sorry, I guess I went overboard, but only because I didn't want to put you on the spot. Dammit, I'm not some craven opportunist, pressing my home-court advantage for a quick sexual conquest. I decided if something physical happened between us on my turf, it had to be your idea. The ball was in your court. Does that make sense?" His expression pleaded for understanding.

"I guess I should be grateful that you have such regard for my honor." She took a step toward him. "There must be some way I can show my appreciation for such chivalrous behavior."

His blank expression told her he didn't comprehend, so she took his hand and led him to the stairs to the loft, astonished at her own boldness.

The king-sized bed in the loft was directly under a skylight. They stood next to it and looked up. The clouds had parted and the stars were visible.

"The Pleiades," Jeff said, pointing. "The daughters of Atlas, fleeing from the attentions of Orion the Hunter."

"Poor Orion."

Wordlessly, they turned toward each other. The kiss was tender and unhurried. Then Jeff placed his hands on her shoulders and held her at arm's length.

"Last chance to change your mind. What if you find out you were a nun before the coma?"

"You think a Hail Mary or two would set things right?"

"Sounds plausible to me." He removed his T-shirt and stripped off his jeans. He pointed to his shorts. "White cotton briefs, J.C. Penny."

"*Très chic.*" She peeled off the oversized T-shirt, dropped it at her feet, and stood there wearing only her panties. "Victoria's Secret, compliments of Charlotte and Leia."

"My god, girl, that body is amazing—not even a trace of flab. Makes me feel self-conscious." He pinched the softness around his middle and clucked his tongue.

"Maybe it's time you stepped up your ... physical activity."

He pulled her to him. During the kiss that followed she leaned against him for balance. That turned out to be a mistake. They fell sideways onto the bed and she struck her head solidly on the wooden headboard with a resounding, hollow *bonk!* like a sound effect in a slapstick movie.

"Oh god, Livvy, I'm so sorry! Are you all right?"

She touched the back of her head gingerly. "I'm not in a coma this time. I think that's a good sign."

"I agree." He threw back the covers and slid in. Then he held out his hand in invitation.

The sheets' coolness against her bare legs and torso contrasted with the heat radiating from Jeff's body. He reached for her. The touch of his body against hers felt incredibly intimate, like a full-length kiss. She was luxuriating in the sensation when he flinched.

"What's wrong?"

He tossed back the covers and examined his ankle. Then he reached over and felt the edge of one of her toenails. "Dangerous weapon you got there, kiddo."

"My turn to apologize." She had intended to trim her toenails after her morning shower but she'd forgotten. *What a dummy.*

"Forget it. Now we're even. Hand me one of those tissues?" He took it from her and held pressure on the wound until the bleeding stopped. "I think the prognosis is good," he said, and tossed the wad of tissue at a trash can in the corner, missing by a good four feet. Then he lay back and turned his head to look at her.

The comical aspects of the night's events, culminating in their clumsy attempts at intimacy, reminded her of a pair of clowns smacking each other with rubber bladders until they both fell down. She started laughing. After a shocked pause, Jeff joined in. They held each other and laughed until tears ran down their cheeks.

"I guess we're not great lovers," he said, gasping for breath, "in the classic sense." After his breathing returned to normal, he shifted onto his side, looking serious. "Livvy, surely you've had sex before?"

It was a good question, one she'd asked herself. The answer was hidden within the impenetrable fog, along with the answers to all the other questions. She shrugged. "I'm twenty-five years old. Is it possible I'm still a virgin?"

"Possible, but not likely these days. Not that it would be a bad thing. Doesn't matter to me either way." He took her hand in his. "Would you rather just forget it for tonight? Before we both need medical attention?"

It sounded to her like that would be his preference. "Maybe that's best."

"Let's just snuggle instead, before we go to sleep." He kissed her forehead and lay back.

Her mind whirling with a mixture of disappointment and relief, she lay close beside him, her body cradled between his side and his left arm, her head resting on his shoulder. They lay together in that fashion, not talking, for perhaps twenty minutes.

Just when she was sure he'd fallen asleep, he whispered, "Livvy?"

"Yes?" she whispered back.

"Were you asleep?"

"No. Why are we whispering?"

"I don't know," he whispered. In a normal voice he said, "I was just thinking about how natural this feels."

She turned her head to look at him. "Are you disappointed we didn't make love?"

"Honestly? Yes. But not because I missed a sexual conquest. If all I wanted was sex, it wouldn't be hard to find. Two pieces of meat rubbing together, pleasant friction, a quick release. Just a mechanical exercise, as impersonal as shaking hands and about as significant. When two people make love it should mean something. Otherwise, it's not worth the time it takes."

And that was exactly right. Simply and succinctly, it summed up how she felt about it as well. "I agree."

"If we make love," he said, "it will be when the time is right. It will be a natural physical expression of our feelings for each other."

She found his hand and squeezed it. On her mind's holodeck a brass band played and the virtual night sky lit up with spectacular fireworks.

Conversation at a lull, they lay there under the skylight, each with their own thoughts. With his left hand, Jeff caressed her abdomen in a distracted, offhand manner, his fingertips light as a moth's wings. She was very aware of the touch of his body along the length of her, as if her skin in those areas had become hypersensitive, and there was a sensation of electricity flowing between them. The feeling of closeness was a welcome antidote to the isolation she'd been feeling since waking from the coma. It was all the intimacy she needed.

It boggled the mind, the sequence of unlikely events that had to occur for her to wind up there, lying beside one of the most sensitive, thoughtful, considerate guys in the world. But the chain of chance happenings that had thrown them together, starting with the carjacking—or perhaps the sequence started when she left Boston for Portland—at any rate, if either event hadn't happened, she and Jeff wouldn't have met that September afternoon at OMRI's swimming pool. Of course, she didn't suspect then that he would turn out to be such a—

Her breath caught in her throat ... then caught once more ... and yet again, in syncopation with his caresses, which no longer seemed distracted or offhand. She sat up and leaned over him and looked into his eyes from inches away. The stars above were reflected in the blackness of his pupils. She kissed him.

He said, "I thought—" Another insistent kiss left no doubt about her intention. "Okay, I give up," he said and pulled her to him. His tongue sought hers. She trapped the intruder between her front teeth, and he waited patiently until she released it.

Her sharp intake of breath marked their joining.

It was like the intimacy she had felt lying beside him, magnified a hundred times. A thousand. If just lying next to him could keep the feelings of isolation at bay, this was the cure. An ultimate closeness. They were no longer separate people; they were conjoined, possessing nine limbs, two pair of eyes, three greedy mouths. Time ceased to be a meaningful concept. There was only the timeless *now*. Waves of sensation grew in intensity until at last her body arched and she heard herself cry out as if from a distance. Still entwined, they floated in the euphoric afterglow, energy spent, appetites sated, secrets known.

Jeff was first to speak. "That," he said, "makes what I'm about to say redundant, but what the hell, I'll say it anyway— I love you." He put his index finger to her lips, silencing her response before it could begin. "You don't have to say anything. I just wanted you to know how I feel."

So she took his hand and kissed each knuckle and then pulled him to her and kissed his mouth tenderly. How on Earth had she found such a perfect guy? Was it some sort of cosmic balancing of the scales, with the coma and amnesia on one side and Jeff on the other? If so, the tradeoff was well worth the cost. She was content to lie in his arms, enveloped in his body's subtle musk, which, she drowsily realized, smelled like ... cinnamon. Just as she was dropping off to sleep, she thought she heard him whisper, "I'm going to marry you, Livvy," but it could easily have been the beginning of a dream.

She slept.

This morning she'd been awake for—actually, she wasn't sure how long she'd been lying there, reliving the previous night. It seemed like hours. The light in the loft had increased considerably since she first woke up. Water droplets from the previous night's rain speckled the skylight above the bed, each a tiny prism that projected its rainbow spectrum onto the skylight's interior surfaces. It was really quite lovely.

Her bed partner stirred and she turned her head to look at him. His eyes opened slightly and then closed against the light. "Mmmm . . . timezit?" he asked, yawning.

She raised up and looked at the clock on the night stand. "A little after seven."

He rubbed his eyes with his knuckles and propped himself up on one elbow to face her. "How would you feel about a good-morning kiss?" he asked with a sleepy grin.

"Depends. How do you feel about morning breath?" She figured hers could probably peel paint.

"Not to worry." Jeff leaned across her and opened the drawer of the bedside stand, in the process abrading her bare shoulder with the stubble on his cheek. He removed a container of Tic-Tacs, dispensed one to her, and popped one in his mouth.

"Mmmmm," she said. The peppermint-flavored kiss that followed was sweet in multiple dimensions.

"I guess breakfast can wait a while," he said.

Isolation—what isolation?

36

Karen returned from the restroom to find Detweiler standing beside her desk, looking around for her. "Hey, Carl."

"Woj, you'll be interested to hear that AFIS got a hit on the print C.S.U. lifted from the Indian guy's car. Turns out it belongs to one Jimmy Chapman, thirty-two, a local skell of long standing." He tossed a folder on her desk. "I pulled his jacket."

"Yeah, huh?" AFIS beat CODIS to the punch, as usual. But then, processing DNA always took longer than fingerprints. She scanned the lengthy rap sheet. Chapman was a naughty boy: assault, menacing, auto theft, breaking and entering, and accessory to armed robbery. He'd been a recent guest of the Oregon State Penitentiary in Salem, serving three years for the armed robbery conviction. Released on parole three months ago.

"I reached out to his P.O.," Detweiler said. "Guy named Kincaid; I met him once. Chapman stopped checking in with him a month and a half ago. Kincaid filed a parole-violation report."

Karen studied the photo on the rap sheet's first page. Chapman had feral eyes, the eyes of a predator. "Looks like an upstanding citizen to me, Carl. Hard to believe he's had trouble with the law."

"Yes, indeed," Detweiler said, slipping easily into the familiar routine. "Probably the nicest guy you ever want to meet. I'm sure this is all just a misunderstanding. What do you say we pay Mr. Chapman a visit and clear it up?"

"Indubitably," she said and put on her jacket. She removed the Smith & Wesson from a desk drawer, slipped it into her shoulder holster, and secured the strap. "But I'll faint if his last-known is still good."

In a stroke of perfect timing, the arrest and search warrants were already at the front desk; Karen folded them and tucked them away in an inside pocket of her jacket.

"Shotgun," Detweiler called out as they approached their unmarked cruiser, a maroon Chevy Caprice.

"Be my guest," she said and got behind the wheel. Before she started the car she looked over at her partner. "What say we hit the Subway on Sixth Avenue first?"

After chewing and swallowing a bite of her sub (*From the Low-Fat Menu: "6-inch Savory Turkey Breast on wheat, 280 calories"*), she asked Detweiler, "Remember that hump who used to be in Subway commercials, that Jared guy, you think he really lost all that weight pounding down subs?"

"Beats me. Why?" When she didn't answer he laid down his BBQ Steak & Bacon Melt (460 calories, Karen had informed him). "What's the matter, Woj? You've been pretty quiet today. Something eating on you?"

She snorted. "Ironic you'd put it that way. I'm the one doing the eating. Everything in sight."

"I've said this before—you have a distorted body image. Like one of those anorexic chicks. What's the name for that, 'body morphodite disorder' or something?"

"Dysmorphic. And I'm a long way from anorexic. Light-years."

"You're not fat, Woj. You got curves, that's all. A woman should have curves."

"Everything in moderation. Including curves."

He gave her a look of exasperation and took a long pull on his iced tea.

Karen changed the subject. "You straighten out your PERS problem?

"God, you wouldn't believe all the bureaucratic—what's the word? Obfustication?—whatever you call it, they threw it at me. But I had them by the short hair and they knew it. In the end they saw it my way. So tomorrow I'm going to make an offer on that motor coach I've been looking at."

"You're really going to do it, huh?"

"Bet your ass. Come January one, Maureen and I are going to strike out for parts unknown in our land yacht."

Karen put her fingers to her temples and closed her eyes. "I see . . . Vegas. I see . . . posh RV resorts. I see . . . humongous fuel bills."

Detweiler sighed heavily. "Yeah, but what you gonna do? The goddamn oil companies got everybody by the balls. Maureen and I have been looking forward to this for so long, nothing's going to stop us now. Anyway, the rig I have my eye on is a three-year-old, forty-foot diesel pusher with three slide-outs. Interior like a palace; that's what sold Maureen on it. It's got all the goodies—generator, exterior cameras, sound system, and a control console like the bridge of a starship. She's a beauty." He was like a ten-year-old rhapsodizing about a new Schwinn.

"I'm happy for you, Carl." She swallowed the last bite of her sub and dabbed at her mouth with a napkin, lamenting that the sandwich was already gone. She could easily have eaten the foot-long version; she had done it many times. She'd managed to rein in her impulsiveness this time only because someone was with her.

Detweiler had his pen out and was sketching a bus-like motor home on a napkin, the tip of his tongue at the corner of his mouth.

"Ready, Carl?"

Back in the car, Karen said, "I keep thinking about how the Indian guy was killed. Quick, deadly, professional—like an execution. Most street and parking lot robberies are crimes of opportunity, but Chapman lay in wait behind the vic's car long enough to smoke three cigarettes. Why?"

Detweiler shrugged. "Only one way to find out. Let's go ask him."

"We have to locate him first." She signaled and pulled out into traffic, pointing the unmarked Chevy Caprice toward Alder Street.

"Our suspect's last-known is the Centurian."

She nodded. "A favorite of discriminating skells."

The Centurian Plaza had once been one of Portland's premier five-star hotels. Back then it catered to well-to-do travelers. Now it was a seedy flophouse that rented rooms by the day, week, or month to junkies, juicers, and ex-cons like Chapman, as well as to folks who were too old, too poor, or too sick to live anywhere else. For the denizens of Portland's underbelly, the Centurian beat living under an overpass or in a cardboard box in an alley, but not by much. Nevertheless, the building managed to retain echoes of its former glory. Its edifice was dilapidated, but the structure still had a regal appearance, like a crone in a tattered wedding dress.

She parked the unit directly in front of the entrance. An old woman in a floppy crocheted hat and threadbare sweater slowly pushed a grocery cart half full of bottles and cans down the sidewalk. She nodded at them as they were getting out of the car. "My Mercedes is in the garage," she said, and continued on, cackling.

Detweiler was still chuckling when they entered the lobby, which smelled faintly of Lysol and urine. The hotel clerk was behind thick Plexiglas that had a slot for passing money and keys back and forth. Of indeterminate age, he wore a soiled gray baseball cap and an expression of utter disinterest.

Karen held the photo against the glass. "Good morning, sir. We're looking for this gentleman."

The clerk peered at it. "Haven't seen him for a while." His voice was a high-pitched buzz. "Figured he's on vacation."

"Yeah, maybe he won a sea cruise," Karen said. "Guess what my next question is."

"Can you have a look at his room?"

"I'm impressed. No wonder Psychic Friends Network went bust. Too much competition from freelancers like you."

The clerk shrugged and turned to a wall-mounted rack that had dozens of keys hanging on hooks. He selected one and shoved it through the slot. "Fourth floor. Room four thirty-two."

A crudely printed "Out of Order" sign was Scotch-taped to the ancient elevator's door, so they took the stairs. The stairs' condition wasn't much better than the elevator's. By the time they reached the fourth floor, they were both winded. The room closest to the stairwell was 403. They started down the hallway, dimly illuminated by the feeblest incandescent bulbs in existence, passing several open doors. The rooms' occupants looked at them blankly, without curiosity. A knock on the door to 432 brought no response from within, so she inserted the key in the lock and opened the door.

The room was about what she expected—harsh lighting from a bare overhead bulb, worn carpet, faded curtains, and beat-up furniture. No Chapman to be found, but some of his possessions were there.

"I would've bet money he'd moved out of this dump," Carl said. "I mean, the guy skips out on his P.O. but keeps the same digs? Doesn't make sense."

The shirts, pants, and jackets hanging in the closet were spaced a uniform three inches apart. Clothes were precisely folded and neatly stacked in dresser drawers. On the top of the dresser were a bottle of Old Spice cologne, a gold Bulova watch, and enough cigarette burns to foil any pretense of elegance. In the bathroom the toiletries and shaving gear were all arranged with precision on the well-worn counter.

"Neat freak," Detweiler said.

A half-dozen magazines were stacked on an end table, an opportunity to see what sort of literature appealed to the room's occupant. The magazine on top was titled *Uncut*, and its cover featured lurid photos of two naked women, both of whom, on closer inspection, also had uncircumcised penises. The rest of the magazines had a similar theme, as indicated by their titles: *She-Male, Tranny Time, Chicks With Dicks, Best of Both Worlds*.

"Looks like our boy has a taste for the exotic."

"Curiouser and curiouser," Detweiler said.

A Chicken of the Sea tuna can next to the magazines contained several cigarette butts. Dollars to donuts the DNA on them would match that on the butts found at the crime scene. She bagged and tagged them. "I think we're done here, Carl."

"Yeah," he said. "Nothing to do now but find the bastard."

The walk down the creaky stairs was easier than the climb had been. Back in the lobby she slid her business card through the slot to the clerk, and instructed him to phone her immediately if the tenant in 432 turned up. He assured her he would, in his odd buzzing voice.

Like hell he would. Soon as they got back to the unit, she reached for the mic to call for backup to stake out the Centurian, in case Chapman returned. She and Detweiler would have to stick around to brief them.

She remembered seeing a yellow and brown Winchell's sign a couple blocks from the Centurian. They could grab a couple bear claws and be back before the surveillance unit got there. She put the car in gear.

From a shadowy recessed doorway across the street from the Centurian Plaza, Chapman watched the unmarked police car pull away from the curb. It was a safe bet they would be back soon. If he was going to sneak up to his room and grab the gold watch it would have to be ricky-ticky quick, divine protection or no.

He knew better than to enter through the lobby, so when he was satisfied the coast was clear he walked down the block, crossed the street, and made for the alley behind the hotel.

The look on the clerk's face when he rapped on the Plexiglas told him what he already knew, that the two cops had been looking for him.

"Friend, you wouldn't violate a tenant's privacy by making a phone call?" He smiled at the clerk, his "cobra" smile.

The remaining color drained out of the man's already pale face. "N-no, of course not."

"I didn't think so. You look smarter than that."

"You got nothin' to worry about from me, mister. I mind my own business."

Chapman winked at him and started for the staircase.

37

Livvy and Leia were shopping at Old Navy when the second text message arrived. Livvy's phone vibrated and chimed simultaneously and she nearly levitated. Another cryptic message from 555-505-0447:

```
ive had lotz of xperience w girlz of ur
kind
```

She handed the phone to Leia.

Leia read the message. "Huh? It says, 'girlz of ur kind.' What kind is that?"

Livvy shook her head. "You think it could be from some sort of memory expert? Someone who's worked a lot with people who have amnesia?"

"A memory expert using textspeak like some fourteen-year-old girl? Not likely." Leia frowned in concentration, blond brows knitted. "Was it sent from the same phone number as the first one?"

"Yes, same number."

"Mighty strange. Hope some wingnut hasn't gotten hold of your number. Some perv or something."

"Yeah," Livvy said, "that's all I need." She blanked the screen and stowed the phone in her pocket.

"Maybe Jeff could help you get rid of the jerk. Beat the crap out of him."

Livvy laughed. "I've never seen Jeff in an actual physical altercation, but I have seen him get confrontational with people who tried to jack him around. No one messes with Jeff. Except me."

"Girl, I am so happy for you—for both of you. He's really special."

"I think so too."

"Hey," Leia said. "Maybe you should call that number from a pay phone and see who answers."

"Great minds. I've been wondering if I should. Why not? I wouldn't have to say anything." Livvy gave a decisive nod of her head. "By gosh, I'm going to do it. But where can I find a pay phone? They're almost obsolete."

"I saw one outside the Rite-Aid down the street."

"We'll drive down there after we pay for this stuff."

Leia stopped next to a display. "Hey, look! These tops are on sale, and they're really cute."

"Adorable." Livvy took her by the elbow and steered her toward the checkout line.

Ten minutes later, Livvy deposited a quarter in the pay phone's coin slot and dialed the number. She counted eight rings before a recorded voice intoned, "We're sorry, but your call cannot be completed as dialed. Please check the number and try again."

Leia stuck her head out the passenger's window. "Well?"

Livvy shook her head.

Leia repeated her original theory, that the text messages were from someone who was trying to scam her or sell her something.

Livvy agreed, despite her growing sense of uneasiness. *I'm probably blowing this out of proportion. Chances are, it's nothing to get upset over.*

At least, not yet.

With the cello's scroll resting in the hollow between her neck and left shoulder, Livvy looked around the room. It was a replica of a seventeenth-century Italian music conservatory, complete with baroque decor. Ellie had designed it herself. They had an audience of five: Floyd, Charlotte, Leia, Jeff, and Henry, who lay at their feet with a doggy grin. Livvy swallowed. None of them noticed her hand trembling as she picked up the bow.

Get a grip, for crying out loud.

Her neck and shoulders were tense, and isometric shrugs didn't loosen them a bit. She looked at Ellie, seated at the ebony Steinway, lips pursed as she scanned the sheet of music before her. They'd agreed beforehand to begin with Cello Suite No. 1 in G Major, Prelude by Bach. Livvy couldn't recall the circumstances in which she'd played it before, but it was familiar to her, familiar enough that she had no need to refer to the sheet music.

Another swallow. *Here goes . . .*

Livvy indicated the downbeat with a nod of her head and they began the movement. The immediate sense of familiarity was the same feeling she had when she swam, like she'd done it a million times before. All the technical things involved in playing the instrument—intonation, vibrato, dynamics—were automatic. Her hands seemed to move of their own volition, confidently and unerringly. The cello produced round, pure notes that reverberated in the acoustically perfect space. When the movement's last strains faded, she looked up and smiled. The room's superb acoustics amplified the applause from the small, but enthusiastic, audience.

Livvy felt like clapping herself. Her musical ability was untouched by the amnesia. It was miraculous. She turned to her accompanist. "That was fun, Ellie. You've been playing a long time. I can tell."

"A while. Long enough to recognize how brilliant you are on that instrument."

"Maybe I just got lucky. Want to try another?"

"It would be my honor, dear. It's not every day I get a chance to accompany a cellist of your caliber."

Livvy crossed her eyes at Ellie. "How about another Bach piece? Cello Suite No. 6 in D Major, *The Courante*." Bach had composed the movement for a five-string violoncello piccolo, a smaller cello. Playing something composed for five strings with only four was technically demanding, but playing the Prelude had emboldened her. Besides, she was curious to know the extent of her facility with the instrument. Just how accomplished was she?

Ellie thumbed through her music until she located the chart. "I'll do my best to not get in your way," she said.

"You'll do fine. Let's just have fun." Livvy smiled at the older woman. "If I can pull this off, I'm going to quit while I'm ahead."

She drew the bow across the strings and the staccato opening notes of *The Courante* filled the room. The composition became a timestream of sound that stretched to a vanishing point on a virtual horizon. As the movement soared, she was carried aloft by strings of horsehair and catgut. Floating over the timestream, at variance with its cold mathematical perfection, she willed it to move and breathe. *The Courante* became hers, her personal and unique statement. As the end of the piece approached, she played a flurry of notes, landing with a sonorous, sustained chord.

This time the applauding audience leaped to their feet. She acknowledged them by bowing her head in their direction. They rushed over and surrounded her, still clapping, as an anxious Henry circled the group.

Ellie hugged her. "Anyone who can play *The Courante* that beautifully should be sitting in the first chair of a symphony's cello section."

"Thanks, Ellie," Livvy said. "I'd be happy to land second or third chair."

Jeff put his arm around her waist. "That was fantastic, honey. I'm in awe."

She stood on tip-toe and kissed his cheek.

"Seriously," Ellie said, "if the Oregon Symphony doesn't hire you immediately they're crazy."

Livvy smiled. In due time she would contact the director and request an audition. But not yet. There were things she needed to do to first. Like find a permanent place to live. And her missing memories.

She heard the phone's distinctive warble from ten feet away. Such great timing—just as she was reveling in the knowledge that, whatever else she'd lost, she still had musical ability. She didn't want to look at the phone, didn't want to see another cryptic text message.

No, thank you. Not tonight.

38

Homicide Division Lieutenant Eichler beckoned to Karen and inclined his head toward his office. Karen pointed to Detweiler, sitting at his desk with his back to them, and raised her eyebrows. Eichler nodded.

She walked over and tapped her partner on the shoulder. "Mr. Steed . . . we're needed."

"Right-o, Mrs. Peel," he said and followed after her.

"What's up, L.T.?" she asked, closing the door behind them.

A man she didn't recognize rose to his feet. Early forties, glasses, salt-and-pepper hair brushed back. His mode of dress —white shirt, light blue tie, black wingtips, gray slacks, rumpled gray suit coat draped over the back of his chair, shoulder rig with a holstered revolver—gave him away: He was a fed.

Eichler said, "Special Agent Beach, meet Detectives Wojanowski and Detweiler, the primaries." The trio shook hands. "Special Agent Beach is a profiler with the Bureau. He reached out to us and generously offered to profile our serial."

"I have an ulterior motive," Beach said. "I've got a special interest in serials. I study what makes them tick." His voice was surprisingly deep, the resonance similar to actor Sam Elliot's. In fact, without the glasses he'd have looked a lot like the actor.

"We can use all the insight you can give us," Karen said. She had her own theories about the killer, but she was curious to hear the fed's take.

"Okay," Beach said, "here's my take."

Karen looked at him sharply. It was like he'd read her mind. Spooky.

"To begin with, the perpetrator's a male. A female wouldn't carve up a woman like that, trans or otherwise. At least, that's been my experience. Judging by the degree of savagery, he feels rage toward his victims. Could be he's retaliating for some sort of betrayal, real or imagined. As for the genital mutilation, it's often an indicator of sexual dysfunction, such as impotence. To him, the knife might be a penis proxy. It might be the only way he can get off."

Karen nodded. She'd suspected the killings were sexually motivated, at least in part.

Detweiler raised his hand as though he were in class. "What about the crosses he carves on their chests—is he a religious fanatic?"

"Good question. I'm sure there's a religious component to his motivation, but I have a hunch it's secondary. I think his primary motivation is the gratification he gets from killing and defiling the objects of his rage. The genital mutilation is a sign that something besides twisted religious fervor is driving him. However, religion might be a convenient just-ification for it. I wouldn't be a bit surprised if it turns out he thinks of himself as some sort of avenging angel. The delusion isn't as rare as you might think. There's a thin line between religious extremism and psychosis. Anyway, the answer is, yes, he's probably a religious fanatic. But a self-serving one."

"One thing," Karen said. "Why only trans women?"

"I predict he'll turn out to be a chaser, Detective."

"Chaser?" Detweiler asked. "What's a chaser?"

"Short for 'tranny chaser.' Chasers are sexually attracted to transgender women, often exclusively. For many of them it's an outlet for repressed homosexuality, so they can tell themselves they're straight."

"Interesting," Karen said.

"The way he poses the bodies indicates an almost tender regard for his victims after he's through with them. He takes great pains to stage the whole scene, every detail. That and the precise folding and stacking of their clothing means he's a perfectionist. It's hardly surprising that he'd have O.C.D. along with his other kinks. Unfortunately, it also means he's careful and methodical. He won't make many mistakes."

"All we need is one," Detweiler said.

"Here's what worries me. So far, he's performed the genital mutilation only *after* he killed them. The photos indicate that with each victim the mutilation became progressively more extreme. If he continues escalating, he may ... change the order of things."

"God," she said. It was a horrifying prospect.

Beach sat back and crossed his legs. "Let's hope you bag this guy before he escalates to that point."

"We're going to do our best," Detweiler said.

"That's all I have for you at this time." Beach made eye contact with Karen. "Profiling is just spitballing, with a dash of psychoanalysis. It will be interesting to see how many hits I get." He almost smiled.

Throughout the briefing it had seemed to Karen that the agent had spoken primarily to her rather than Detweiler. That was unusual; men almost always talked to her partner. No possibility Beach would have a more-than-professional interest in her. Not on a day when she looked even frumpier than usual. Besides, why would he, or any man, be interested in a fat tub of goo?

Beach caught her studying him and raised one eyebrow. She looked away, feeling her cheeks grow hot. *Way to go, Karen. Real smooth.*

"Tell me," Detweiler said, "how did you become a profiler?"

"It was kind of a fluke," Beach said. "The Bureau was using psychological profiling extensively, and I had a Ph.D. in psychology, so it was a good fit. Best part, I have something to fall back on if this special agent stuff doesn't work out."

That got a laugh from the group. Eichler signaled the meeting was over by standing. She and Detweiler shook hands with Beach and thanked him for his insights. Detweiler held the door open for her and then followed her out.

"Fascinating stuff, hey, partner?" he said when they were out in the hall.

"It made a lot of sense, Carl. I was impressed."

"I'll be interested to see how accurate his profile turns out to be." He paused by the restrooms. "You go ahead, Woj, I'm going to hit the can."

Karen stopped at the drinking fountain on the way to her desk. When she bent over to drink, she saw a pair of black wingtips behind her worn brown Hush Puppies. She straightened up and turned around.

"Detective." Special Agent Beach held out his business card. "You should have one too. Just in case you want to bounce something off me."

"Oh. Thanks."

"It's a fascinating case, so please give me a call if I can be of further assistance."

Back at her desk she couldn't stop thinking about Beach's warning that the killer might escalate and the unimaginable suffering it would mean for his victims. Karen had been in Homicide Division for ten years, so it took a lot to make her shudder, but that did the trick. If it was the last thing she did, she'd make damn certain the sick bastard was out of commission. Permanently.

39

Detweiler closed a file folder and stood up and stretched. "Going to the press conference, Woj?"

"Thought I'd look in on it. You?"

Detweiler shook his head. "I hate those things. I'll catch up on some paperwork instead."

Karen finished putting on her jacket. She wasn't looking forward to the press conference herself. Cops had a love-hate relationship with the media. More often than not, they hampered an investigation. But the public's right to know trumped law enforcement's effectiveness.

The first-floor press room was already packed and noisy when she got there. Television crews from KOIN, KGW, and KATU, the three local network affiliates, as well as KPTV, the Fox affiliate, were busily setting up equipment. She recognized stringers from AP and UPI and a reporter from *The Oregonian* among the crowd. She was mildly surprised to see a reporter—she applied the term loosely—from *Inside Scoop*, Portland's infamous tabloid. Hard to believe he had actual press credentials. She wondered who all the onlookers were. One thing was clear: This was big news, national stuff. She found a chair at the very back, near the door.

Dick Cantwell, the department's press officer, was behind the podium making a last-minute note before beginning. Late forties, balding, with rimless bifocals, Cantwell looked more like a tax preparer at H&R Block than a police officer. But he was adroit at handling the press, no argument about that. She didn't envy him the job; she wouldn't have it at double the pay. Cantwell cleared his throat and waited until the hubbub subsided; then he tipped his head back slightly and peered through the bifocals' bottom half at the prepared statement.

"Over the past four weeks," Cantwell said, enunciating each word with precision, "four area residents have been murdered, three in Portland, one in Vancouver. We are working closely with the Vancouver police to investigate these homicides. All four victims were in their twenties, all were prostitutes, all were transgender. Only two had undergone gender reassignment surgery."

Cantwell waited patiently until the rising din from the reporters died down before he continued. "All the victims were killed with a knife or other sharp implement, and their bodies were moved to where they were found. We're treating the murders as hate crimes."

A collective murmur from the reporters rose and then tapered off.

"The victims' names are being withheld pending notification of next of kin. The investigation is continuing. That's all I have for you at this point in time." Cantwell said. "I'll take questions now."

The room erupted, the reporters shouting questions and waving their arms in the air, trying to get Cantwell's attention. He pointed to the AP reporter, a large man with bushy red hair.

"We've heard rumors that the victims' bodies had been mutilated," the reporter said. "Can you confirm this and, if so, were they mutilated before or after they were killed?"

Karen saw Cantwell press his lips together, a clear sign he was irritated. The department always did its best to keep details of a crime out of the press. The fewer details the public knew about a case, the easier it was to filter out the false leads and confessions that inevitably flooded the department in sensational cases. Cases like this one.

"Yes," Cantwell said, "the victims bodies were mutilated. It was done after they were killed, according to the medical examiner."

"It's also rumored that some of the mutilation involves religious symbols," the AP reporter persisted. "Do you think the killer's a religious nut?"

Karen wondered who the source of the leak was. Unlikely that it was in the department or the coroner's office. Probably an onlooker who saw one of the bodies before the police arrived on the scene.

Cantwell shook his head. "I won't comment as to the nature of the mutilation." He pointed next to a woman in the front row, a reporter for KOIN, the local CBS affiliate.

"Thank you," she said. "Had any of the victims been sexually assaulted?"

"The autopsies found no bruises, abrasions, or seminal fluid in or on the victims."

Karen had to admire the way Cantwell threaded the needle. His answer was technically true, but what happened to those transgender women definitely constituted sexual assault. The fact that it occurred postmortem and the attacker used a sharp knife instead of his wang didn't mean the assault wasn't sexual in nature. But the department was withholding those suppositions from the press at this point in the investigation, so Cantwell deftly sidestepped the question.

The press officer pointed to KPTV's reporter, a well-groomed fellow who also anchored the evening news. He spoke in a deep, well-modulated voice. "Have you questioned any of the victims' . . . co-workers to see if they can provide any useful information?"

Cantwell replied, "Yes, we're in the process of interviewing area transgender prostitutes in connection with the killings."

"He means she-male hookers," the reporter from *Inside Scoop* said *sotto voce*, but loudly enough to be heard by everybody in the room. Several people laughed.

What an asshole. Karen wanted to shout it at the top of her lungs.

Cantwell ignored the outburst and pointed to the reporter from *The Oregonian.*

"Do you think the killer is targeting prostitutes only," he asked, "or transgender women in general?"

"Since only prostitutes have been murdered so far," Cantwell said, "that would seem to indicate that transgender women who aren't involved in the sex trade are not being targeted, but it would be premature to say with any certainty."

"Women? Hah! That's a stretch!" The *Inside Scoop* jerk again, and he wasn't even trying to keep his voice down.

"Socially and legally they're women," *The Oregonian's* reporter said, glaring at him. "Whether you like it or not."

The tabloid reporter feigned a loud sneeze that sounded like "Bullshit!" and grinned at the other reporter.

KGW's reporter was next be called on. "How much progress have you made with the investigation?"

"At this point we're following up several promising leads," Cantwell said.

Which was complete horseshit, of course. At this point they had pathetically little to go on, other than the possibility that the killer might have driven a dark-colored car with tinted windows—this from working girls she and Detweiler had interviewed on Belmont. But "following up several promising leads" was all the specificity the media got.

Cantwell closed his notes and nodded once at the roomful of reporters. "Thank you, everybody." A fusillade of questions followed him out of the room.

Karen was first out the rear exit.

Sarah switched off the television after the local news. She was taking a first sip of wine when her phone trilled. She answered it, hoping it wasn't some type of medical emergency. She really, *really* wanted to stay home and relax.

"Sarah?" It was her friend Kate. "Have you been following the news? About the murders?"

"Hard to avoid it. *The Oregonian* is giving it front-page treatment. And I just watched a report on channel six."

"They're calling him 'The Tranny Killer. It's a damned circus."

"Sensationalism sells."

"Even Public Broadcasting is getting into the act. OPB is running an announcement on channel ten about a program that will air next Sunday titled 'Transgender.' It'll be a panel discussion."

"Be glad the title isn't 'Transgenders.' I hate when it's used as a noun instead of an adjective. Did they say who's going to be on the panel?"

"It'll be a potpourri. Some Ph.D. from Berkeley, supposed to be heavy hitter in gender studies, never heard of her. Richard Ronson from the Family Morality Council, to provide the evangelical viewpoint."

"Wonderful," Sarah said, wrinkling her nose.

"And none other than high-profile transgender filmmaker Melissa Beauchamp. She'd never miss a chance for some free promotion."

"Cut her some slack, Kate. She's a publicity hound, but we could do worse."

"Speaking of doing worse, you know Amanda Tyler, of the Rose City Gender Consortium? Flamboyant late-transitioner with a voice like a didgeridoo?"

Sarah winced, but Kate's description was accurate. "Sure, I know who you mean."

"She'll be there in all her glory, no doubt wearing a miniskirt and strappy platform heels, as is her wont."

"Maybe she'll dial it back."

"Don't count on it."

"It's a minor concern, compared to those poor murdered girls. If only trans sex workers would stay off the streets while that wackjob is still at large."

"They don't have that choice, most of them."

Sarah sighed. "Well, now that I'm thoroughly depressed, I think I'll say goodnight and try to get some sleep."

"Hang in there, girl," her friend said.

After ending the call, Sarah started to empty the nearly full glass of wine into the kitchen sink, but stopped short. No sense wasting perfectly good cooking wine. She took some plastic wrap, covered the glass, and put it in the refrigerator. Then she went to bed.

40

The basement television viewing room was a quarter-scale vintage theater, complete with authentic decor. Livvy and Jeff gaped at the wall sconces, the thick carpet, and the velvet curtains flanking what had to be the largest flat-screen television in existence.

"One hundred fifty-two inches, in case you're wondering," Floyd told them. "Plasma."

Other than size, the only departure from an authentic vintage theater was the seating, a concession to comfort. Instead of fixed chairs there were a dozen recliners, three rows of them, four recliners to a row, all upholstered in the same sea-green velour. They chose the middle two chairs in the center row and sank into the soft cushions. Charlotte and Leia entered the little theater engaged in animated conversation, accompanied by Henry the dog, who flopped down in the aisle.

Floyd leaned forward from the back row. "Glad you two could join us. One of my clients is a guest on tonight's program. Should be interesting."

"Phillipe Labrecque," Ellie said, "looks like he could be George Clooney's brother, and he has the most delightful French-Canadian accent. He commissioned Floyd to design a house for him in Montreal, something ultracontemporary. So Floyd designed the most incredible—"

"Excuse me, dear," her husband said. "The program's starting." He tapped a touch-screen tablet.

The lights dimmed and surround sound from hidden speakers filled the small theater.

"This Oregon Public Broadcasting program is made possible by contributions from the Echelon Foundation, Alvin B. and Katherine T. McNulty, Floyd and Elinor Conover, and from viewers like you."

Phillipe Labrecque did not want to be there. As far as he was concerned, it was a colossal waste of time. He would much rather finish a paper he was writing for *Neuroscience Journal*, but Floyd Conover had asked him to do the program, and Phillipe wasn't about to refuse him. He would sooner turn down a request from the Canadian prime minister.

He could see a monitor from where he sat. The program title was superimposed over a wide shot of the moderator and the panel, comprised of three men and two women seated in a semicircle. Phillipe was on one end, on the right side of the monitor's screen. The moderator, silver-haired and impeccably attired, sat at the center of the semicircle, facing them. The title dissolved to a closeup of the moderator.

"Good evening, I'm Charles Masters. Welcome to the third installment of our *Diversity* series, promoting understanding of diverse aspects of our society. The title of tonight's program is 'Transgender,' and it's especially timely in view of recent tragic events here in the Portland-Vancouver area. We'll talk about that, and about the prevalence of violence directed at transgender people. Right now, let's meet our panel.

"We're pleased to have with us this evening Dr. Esther Weissmann, professor of psychology at UC Berkeley and author of *The Gender Continuum*." Close shot of Weissmann, sitting on the far end of the panel. A sharp-featured woman who looked to be in her sixties, she wore a checked pantsuit that caused dizzying moiré patterns on the monitor.

"Richard Ronson, director of the non-profit Family Morality Council, and author of *Abomination* and *Pathway To Normal*." Closeup of a tight-lipped man with wire-rim glasses and a red, white, and blue bow tie. His thin face wore a permanent I-think-I-smell-shit expression.

"Melissa Beauchamp, a Seattle filmmaker and Spirit Award nominee last year for her acclaimed documentary *Rockin' Your Gender*." Beauchamp was thirtyish, tall and slender, with long, straight, strawberry blond hair parted in the middle. She held herself like a woman who knows she's attractive.

"From Oregon Senate District thirty, Republican State Senator Ken Culbertson." The heavyset, florid-faced man sitting next to Phillipe acknowledged the introduction with a curt nod. His hair was parted just over his ear, and long, thin white strands from the side and back were creatively swept over the top and lacquered in place in a hopeful attempt to disguise his baldness.

"Dr. Phillipe Labrecque, professor of neuroscience at Université de Montréal, and author of *Brain Gender*." Phillipe looked away from the monitor, but not quickly enough to avoid seeing a closeup of himself. As usual, he was embarrassed to see that stalwart face on the screen. It belonged to a Miami news anchor, perhaps, or a professional golfer. Certainly not a neuroscientist. But then, few scientists had a year-round tan like Phillipe's, a result of tennis in the summer and skiing in the winter.

"And a last-minute change—Amanda Tyler from the Rose City Gender Consortium will not be joining us this evening. To the rest of you, welcome. We begin tonight's program on a troubling note. In the past two months, four transgender women, all sex workers in Portland and Vancouver, were brutally murdered. Dr. Weissmann, in an article that appeared in yesterday's *Huffington Post*, you wrote that the murders reflected an increase in violence directed at transgender individuals, particularly transgender women. Would you speak to that?"

"Yes, certainly," Weissmann said. "Hate crimes against transgender people have been increasing yearly at a double-digit rate. Transgender individuals in the U.S. today have a one-in-twelve chance of being murdered, one chance in eight for transgender people of color. By comparison, the average person's chance of being murdered is one in eighteen thousand. Several hundred transgender women are murdered every year. The actual number is undoubtedly higher, since many of the slayings are not reported as hate crimes. The incidence of beatings, rapes, and other serious abuse is higher still."

"Alarming," Masters said. "In your article, you said transgender sex workers are targeted more than other groups. But that doesn't seem to deter them from engaging in that type of work, as one would assume it would. Why not?"

"The reality is, most of them have no choice. Transgender people are stigmatized and marginalized by society. And the younger they are, the fewer choices they have. Shunned by their families, ostracized by their peers, discriminated against, and unable to obtain jobs, they turn to sex work. In fact, over half of transgender youth sell their bodies to survive."

"It's tragic," Masters said, "that a homicidal maniac is preying on this vulnerable group here in Portland."

"We need to keep in mind that these individuals were not murdered because they were prostitutes. They were murdered because they were transgender. Because of their gender identity."

The large man next to Phillipe snorted loudly, drawing everyone's attention. "Well, what did they expect?" he said. "If they hadn't pretended to be something they're not, they'd probably still be alive."

"Senator," Weissmann said after long seconds of shocked silence, "Surely you're not blaming the murder victims?"

"They were asking for trouble and they got it. That's all I'm saying."

Masters looked at his notes. "Senator Culbertson, in the last legislative session you introduced a bill to prevent transgender individuals from having their Oregon birth certificates changed to reflect their new, legal gender following surgery. The bill failed to pass. Why did you feel there was a need for such legislation?"

"Government should not be endorsing alternative lifestyle choices."

Weissmann leaned forward. "Please elaborate, Senator."

After loosening his tie, Culbertson stuck out his chin and said, "Well, those—those people are not what most Americans would call 'normal.'"

Phillipe gritted his teeth. *How did that idiot get elected to public office?* But he knew the answer: The senator represented a rural district, where a majority of voters think much the way he does.

"I think," Ronson said, "we should thank God for common-sense lawmakers like Senator Culbertson." He punctuated his opinion with a "So there!" nod of his head.

Weissmann's face expressed her disgust. "Thanks to education, society is becoming enlightened about this complex subject. More and more people understand that being transgender is not a 'lifestyle choice.' Nature made a mistake, one that's correctable. Medical technology can bring their bodies into alignment with their minds, in harmony for the first time in their lives."

Clearly agitated, Ronson said, "Excuse me, but that's a load of liberal poppycock. God makes you either male or female, no 'correction' needed. Changing what the Lord has wrought is not only wrong, it's blasphemous. God doesn't make mistakes."

"Yeah, right." Beauchamp said. "Try explaining that to children born with cleft palate, club foot, spina bifida, heart defects, or other congenital abnormalities, Mr. Ronson. Tell them it's wrong to correct those conditions, and they'll just have to live with them."

"Don't be ridiculous. That's different."

"Why? Because those conditions don't involve the genitals?"

"The difference is, there's nothing wrong with the genitals these transgenders"—he pointed at Beauchamp—"are born with!" Ronson's voice rose in pitch and volume. "They mutilate perfectly healthy body parts!"

Beauchamp's reply was measured. "That's not how we see it, Mr. Ronson. To us, it's aligning our bodies with our minds, as Dr. Weissmann said."

"Then you're mentally ill. You need psychiatric help."

"Gender dysphoria is classified as a correctable *medical* condition, not a mental illness."

Ronson looked smug. "Correctable with hormones and surgery? What about your DNA? Males have XY chromosomes and females have XX. And I know this for a fact: Chromosomes can't be changed. Which means gender can't be changed. That should be obvious."

That was Phillipe's cue to jump into the fray. "Excuse me," he said, "but it's not as simple as that. There are numerous exceptions to the norm. Are you familiar with Androgen Insensitivity Syndrome? No? Many individuals with AIS are born phenotypically female, despite having a male karyotype. They don't develop as male because their bodies are resistant to testosterone."

"But something like that has to be very rare," Ronson said.

"Not as rare as you might think. In the United States alone there are thousands of XY females with AIS and XX males with de la Chapelle syndrome, the counterpart to AIS. Usually, people around them are totally unaware of their condition. Often, they're not aware of it themselves."

"Dr. Labrecque, surely you're not saying that all transgenders have some type of biological abnormality? It's my understanding that most were physically normal males before they . . . had their willies chopped off."

Beauchamp was quick to object. "That's an offensive way of putting it, Mr. Ronson. It's more accurate to say the tissues are surgically rearranged. Reconfigured."

Ronson waved one hand dismissively. "Whatever."

Calmly, Phillipe continued: "To address Mr. Ronson's question, research indicates there's likely a biological basis for gender dysphoria, even when no chromosomal irregularities are present. Scientists have found that certain structures in the brains of male-to-female transgender individuals are more consistent with female brains than male brains. Simply put, their brains seem to be 'wired female,' like their non-transgender counterparts. My own research corroborates these findings."

Ronson seemed undeterred. "We can argue all night about these side issues, but I'm sure about one thing: Transgenders can be cured. The Family Morality Council sponsors an outreach to troubled transgenders, which we call Reclamation. Using biblical-based counseling, we have helped many former transgenders to reject effeminate behaviors and reclaim their manhood. I describe the process in depth in my new book, *Pathway To Normal*."

"Excuse me," Beauchamp said. "I'm familiar with your so-called 'cure,' Mr. Ronson. It's a despicable hodgepodge of religious indoctrination, guilt-tripping, shaming, and aversion therapy, none of which has ever been demonstrated to cure anything, except peace of mind. Two of the individuals featured in your book have disavowed Reclamation, and another is currently institutionalized and receiving treatment for schizophrenia."

Ronson's pale cheeks reddened. "That's a crock of sh— pack of lies! Reclamation *does* work. We offer transgenders hope."

"Right. The same way that lobotomies offered hope to people back in the Fifties."

"Here's the unvarnished truth, even if you don't want to hear it: Transgenders are abominations." Ronson pointed an accusing finger at Beauchamp. "Your lifestyle is twisted and sinful. The holy bible tells us so."

"Only if you cherry-pick and distort certain verses in the Old Testament to support your bigoted claims."

"Nonsense!" Senator Culbertson bellowed. "It's an outrage that gullible people are taken in by your atheistic, liberal claptrap. It's all part of you people's agenda to destroy this great country from within. But decent, God-fearing Americans will not let that happen. Be forewarned, many more transgenders are going to end up dead, just like those she-male whores."

Silence fell over the studio. Off in the distance the plaintive wail of a lone siren rose and fell.

Beauchamp threw up her hands. "Well, there you have it—the social conservatives' solution: Murder all transgender people."

"Now just a goddamn minute!" Culbertson shouted. "Listen here—"

Weissmann cut him off. "Excuse me, Senator, but there's almost certainly a direct correlation between the rise in violence toward transgender people and the type of hate-filled rhetoric we've heard tonight from you and Mr. Ronson. Such inflammatory talk isn't just deplorable, it's downright dangerous. It can incite unbalanced individuals to violence."

"That's exactly what these bigots have in mind," Beau-champ said. "Encourage violence toward transgender people and let the sickos get rid of them."

"That's a baseless accusation," Ronson said. "Don't blame us for what your sinful ways have wrought."

Beauchamp wouldn't let up. "If you're wondering why so many transgender people are beaten, raped, and murdered, look no further than these two men and their fellow bigots. Their irresponsible rhetoric inflames unhinged individuals, encouraging them to do violence."

Ronson and Culbertson leaped to their feet in protest, their faces flushed, both men gesticulating and shouting incoherently. Beauchamp and Weissmann joined the melee.

Although he could barely be heard above the commotion, Masters said, "I'm afraid we are out of time. I'd like to thank our panelists for the ... spirited discussion. On behalf of *Diversity*, I'm Charles Masters. Good night."

The studio director's voice came from a speaker: "*Hold for credits.*" On the monitor, credits rolled over a wide shot of the panelists. Except for Phillipe they were all on their feet, pointing their fingers at each other and shouting. Masters was blotting his forehead with a handkerchief. "*Okay, everyone,*" the director announced, "*we're out.*"

Phillipe stood and stretched. He couldn't wait to get the hell out of there.

"Well," Jeff said, "that was very enlightening." He looked over at Livvy. "Hey, what's wrong?"

"I'm not feeling well. I think I need to go lie down for a while."

"I'll walk you up to your room, hon."

"No, please don't bother. You stay and visit." She patted his arm and stood up. "I should be feeling better by dinner time." She said goodbye to the others, and assured them there was nothing to be concerned about.

In her room she lay on her bed with a comforter over her, yet she was shivering uncontrollably. The queasiness she felt in the little theater had subsided, leaving in its wake a feeling of unspecified, minor-chord dread.

She focused her attention on her breathing, forcing herself to take slow, regular breaths, and in a while the shivering eased off.

41

The article was featured on the front page of the *The Oregonian*, above the fold:

Local Transgender Activist Murdered

The unclothed body of local transgender activist Amanda Tyler, 56, was discovered in Montavilla Park at NE 82nd Avenue and Glisan Street by a jogger early Thursday morning.

Portland police spokesman Dick Cantwell said, "Amanda Tyler is the fifth victim of a killer who has been targeting transgender women in the Portland-Vancouver area. The first four victims were all sex workers, but Ms. Tyler's murder indicates that the killer has expanded his focus to include transgender women in general. Area transgender women are advised to exercise extreme caution while the killer is at large."

Investigators are certain that the same killer is responsible for the latest slaying, Cantwell said, because all five murders had certain elements in common. Those details are being withheld during the active investigation, to eliminate the possibility of a "copycat," an imitator.

Tyler was to have participated in an Oregon Public Broadcasting program on Wednesday night but failed to show up. Medical Examiner Jon Wu confirmed that Ms. Tyler's time of death corresponded approximately to the time the live program was broadcast.

Sarah folded the newspaper and put it aside. She took a tissue from her pocket and blew her nose. Mixed in with the sorrow was guilt and regret that her voice had been among those critical of Amanda. The consensus of the so-called "transgender community" was that she did more harm than good, by presenting an image of a transgender woman that bordered on caricature. It wouldn't have mattered had Amanda not been so high-profile. But transactivism was her passion, and she approached it with zeal.

Many late transitioners pass well, blending in perfectly with other women their age, but Amanda was not among their ranks. The problem wasn't her age or her physical features; it was her presentation: Amanda seemed to be going through a delayed adolescence. She shopped for her clothes at stores like Old Navy and Forever 21, and her ensembles could be attention-getting, even startling, on a woman her age. Add a teenager's approach to hair and makeup and a bass-register voice, and you had a walking spectacle. The pointing and snickering was painful to watch, but if Amanda noticed, she didn't let on. Her apparent obliviousness enraged the less charitable members of the transgender community. Sarah viewed it with resignation and tolerance. Which is not to say she hadn't been concerned about public perception.

That concern—had it been elitism in disguise? Was she an elitist who had cloaked her bigotry in "concern"? She groaned at the thought. But it didn't seem likely. An elitist would feel superior to late transitioners, would she not? Sarah didn't, and hadn't. She knew full well that the deciding factor in her outcome and theirs was opportunity. She'd gotten the opportunity to transition early; they had not. Her concern about public perception was legitimate. No elitism in the equation.

Had Amanda lived long enough, her presentation would undoubtedly have evolved into one more age-appropriate. With a little vocal work—okay, a lot of vocal work—she would have assimilated into society. But she died without having experienced fitting in as a woman, and that was nothing short of tragic.

Rough edges aside, the fallen sister deserved respect. And admiration. Transitioning at Amanda's age took courage and an iron-willed determination to not reach the end of her life full of regret about the road not taken. She'd had the fortitude to take that road, and when people pointed and snickered, she gave no indication that it fazed her in the slightest. You had to admire that alone.

The mantel clock chimed, jarring Sarah from her somber reflection. It was 9 p.m. She looked out through the living room window at the expanse of city lights puncturing the blackness. The view at night was usually calming, but tonight it had the opposite effect. Somewhere out there in the darkness a homicidal maniac was on a rampage. For all she knew, he was lurking outside her door.

Sarah got up from the recliner, walked into her bedroom, and opened the top drawer of her dresser.

The Smith & Wesson Ladysmith revolver felt cold to the touch. Friend and colleague Leon Wasserman had helped her pick it out at a sporting goods store over on Stark. After that they went to a local indoor range where Leon showed her how to load it, fire it, and clean it afterward. Knowing the gun was in the dresser drawer, hidden beneath her underwear, made her feel safe. Safer anyway. She checked to make sure it was loaded and then put it in her purse.

She would not be a victim. Not if she could help it.

42

Karen was in line at the Subway on 6th Avenue, looking at the menu on the wall and thinking how delicious the Chicken & Bacon Ranch Melt looked in the photo. It was tempting—*God*, but it was tempting—but she knew she'd order either a Turkey Breast or Veggie Delite, as usual. Six-inch, of course; foot-long subs were a thing of the past for her. Sticking to the diet was tough, but she'd borrowed an affirmation from Alcoholics Anonymous: One day at a time. And it was working, well enough to knock off twelve pounds so far.

A deep voice behind her said, "Hello, Detective."

She turned around. The man was wearing a gray hoodie, jeans, and Reeboks. Momentary blank; then recognition clicked on. "Unless the Bureau has relaxed its dress code, Special Agent Beach, you're out of uniform."

"Hey, even feds get a day off now and then. And please call me Gil."

"Okay." She pointed to herself. "Karen."

It was her turn to order. She went with the turkey: Nine-grain wheat bread, pepper jack cheese, lettuce, tomatoes, black olives, extra banana peppers, light mayo, no oil or vinegar.

"Impressive," Gil said. "You rattled that off like a Subway veteran."

She laughed. "It's my home away from home."

"I'm an Arby's man myself. I'm slumming."

"Sometimes I go to Arby's for a change of pace. Their Market Fresh sandwiches are pretty good."

"Listen to us—our conversation is about fast food. Are we the two most boring people on the planet?"

She laughed again. "Fast food is a subject near and dear to a certain cop who rarely brings her lunch."

He gave his order to the girl behind the counter. "I'll have what she's having." To Karen he said, "*When Harry Met Sally* is one of my favorite movies. Different circumstances, of course."

"Very different."

After they paid for their sandwiches and drinks, it was inevitable they would share a booth. They picked one next to a window.

"So how long have you been on the job?" he asked her after chewing and swallowing a bite of his sandwich.

"Twelve years. Third-generation cop. How about you?"

"Sixteen years next month." He took a drink of his Coke. "Third-generation, you said. All here in Portland?"

"Boston, mostly. I've only been out here a little over five years."

"That explains your Boston accent. I get the impression you enjoy the job."

"I do. Most of the time."

"Any luck tracking down your serial?"

She shook her head. "We could use a break in the case."

"Better not underestimate this guy, Karen. He's careful and crafty. He'll be hard to catch."

"I won't underestimate him, but he's human. He'll slip up sooner or later."

They stopped talking for a time, concentrating on their sandwiches. She wished she had worn something more presentable than a shapeless knit top, baggy slacks, and worn brown shoes. It wasn't like she didn't have better clothes. She'd splurged and bought some tops, bottoms, and shoes as a mini-reward for losing the twelve pounds, but she had yet to wear any of them; too busy with the job. Anyway, snazzier clothes probably wouldn't make any difference to the ag—to Gil. Fat chance he'd be interested in her.

"Did you happen to catch the OPB program last night about transgender women?"

"I did," she said. "Pretty interesting, huh?"

He nodded. "Especially at the end, when it turned into a free-for-all."

"I did some shouting at the TV when those two bozos—" she halted mid-sentence, realizing she had no idea where her lunch companion stood politically. What if he were a hard-core right-winger? If so, he might not appreciate her taking shots at the evangelical Christian and the Republican state senator from the sticks. But if Gil turned out to be a rightie, it would be a deal breaker, even for a casual friendship. Which was almost certainly where this relationship had been headed.

"I know what you mean," Gil said. "If you ask me, those two clowns are dangerous characters. The psychologist on the panel had it right—the extremists' brand of hate can incite unhinged folks to violence. For all we know, your serial was motivated by that kind of talk."

"Wouldn't surprise me in the least." So Gil wasn't a rightie, thank heaven. Nice to run into someone on her wavelength; encountering a kindred spirit always brightened her day. Her colleagues on the job, a large percentage of them, leaned to the right. When they parroted crap they heard on Fox "News" and right-wing talk radio, she tuned them out in disgust.

Gil wiped his mouth with a paper napkin. "Excellent sandwich, I must say."

"And relatively low-cal." She patted her stomach. "Watching the diet."

"Women," he said, shaking his head. "Every woman I know seems to be on a perpetual diet. Even when they're the perfect weight."

That made her laugh. "I certainly don't fit *that* profile."

"Oh? Could've fooled me."

"I'm at least twenty pounds too heavy. My ass has its own zip code."

"Nothing wrong with that." It was the first time she'd seen him smile. It was a disarmingly shy smile, as if smiling embarrassed him.

She finished her sub and drained the last of the Diet Coke. "Shall we?"

After they disposed of their sandwich wrappers and empty paper cups, Gil opened the door for her. It was cold outside, but it wasn't raining, thank God. Only two cars were in the parking lot, both VW Passats. The silver one was hers; she'd bought it new last year and loved it. The midnight blue one with the temporary license sticker in the back window turned out to be Gil's.

"It's the diesel model," he said. "Had it only a week, long enough to learn that dark blue shows every last fingerprint and speck of dust."

"It's pretty, though."

Gil shifted from one foot to the other several times. Finally, he said, "Karen, would you like to ... maybe have dinner with me sometime? Preferably someplace where they don't serve the food in paper wrappers?"

She couldn't answer. Brain vapor lock.

He quickly added, "Maybe you're seeing someone, in which case, I—"

"Sure, Gil," she finally managed to say. "That would be nice."

The serious look on his face gave way to another shy smile. "Great. Think you'll have a free evening in the foreseeable future?"

She wrote her cell number on the back of her department business card and held it out to him. "I'll be a little busy until we collar this psycho, but after that ..."

He took the card. "We'll celebrate after you bag him."

She fished out her keys and unlocked the driver's door of her car. Gil backed his sleek blue car out of the space and waved to her and then exited the parking lot onto 6th.

Karen was almost home when she remembered she needed groceries. She had to brake hard so she wouldn't overshoot the entrance to Safeway. The driver of the car behind her leaned on his horn in protest and flipped her off as he sped by.

Miraculously, the first shopping cart she picked didn't pull to the side or have wheels with corners. She wanted to expedite the process and get home.

In the slow-moving checkout line, she inventoried the contents of her cart: salad makings, fruit, a liter of Diet Coke, and a dozen WeightWatchers Smart Ones microwavable dinners that were on sale. No cookies or cakes, and especially no Häagen-Dazs coffee ice cream, her favorite; she'd been known to eat an entire pint in one sitting. The days of such indulgence were over. It was diet-or-die time.

Her eyes scanned the magazines and tabloids that lined the checkout aisle. *Cosmopolitan* inquired, "How Can You Be Sure He's Not Cheating?" *People* and *Us* breathlessly promised to dish plenty of delicious dirt about celebrities she'd never heard of. And then a bold headline on *Inside Scoop*, Portland's notorious tabloid, caught her attention. She removed it from the rack, intending to speed-read the article in the line, but she was next to be rung up, so she tossed the tabloid in her cart. She could always give it to Mrs. Zapeda next door, to line her parakeets' cage.

At home, after putting away the groceries, she sat down at the kitchen table with the tabloid and opened it to the cover article:

Tranny Beauty Has Amnesia and Can't Remember Being Male

From the Now-We've-Heard-Everything Department:

At the beginning of September, a patient at a Portland hospital who was known only as "Jane Doe" woke from a coma with almost total amnesia, unable to remember who she is or anything about her past. Her first name—that's the only thing she can recall.

Not exactly newsworthy, right? Well, keep reading, because it gets more interesting. In fact, we think you'll agree that it gets downright fascinating.

It turns out that the lovely young woman had a shocking secret: She's a tranny, a "she-male." Hard to believe, because, to look at "her," no one would ever suspect "she" is not a genuine female. However, chromosome tests don't lie.

That's not all. A juicy twist to this story made even *Inside Scoop*'s most jaded reporters shake their heads with amazement: The amnesic patient has no idea she's a tranny. For reasons unknown, her doctor has withheld this information from the hospital—and from her. So she assumes she's just an ordinary young woman. Fortunately for readers of *Inside Scoop*, the man who discovered this unusual situation, a former hospital employee, felt the story needed to be told.

Inside Scoop asked transgender filmmaker Melissa Beauchamp for a comment. She told us, "Talk about deep stealth! Amnesia would be the deepest stealth of all." In the transgender community, "stealth" means to blend into society so completely that nobody suspects one's transgender history. And we have to agree with Beauchamp. To not even suspect you were once a dude would be "deep stealth" indeed.

Amnesia expert Dr. Warren Fenstermacher of Idaho State University said such extensive memory loss is almost unheard of. "Gender is such a basic aspect of one's self-image, it's difficult to accept that someone is unable to remember having once been another gender," Dr.

Fenstermacher said. "But then, I can't recall a case of amnesia that involved a transgender individual, so it's uncharted territory."

This story is still unfolding, dear reader. You can be sure that *Inside Scoop* will stay on top of it, so you'll want to stay tuned!

Karen scowled and tossed the tabloid down on the table. She despised tabloids in general and *Inside Scoop* in particular. The unfortunate transgender girl in the article had enough troubles without being hounded by that pack of jackals.

So a "former hospital employee" had given them the story. She wondered how much the tabloid had paid for it. And which hospital it was. And why the employee was former instead of current.

A cop's curiosity has no "Off" switch.

43

Sarah slowed the car and pulled into the Red Robin's parking lot just as the rain turned into a downpour that bounced off the asphalt. Just her luck, to be caught in a damn deluge without an umbrella. To make matters worse, she was five minutes late. The only parking spaces available were at the far side of the lot. She parked and pawed through the glove compartment until she found the folded clear plastic scarf. After tying the strap under her chin, she zipped up her parka, grabbed her handbag, and ran for the entrance.

Inside the restaurant she was met by a smiling hostess and atonal strains of "Happy Birthday" from the dining area, followed by cheering and applause. Sarah pointed to the bar. "I'm meeting someone."

The bar was less than half full and relatively quiet, the patrons nursing their drinks and talking quietly. She spotted her friend Petra at a table in the back.

"Sorry I'm late." Sarah unzipped her parka and draped it over a chair and then sat down. "Traffic."

"No worries," Petra said. "Just got here myself."

Sarah was still wearing that day's hospital garb and minimal makeup, her hair pulled back into a bun. In contrast, Petra's hair and makeup were flawless, and she was dressed stylishly, as befitting a buyer for Nordstrom's. But on closer inspection, concealer hid circles under her eyes.

"You okay, Pet?"

"I've been better, actually."

Before Sarah could ask her what was wrong, a waiter with his blond hair in a frizzy ponytail stopped by the table to take their drink order. They both ordered margaritas; the Red Robin made great margaritas. After the waiter left, she said, "Okay, let's hear it."

Petra played with the salt shaker. "I let myself be talked into going to a family reunion. Big mistake."

"Uh-oh—problems with pronouns?"

Petra nodded. "But pronouns were the least of it. Sare, I was an object of curiosity. A figure of fun. Not to mention, a target of hostility."

"I'm sorry, Pet. What happened?"

"It started off with one of my cousins' wives following me around and assuring me she had no problem with me. None whatsoever. Not even the a teensiest bit."

"But you weren't convinced?"

"Not so much. Another cousin's husband told me I looked 'really good.' I thanked him politely, and he said, 'No, I mean it, you look really good.' And to make very sure I understood, he repeated it three or four more times."

"Good grief."

"That was just a warmup. Things really started rolling when my uncle Dallas got toasted and started calling me a 'she-male' with his customary bray, to the amusement of everyone but me."

The ponytailed waiter appeared with their margaritas and then retreated.

"Pet, that's awful."

"I got in some licks of my own, though. My cousin Debbie, a radical lesbian feminist, cornered me and started honking about how I wasn't a 'real woman' and had no right to 'invade women's space'—that's what she kept calling it, 'women's space'—and she said my 'change' was yet another example of 'male privilege.'"

"So what did you say to her?"

Petra's laugh had a bitter edge. "I told her I could make a good case that I had more right to 'women's space' than she did. 'After all,' I said to her, 'you didn't have to do anything to attain it. It was handed to you on a silver platter, while I had to overcome incredible obstacles to get here.'"

"Let me guess—that didn't sit well with her."

"She was apoplectic. I thought she was going to have a stroke. She called me every name in the book, including 'freak' and 'pervert.' That's when I decided I'd had enough and departed the festivities."

"So why did you go in the first place?

"Optimism. I had hopes that, after all this time, they could see me as a woman."

Sarah shook her head slowly. "Pet, your family and your old friends can never see you as a woman, even if they wanted to. Their imprinting is too strong."

"Imprinting? What do you mean?"

"Gender is one of the most primary aspects of a human being. The first thing we do when we meet other people is gender them as male or female. It precedes classifying them as friend or foe, attractive or ugly, black or white. When we gender someone, a process known as 'imprinting' occurs. It's permanent; it can't be changed. Trying to change it—and they do try—ends up causing cognitive dissonance. The most determined can train themselves to get the pronouns right, to be polite. But despite the fact that the rest of the world sees you as an attractive, twenty-something female, your family and old friends still see you as male. Imprinting."

"Imprinting," Petra said, tasting the word. "It explains a lot. Depressing as hell, though.

"There's an upside. The people who know you only as a woman are incapable of seeing you any other way."

"Well, that's some consolation."

"Understanding imprinting won't make family reunions more pleasant, but at least you won't have unrealistic expectations when you go to one."

"I always learn something from you, Sare."

Sarah took a sip of her margarita and thought about her last visit home, a "family reunion" of sorts.

Home was Kamphaeng Phet, a small town about 150 kilometers north of Bangkok. Her father and mother operated a dry cleaning business there. Like most Asian cultures the Thai place great importance on "face," the respect of others, and her parents were no exception. Sarah was a great embarrassment to them. After she transitioned at thirteen, still prepubescent, they quickly arranged for her to go live with Yaai, her grandmother, in Chon Buri, twenty kilometers south of Bangkok.

Unlike her parents, Yaai was proud of Sarah. Besides footing the medical bills for her gender reassignment, she put Sarah through university and medical school in Thailand and supported her move to the United States for residency training. Whenever she got the chance, Sarah flew back to Thailand to visit her. And when Sarah opened her practice at OMRI, Yaai's delight knew no bounds. When Yaai died, her estate was divided equally between Sarah and her mother, which only widened the gulf between her parents and her. They spurned Sarah's hopeful attempts to reconnect with them.

Five years passed before Sarah returned to Thailand and Kamphaeng Phet. She found the passing of time had not softened her parents' attitude. She'd hoped to establish a relationship with them that was, if not affectionate, at least cordial. It was not to be. Interactions with them remained icily formal. It was hard to say which was more responsible for their intransigence, their imprinting or their need to save face. Sarah respected her parents, but she couldn't say she missed them. She did, however, greatly miss Yaai—

"Earth to Sarah." Petra snapped her fingers twice. "How was your trip?"

"Sorry. Lost in thought."

"I was saying that imprinting explains why our family and friends don't accept us as women, but it doesn't account for their hostility. Or the hostility society has for trans women in general. Far more than trans men. What's behind all the animosity?"

"At its core is misogyny," Sarah said. "Excluding radical lesbians, show me someone who's hostile toward trans women and I'll show you a misogynist. In a patriarchal society like ours, where male privilege and misogyny are so deeply ingrained they're invisible, renouncing maleness is regarded as heresy. As the ultimate betrayal. Hence, the hostility."

"I can see how a man might feel that way, but it doesn't make any sense that a woman would."

"Don't kid yourself, women can be as misogynistic as men. From birth, women are bombarded with the message that females are inferior to males, and on a subconscious level they accept and perpetuate it."

"So why didn't *we* accept it?"

"We've seen the other side," Sarah said, smiling. "We know for a fact that males aren't superior."

"It explains why trans men don't have to deal with as much hostility as trans women. By becoming male, their status is elevated. Maleness is a step up; femaleness is a step down."

"Exactly."

"It's not fair."

"No, but you knew the mission was dangerous going in."

"Think it will always be that way?"

Sarah shrugged. "Education is changing attitudes, but it's a slow process. Every so often a lawmaker proposes legislation to correct a glaring injustice, but it meets with furious push-back from the right. Over the long run, though, the problem will just . . . go away. The hard-core misogynists, transphobes, and homophobes—in other words, most of today's right wing —will die off, making way for more progressive-minded people, with more enlightened views. In the meantime, unless there's a massive coordinated effort, which would take some serious financial backing, we'll just have to be patient and do the best we can."

"Have you ever considered becoming a transactivist, Sare? I don't know anyone who's more articulate about this stuff."

"And give up my privacy?" Sarah shook her head. "No thanks. I'm looking for a way I can contribute while remaining stealth. I just haven't found the right fit yet."

But something would come along by and by, something tailor-made for her talents and abilities. She was sure of it.

Livvy was brushing her teeth when her phone sang the distinctive little ditty that signaled a new text message's arrival. She expelled a frothy mouthful and picked up the phone. As expected, it was from the anonymous sender:

```
im hot on ur trail u can run but u cant
hide
```

She stabbed a button and the screen went dark. The cryptic text messages had gotten progressively creepier, but this one was almost threatening. If it was a prank, it was long past the point of being funny. Perhaps it was time to involve Verizon, ask them to trace the calls, find out who made them. It was probably some kid with too much time on his hands. Or it could be someone with mental problems.

She sighed, shaking her head. Wasn't the amnesia enough to deal with? The phantom texter's nonsense was as welcome as another knock on the head.

44

At her desk after the squad's morning briefing, Karen picked up Jimmy Chapman's rap sheet. As usual, she was struck by the reptilian look of his eyes in the photos on the first sheet, how they complemented the snake tattoo on his neck. He was lying low now, but sooner or later they would find him, and he'd go down for the murder of Sanjit Rajaragavan—

Who had worked at a hospital.

Who had gotten Stingler fired.

From his job at a hospital.

She felt a familiar rush. It was the excitement she always felt when she sensed she was closing in on something important. She scanned the sheet, not knowing what she was looking for but sure something was there. Priors, contacts, relatives . . . The only relative listed was an older sister, Lena Weber. Karen paused. The sister had a Tigard address, and it looked familiar.

"It can't be." She opened her notebook and flipped back through the pages.

And there it was. She'd been to that very address, to question Dennis Stingler in connection with his former co-worker's murder. Stingler lived in the basement, his mother in the house above.

So Chapman was Stingler's uncle.

It happened that way sometimes. There might be several pieces of seemingly unrelated information and something, some sixth sense, will enable her to suddenly see the connections. Like pieces of a puzzle falling into place. At such times she loved the job.

"Got something, Woj?" Detweiler asked from behind his desk. "You have a cat-ate-the-canary look."

"Carl, you're not going to believe this. Grab your jacket. I'll fill you in on the way."

"Where are we off to, if you don't mind my asking?"

"I thought we'd take a run over to Tigard."

The first thing Karen noticed when they drove up was the yellow Porsche Boxster parked in the basement apartment's driveway, instead of the 20-year-old Corolla that had been parked there before. She was about ready to knock a second time when the door opened six inches. Stingler didn't look happy to see her.

"Hello again, Mr. Stingler," she said, her manner extra-friendly. "Detective Wojanowski, in case you forgot. This is Detective Detweiler."

A micro-expression, unmistakably a sneer, flickered over Stingler's face. "What can I do for you, Detectives?"

She pointed at the yellow sports car. "You win the lottery or something?"

"Made some money with some software." He mumbled it.

"May we come in?"

"Uh, sure, I guess." Stingler stepped aside to let them enter. "What's this all about?"

"Hope we're not interrupting anything important."

"Just watching some television." Stingler picked up the remote and muted the TV. "What's on your mind, Detectives?"

"This software you made some money with, was it Marauder, by any chance?" Karen watched his reaction.

He laughed, but it sounded forced. "How could I make any money with a simple hack like that?"

"You tell me."

His close-set eyes darted around the room, the eyes of a rodent in a trap.

"I can think of one way," she said. "Using your 'simple hack,' you uncovered some patient medical information—confidential, private information—which you sold."

Stingler's mouth opened and closed several times; then he said, "That's crazy talk."

She unfolded the *Inside Scoop* and handed it to him. As he read it his coloration gave him away. Pale gray for guilt.

He looked up, a sullen expression on his face. "So?"

"So I want everything—what information you gave them, how much they paid you, who else knows about it—you know, all the pertinent details."

"I think maybe I need a lawyer," Stingler said.

Karen gave Detweiler an almost imperceptible nod, his cue to jump in.

"Look, kid," Detweiler said, smiling, "you're an accessory to murder. Hope your little software program made you a lot of money, because a criminal lawyer is going to cost you a fortune."

"Accessory to murder?" Stingler's voice rose an octave. "What are you talking about?"

"You're related to an ex-felon named James Chapman." It was a statement.

Stingler nodded. "He's my uncle."

"And of course you have no idea where he is."

"Not right now I don't. He shows up when he wants something."

Detweiler looked skeptical. "When was the last time he wanted something?"

"Couple weeks ago. He needed a reference for a job managing one of those storage places. I don't know which one, but he told my mom it was on the east side. I guess he got the job."

Detweiler winked at her out of Stingler's view and continued the prearranged routine. "Here's what we think:

We think you asked your uncle to kill the little Indian guy for getting you fired. We think that's the 'accessory to murder' part. And we think you're coming downtown with us."

Stingler looked alarmed. "Wait a minute! I—I didn't . . . If Jimmy killed Sanjit, he did it on his own. I swear I didn't even find out about it until I saw the news on TV."

"Sure, kid," Detweiler said, and produced a pair of handcuffs. It was a nice touch. He turned to Karen. "Will you Mirandize him while I cuff him, partner?"

It did the trick. Stingler became the open-mouthed man in Edvard Munch's *The Scream* (a painting Karen had actually seen, at the Museum of Modern Art, during a trip to New York). He was ready to spill it all.

"Wait a minute, Carl," she said. "Let me talk to Mr. Stingler alone."

"I'll be right outside." Detweiler glared at Stingler before stepping outside and closing the door behind him.

Karen crossed her arms. "Okay, Dennis . . . suppose you start at the beginning."

Stingler's shoulders slumped.

Twenty minutes later, Karen was back in the car with Detweiler.

"I got it all, Carl," she said, waiting for a chance to pull out into traffic. "The intercepted email, all the information on the amnesia patient, her medical records, her photo, everything. Stingler was anxious to please. You scared the crap out of him."

"That was the idea. Hey, that guy looks kind of like a ferret. You notice that, Woj?"

"Listen to this . . . *Inside Scoop* paid him ten grand for his information, an advance on future installments. Know what the sap did? He blew it all on a down payment on that yellow sports car, counting on the money rolling in, never anticipating we'd queer his play."

Detweiler laughed at that. "What about Chapman?"

"Stingler swore on his mother he didn't ask Chapman to whack Sanjit, didn't have anything to do with it. I believe him. He was scared shitless; he would've confessed if he was guilty. He thinks his mother told Chapman about Sanjit getting him canned and then Chapman did his nephew a favor, unasked. A family honor thing."

"I could buy that," Detweiler said.

"There's something else. Chapman got a chance to use Stingler's computer when Stingler wasn't there. We have to assume that Chapman saw all the information I got from Stingler, so he knows all about the transgender patient. Remember those magazines in Chapman's room at the Centurian?"

"You're thinking he'll stalk her?"

"I am indeed. Call it a hunch." Then she put the cherry on top. "Carl, I like Chapman for the transgender killings. I think he's our serial."

It didn't take Detweiler long to add it up. "Holy Christ," he said. "I can see it."

"We didn't make the connection sooner because we were looking for whoever killed Sanjit—a man, not a transgender woman—and because Sanjit's killer was sloppy, leaving cigarette butts and a print behind at the scene. We figured our serial would never be that careless. Something must have rattled Chapman to make him screw up so bad." She sighed. "I can't help but look back now, at how neat he kept his hotel room, at his choice of magazines . . . those things should've tipped us."

Detweiler snorted. "Mighty sharp hindsight you got there. You put it together, Woj, that's what counts. Now what do you say we locate Mr. Chapman and inquire what spooked him when he snuffed Sanjit?"

"Splendid idea. What say we canvas the mini-storages on the east side? There are a slew of them, but the day's still young, maybe we'll get lucky."

"I'm feeling lucky," Detweiler said, "And it's not as if we have other leads coming out of the woodwork."

"Sadly true. By the way, I've got another hunch for you to chew on. A certain partner of mine is probably going to retire on a high note after collaring a notorious serial killer."

That brought a grin to Detweiler's face. "I wouldn't mind that at all, partner."

45

Detweiler grunted and pointed through the windshield. "There it is, Woj. Access Mini-Storage. Quite a setup, too."

It was a larger operation than they'd expected, probably four hundred storage units of various sizes and a large area with RVs and boats in formation. And an on-site manager who turned out to be a homicidal maniac.

Karen parked in an empty space labeled, "Reserved For Manager." A patrol car rolled up just as they were getting out of the car. It was Evans and Simmelink. The four of them started up the outside staircase to the manager's apartment, the two uniforms in the lead.

"Fat chance Chapman's going to be here," Detweiler said. "The owner said he's been trying to catch him here for the two weeks. He was pissed as hell when he found out that Chapman had the lock changed."

The stick-on sign on the door said, "MANAGER." She nodded to Simmelink.

He stood to one side and knocked on the door using the butt of his Mag-Lite. In a commanding voice he called out, "James Chapman. Police. Open up."

No response.

Simmelink knocked louder and called out a second time. He looked at Karen, eyebrows raised in inquiry.

"Go ahead," she said.

Evans wielded the portable battering ram and the door flew open with the first blow.

The studio apartment had a small refrigerator, two-burner stove, daybed, bedside table, dresser, free-standing closet, and a small kitchen table with two chairs. El-cheapo furnishings.

She opened the refrigerator and saw an unopened jar of ranch chip dip, a six pack of Pabst Blue Ribbon with two bottles remaining, and a pizza box that contained three curled, desiccated slices of pepperoni pizza. Chapman wasn't into health food, apparently. The cupboards were bare, and the closet contained only empty wire hangers. Everything pointed to a single conclusion: Chapman was long gone.

In the bathroom the usual toiletries were missing. The waste basket contained an empty can of Right Guard deodorant spray and a toilet paper tube. Threadbare towels and washcloths were neatly hung on towel racks, draped and spaced perfectly. The white porcelain tub was surprisingly large for a studio apartment. She shined her penlight down the drain and mused that the tub would be a perfect place to let a body bleed out. C.S.U would give it their complete attention when they processed the scene, but she wanted to peek anyway. It looked revoltingly slimy down there.

"Tranny magazines," Detweiler called out from the other room. He was standing by the bedside stand, pointing to an open drawer. "Chapman must've cleared out in a hell of a hurry, to leave his precious magazines behind." A clean brass ashtray was on the tabletop, a book of matches beside it. On the cover:

MEDALLION CLUB
Exotic Dancing
No Cover

3057 Belmont Ave.
555-255-3057

"Tranny bar," Detweiler said. "It's probably his hunting ground."

"The department stepped up patrols in that area after the bodies started showing up. Not enough to be very effective, though."

"The department has to prioritize the allocation of resources for patrols. Budget cuts got us spread pretty thin."

"I have to wonder how priorities would have shifted if Chapman's victims hadn't been transgender."

"Beats me," Detweiler said. "One thing I do know, our suspect's in the wind. He could be in Montana by now."

"He could, but I don't think he is. I think he's still in the area, lying low."

"Yeah, huh?"

"He's after Livvy, the transgender girl with amnesia. And that's how we're going to catch him."

"It's your show, Woj. I'm just along for the ride."

"I just heard car doors. Probably the C.S.U. team. Let's get out of their way so they can do their thing."

They were halfway back to the House, Detweiler behind the wheel, when their unit's call sign came over the radio. Karen keyed the mic and echoed the call sign.

Dispatch said, *"Suspect vehicle, black 1967 Chevrolet Camaro, Oregon plate Ocean Charles Ida eight six four, located in Lloyd Center parking lot, Northwest corner."*

"On our way," she said as Detweiler switched on the lights and stepped on it.

Ten minutes later they were window-to-window with a patrol car, Mannheim and Phipps inside.

"Hey, Woj, Carl," Phipps said. "We were on our way to have lunch at Arby's when Mannheim spotted the Camaro."

"Good eye, Mannie."

"Gonna buy me lunch, Woj?" Mannheim winked at her.

She and and Detweiler got out of their car and walked over to the Camaro. With its jet-black paint and extra-dark tinted windows, it looked sinister. It seemed to crouch there, a predator like its owner.

Detweiler clucked his tongue. "Phipps, you better cite the owner of this vehicle for those windows." He walked around to the rear of the car and bent down. "Tailpipe's cold as can be. It's been here a while."

"Don't look for the driver to be back anytime soon," Karen said. "This car was ditched."

Detweiler pantomimed to Phipps that he should pop the lock. The patrolman got a Slim-Jim from his patrol car and had the driver's door open in less than ten seconds. The interior was empty—nothing in the glove box, nothing under the seats. By then Phipps had picked the lock on the trunk. Except for the spare and jack, it was empty also. But no telling what the lab boys would come up with when they gave it a good going-over.

"The car hauler ought to be here any minute," Detweiler said.

Karen managed to restrain herself from hounding the lab techs for the results. Finally, Ian Remmick called and told them to come down to the lab.

Detweiler trailing her, she pushed open the lab's door five minutes later. "Please tell me you found something, Ian."

"I'll say this," Remmick said, "the guy that owned this car was a fanatic about keeping it clean."

"Yeah, he's a neat-freak," Detweiler said.

"But clean as it was, he still overlooked a few things," Remmick said. "We found three hairs in the trunk. Two were black and belong to the suspect. But the third one, the longest one, was blond. It's a DNA match with one of the transgender victims. And just in case that's not enough, we found a small piece of clear polyethylene plastic sheeting that had caught on the trunk latch, a tiny fleck of blood on it. The blood belongs to a different transgender vic. Looks like the guy transported their bodies in the trunk, wrapped in plastic tarps."

"Nice work, Ian," she said.

"One more thing. The bathtub in the suspect's apartment —we found traces of several types of blood in the P-trap. If I had to guess, I'd say that's where he killed them. Makes sense. Let them bleed out down the drain. No mess, no fuss."

Detweiler turned to her. "Another bull's-eye, partner."

"Yeah, but now we have to find the creep," she said. "Hopefully, before he finds another victim."

"Any ideas?"

"I think I'll pay a solo visit to the Oregon Medical Research Institute. I want to talk to one of the doctors there."

46

After grabbing a late lunch in the hospital's cafeteria, Sarah returned to her office to find a woman waiting at her door. Her bearing gave Sarah the impression she was there on official business. Her clothes—tailored herringbone sport coat with leather elbow patches, khakis, comfortable-looking brown shoes, no purse—reinforced it.

Had the hospital found out about the clandestine karyotyping and called the police? Unlikely. OMRI's administration would handle the matter internally, at least at the outset. So what did the woman want? Sarah had an ability to adopt an impassive mask that concealed inner turmoil. She wore it now. "May I help you?"

"Dr. Soong? Detective Wojanowski, Portland Police," the woman said and flipped open a wallet to show a badge and police I.D.

Sarah unlocked the door and held it open for her visitor. Inside, Sarah asked her, "What can I do for you, Detective?"

"I'd like to talk with you about one of your patients. Livvy Covington."

"Livvy?" Sarah felt the mask slip, but quickly recovered. "Has something happened to her?"

"She's fine," the detective said. "I want to make sure she stays that way."

"I don't understand."

"Miss Covington might be in danger."

Sarah swallowed. "What kind of danger?"

"Dr. Soong, surely you're aware that a serial killer has been murdering transgender women in Portland and Vancouver?"

"Yes, of course."

"I believe the killer has targeted Miss Covington."

"How could the killer—" She broke off, realizing what she was about to ask.

"—know that she's transgender?" The detective walked to the window and looked out.

Sarah hoped the surprise she felt wasn't apparent. "Right. And how is it that *you* know?"

The detective turned away from the window. "It seems some of your private email concerning Miss Covington was intercepted by a former hospital employee named Dennis Stingler. He worked in the IT department. Know him?

Sarah shook her head. "No."

"He was fired for invasion of privacy and unauthorized use of hospital property."

Sarah was silent as she considered the implications of someone—of anyone—seeing the email she'd written about Livvy. A shudder ran up her spine and back down.

"If it's any comfort," the detective said, "the hospital is unaware of Miss Covington's ... situation. They didn't see the contents of the email. But the fact remains, Stingler knows."

"Stingler is the killer?"

"No."

"Then who is?"

"Stingler's uncle, an ex-felon who had access to his nephew's computer. I think he saw the intercepted email. I'm acting on the assumption he did."

She and the detective had been standing in the middle of her office. Sarah walked around the desk and dropped into her chair. The detective sat down in one of the chairs in front of the desk.

"I'm afraid it gets worse." The detective handed her a tabloid newspaper across the desk.

The headline made Sarah forget all about maintaining a mask. She read the article and then closed the paper with disgust. "Jesus."

"Fortunately, they didn't reveal her name. But we should be glad they ran the article. If they hadn't, I wouldn't have suspected Stingler's uncle was the serial killer or realized that Miss Covington was in danger."

"So what do you need from me?"

"Do you know how to contact Miss Covington?"

"Sure, I have her phone number. She's staying with some friends she met in the hospital. I've got their address."

"That would be very helpful."

Sarah hesitated and then asked, "Are you going to inform the hospital administration about this? About Livvy, I mean?"

The detective shook her head. "I don't see any reason to involve the hospital, since Miss Covington is no longer a patient."

"So . . . what are you going to say to her?"

"I've been wondering about that myself. How do I inform her she's in danger from a serial killer who murders only transgender women without her realizing she's transgender herself?"

"I don't know. I was hoping she wouldn't have to find out so abruptly." *Or at all.*

"Any ideas?"

Sarah shook her head

"Guess we will have to play it by ear, then." The detective folded the tabloid and returned it to an inside pocket in her jacket.

"We?"

"I was hoping you would go with me to talk to her. She might need support and reassurance after we break the news to her. As her doctor, you're the logical person to provide it."

"Well . . . okay. I guess." But she was not looking forward to it.

"Thanks, Doc, I appreciate it." The detective smiled. "One more thing . . . I think it would be better if you were the one to call her and set up the meeting. Now, if possible."

Sarah shrugged off her misgivings and reached for the phone.

47

It wasn't a Harley, which would have been Chapman's first choice, but the Honda would do just fine for his purposes. His friend Dozer had taken it as payment from a guy who owed him money. True, the ancient CX-500 was uglier than a warthog, but its odd-looking engine sounded solid. He revved it several more times and then shut it off.

"Dozer, man, I really appreciate it. It's just until I can find another set of wheels."

"No problem. Jimmy, are you sure you want to use that full-face helmet? I have a cool little skid lid you're welcome to borrow instead."

"Thanks anyway, but I want to fly under the radar. Be as anonymous as possible." He put on the helmet and buckled the chin strap.

"I dig. Take care, man."

"I owe you one, my brother." He gave Dozer a fist bump and thumbed the engine back to life. After engaging the clutch he tapped it into first gear with his toe, and eased down the driveway and out into the quiet street. The Honda engine felt smooth as an electric motor as he accelerated. It was surprisingly peppy, which was good. He wouldn't have any problem keeping up with traffic on the thoroughfares.

As he rode down Division Street he felt his luck had turned for the better.

Last night it seemed to be going sour. He'd been at the Linger Longer on Burnside, drinking a Pabst Blue Ribbon and watching the television over the bar. So far he'd managed to stay one step ahead of the cops. Ditching his beloved Camaro had been tough, and he was feeling bad about it, but of course he'd had no choice. Without a doubt, they were looking for the car. Before dropping it off at Lloyd Center he'd given it an extra-thorough cleaning, so it was unlikely they'd find anything in it.

But he wasn't home free, not by a long shot. There on the television, bigger'n shit, was his mug shot. The volume was down, but he could make out a few words and phrases: *"... wanted for murder ... armed and dangerous ... do not attempt ..."*

He glanced around. Only four other people were in the tavern at the moment: a geezer nursing a beer by himself at a corner table, a guy talking football with the bartender at the end of the bar, and a grandma type in a lime green jogging suit, hunched over a video poker machine against the wall. None of them were paying any attention to the television. He wasn't going to wait around to see if they would. He slid off the stool and slipped out of the tavern unnoticed.

Chapman walked on east on Burnside at an unhurried pace and took stock of his situation. He had to get some wheels, and soon. Being mobile was a necessity. He could always steal a vehicle; it wouldn't be the first time. That was a fall-back; better to borrow one. Then he thought of Dozer, who lived just off Burnside, within walking distance. That was a stroke of good luck.

So he'd crashed at Dozer's for the night and borrowed the Honda he was now riding. The motorcycle gave him freedom to move around inconspicuously. The cops wouldn't be looking for a biker. He scrupulously obeyed speed limits and traffic lights to avoid being pulled over. A traffic stop would force him to use something else he'd borrowed from Dozer: the 9mm Beretta tucked in his waistband, and that would attract the kind of attention he wanted to avoid at all costs.

A hunter's first order of business is to locate his prey. He needed to find a Kinko's and print out a Google map to help him find the place in the Southwest Hills where she was staying. Chapman remembered passing by a Kinko's on Northeast 7th when he'd ditched the car at Lloyd Center. After signaling properly he turned right on Grand Avenue and rode north at precisely the speed limit.

It felt good to be back on the hunt.

48

Livvy escorted her two visitors through the house to the side deck, where they could talk in private. The police detective—was she there to inform her in person that they'd caught the thief who stole her car (and her memories)? But why was Dr. Soong with her?

The deck overlooked the Conovers' private park, which, in addition to the expansive lawn and plantings, had its own pond and putting green. The bright October day was on the verge of being cold; Livvy had on a light sweater and the two other women wore jackets. They found a table shaded by an umbrella and sat down. Livvy crossed her arms and waited.

The detective pointed to a huge tree about two hundred yards away. "Is that a treehouse up there?"

"It is. Floyd—Mr. Conover—built it with his own hands. He says he does his best thinking up there."

"Doesn't Mr. Conover use a wheelchair?"

"It has an elevator. It's not an ordinary treehouse."

"I guess not."

"So," Livvy said, "have you caught the jerk who assaulted me and took my car? Isn't that why you're here?"

The blank look on the detective's face lasted only a moment. "Your car? Oh, right, right. No, we haven't. I'm here about a different matter."

"Oh."

"I'm here to warn you that you may be in grave danger." The detective took some folded papers from an inside pocket of her coat. "We're looking for an ex-felon who's killed five women so far. I have reason to believe he has targeted you."

Livvy gaped at her. "Me? Why me?"

The detective slid a sheet of paper across the table to her. "Ever seen this man? His name is James Chapman."

The man in the mug shot stared into the camera with bored indifference and a hint of a sneer. Livvy shook her head. "Never seen him before."

"And if I do my job right," the detective said, "you never will."

"I'll ask again. Why me?"

The detective glanced at Dr. Soong before she answered. "The important thing right now is keeping you safe. So think hard, have you noticed anything out of the ordinary lately—someone acting strange or something that struck you as odd?"

"Actually, there *is* one odd thing," Livvy said. "I've been getting weird text messages." She took her phone from a pocket, entered her security code. "And they're starting to really bug me." She located the messages and handed the phone to the woman.

The detective read though the text messages and looked up. "I'd hoped they wouldn't be from our suspect," she said, "but they are. No doubt about it." She handed the phone to Dr. Soong.

"Wait," Livvy said. "A serial killer has been texting me?"

"I'm afraid so. Hope you can get along without your phone for a day or so. I'm going to have the lab analyze those messages."

"Sure, I guess. So what happens now?"

"As I said, our first priority is to keep you safe, so until we catch this nut you'll have round-the-clock police protection. You'll need to stay put, I'm afraid." The detective craned her neck to look at the house. "That shouldn't be too much of a hardship in this setup."

Livvy groaned. Being a prisoner, even in this idyllic place, for God knows how long, wasn't an appealing prospect. It meant she and Jeff would have to ditch their plans to fly up to Colby tonight or tomorrow—

But maybe not. "What if I were to leave town and stay away until you catch him?"

"Leave town? Where would you go?"

"The guy you met when you arrived, Jeff Longcypher? He lives up the Columbia Gorge about ninety miles from here, in a little town called Colby. Jeff owns and operates the airport there. We were planning to fly up there together today anyway."

The detective looked thoughtful. "I've driven through Colby," she said. "It's fairly remote, which is good. You'd be out of danger, with no need for police protection. I like it."

"That's a relief," Livvy said. "I'll pack a suitcase after you leave. We'll leave right after the barbecue."

"Perfect. Problem solved. If there's any hitch, just let me know and I'll arrange for police protection. The main thing is to keep you safe."

Livvy's curiosity was in high gear. Things didn't add up; there were too many missing pieces. What was up with the covert looks between Dr. Soong and the detective? For that matter, why was Dr. Soong even with her? How did the detective find out the killer was after her? And the big question: Why had the killer chosen her? Answers, she wanted answers. "Detective, the text messages, what do you think they meant?" A circumspect approach.

The detective and the doctor exchanged looks again, more evidence that something seriously strange was going on.

"Hard to say what they meant until we analyze them further," the detective said.

Time for a more direct approach. "You said this man has killed five women. Were they just random killings, or was there some connection between them?"

Sure enough, the detective and Dr. Soong glanced at each other.

"We're still looking into that," the detective said.

The elusive thing that had been nibbling away at Livvy's awareness suddenly materialized front and center. On the OPB program she saw the other night, the panel had discussed local murders by a serial killer—

She had to ask. "The women he killed . . . were they transgender women?"

"Told you," the detective said, looking at the doctor.

Dr. Soong said, "Would you excuse us, Detective? I'd like to talk with Livvy alone, if you don't mind."

"Not at all," the detective said and stood up. "I'm going to take a walk and admire these lovely grounds." She stepped down from the deck and looked back at Livvy. "But I want to go over your plan again after I get back."

They watched her walk away, toward the pond.

"She had a feeling you'd put things together."

Livvy turned to face her squarely. "I want to hear you say it."

49

The doctor regarded her for several long seconds before she spoke. "You're a transgender woman, Livvy."

Livvy sat motionless, gazing out over the pond. A dozen honking Canadian geese were circling it at low altitude, looking it over. It met with their approval, apparently, because individual geese began peeling off from the flock, gliding down to execute graceful water landings. Once they were all on the water, the armada sailed around the pond in stately fashion.

Dr. Soong touched her arm. "Are you okay?"

Livvy shrugged. She had braced herself, expecting to be reeling. Instead, she felt a strange calm. Shell shock.

"Did you have any any clues, any indications?"

"Well .. there were dreams." Dreams that were now starting to come into focus.

The doctor nodded. "Amnesia usually doesn't affect the subconscious, where dreams are from." She cocked her head to one side. "This development had to come as a shock, but you seem to be taking it in stride."

Livvy snorted. "Yes, I'm handling it so well."

"Finding out you're transgender is no cause for rejoicing, Livvy, but it isn't the worst thing in the world."

"Know what I feel, Dr. Soong? I feel *dread*. But it's not dread of being a transgender woman. It's a pervasive feeling that something incredibly painful happened to me *because* I'm transgender, and I'm dreading the possibility I'll remember what it was."

"You don't have any idea what it might be?"

Livvy shook her head. "It's ... indistinct. A shadowy thing. I can sense its presence, but that's all."

"Hurtful memories. Given a choice, many people would choose amnesia if it meant blocking the pain of those hurtful memories."

"But I wasn't given a choice." Livvy picked at a cuticle. "Know what's strange? Yesterday, other than having amnesia, I was just ... a normal woman. And now—"

"And now you're still a normal woman. A young, attractive, *normal* woman. Nobody in their right mind could look at you and think otherwise."

"Well, there's one major difference between other women and me—they don't have to contend with being transgender."

"If it had been up to me, you wouldn't either."

"When did you find out, Dr. Soong?"

"Remember when I swabbed the inside of your cheek? The test was conclusive. But I was the only one who saw the result."

"Why is that?"

"I thought you deserved a chance at a life free of baggage. A fresh start. I envy you that, because I have baggage of my own. All women like us do, to some degree."

"Women like us?" Livvy scanned the doctor's face. "You mean—are you ... ?"

"Yes," the doctor said. "Surprised?"

Livvy stared at her open-mouthed and wide-eyed. "I would never have guessed."

"That's because, like you, I transitioned young. We didn't have a male puberty, so our bodies weren't masculinized by testosterone. Our puberty was female; estrogen had the same effect on us that it has on any adolescent girl. It gave us a feminine morphology—narrow shoulders and ribcage, wide pelvic structure, slender hands and feet, small jaw, smooth forehead, breast development, and higher-pitched voice. As a result, we're undetectable. Unclockable, we call it."

"I guess I should feel fortunate."

"Yes, you should," the doctor said. "Except for the fact that you can't get pregnant, you're physically identical to other women in every way that matters—including your genitals. The surgery is so sophisticated these days that even a gynecologist couldn't tell without looking closely."

"Really?"

"Even then, a gynecologist wouldn't necessarily conclude you're transgender. Lots of women have labiaplasty surgery, which leaves scars that are similar to ours and all but invisible."

"So unless I inform someone about my ... situation, there's no way they would know?"

"That's right. As a general rule, I don't disclose. Not even the hospital is aware of it. The only reason I'm telling you is to show you it's possible to assimilate into society and lead a completely normal life. It's entirely up to you."

"A normal life is all I want."

"You've got a head start. Amnesia has an upside—it gives you a clean slate."

"A clean slate. This isn't the first time I've heard someone describe it that way."

The doctor touched her arm. "Livvy, you might feel compelled to tell your new friends about this aspect of yourself, seeking support. Don't. Not right away. Wait a while, until you've gotten your bearings and had a chance to think the matter through. It's a very personal thing. You might decide that no one else has a right to know, that it should remain private. Anyway, think about it first, so you won't regret your actions later. That's my advice to you."

Her advice made sense, but Livvy couldn't imagine withholding the information from Jeff. "What about relationships? Surely you shouldn't keep something like this from your ... significant other?" She almost said "boyfriend," but in the present context it sounded juvenile.

"That's a good question, Livvy, but I don't have an answer for you. It's a personal decision."

As far as Livvy was concerned, the decision had been made. She couldn't withhold such an important aspect of herself from the man she loved. After they were in Colby, that's when she would tell Jeff. She was certain it wouldn't make any difference to him.

"You're back," the doctor said, watching the detective climb the steps to the deck.

"Beautiful grounds," the detective said, slightly out of breath. "Like a park." She sat down at the table. "Okay, let's go over this again, Livvy. Right after the barbecue you and Jeff are going to fly directly to Colby, and you won't come back until the danger is over, correct?"

"Correct."

"Good. What airport will you be leaving from?"

"The one in Troutdale."

Dr. Soong said, "I know a couple of doctors who hangar their planes in Troutdale."

The detective nodded. "I'll check back with you in a while to make sure there were no hitches. And I'll arrange for a surveillance unit to keep an eye on this place after you're gone, in case the suspect shows up looking for you." The detective slid a card across the table to her. "Here's my cell number. Call me if you have any questions or problems or if you think there's something I need to know about. Okay?"

Livvy nodded. "I will."

The detective looked at her companion. "Dr. Soong, shall we?"

The doctor stood up and gave Livvy a hug. "Call me any time you want to talk."

Livvy showed them to the side footpath that would take them to the parking area. After they disappeared around the corner she turned and slow-walked, zombie-like, into the house.

She didn't see him at first.

Just inside, on a chair near a window open to the deck, sat Jeff. He jumped to his feet, obviously embarrassed. "Hi," he said, and then he seemed to realize how inane it sounded.

"How—how long have you been there?" She had trouble getting the words out.

The look on his face, a mixture of guilt, embarrassment, and confusion, said it all. "A while," he said. "I was walking by the open window, and I was curious what those two were doing here—Oh Jesus, that's no excuse. I had no business eavesdropping on your private conversation. I'm very sorry."

"How much did you hear?"

His eyes were downcast. "I heard most of it, I think."

She felt her gorge rising. "Excuse me," she said and made a dash for the bathroom in the hall. She managed to make it, if only by seconds, before that morning's breakfast was expelled violently in a paroxysm of gagging and coughing. She spat out the last of it and flushed the toilet and used tissue to wipe errant flecks of vomit from the porcelain rim. After washing her hands she bent over the basin and splashed cold water on her face. Then, utilizing the faucet as a drinking fountain, she rinsed the sourness from her mouth.

After she dried her face she examined her reflection in the mirror. She couldn't see any difference; she looked just the same as before. But the way Jeff had looked at her—so sad and so ... shocked, like someone who had just witnessed a horrifying event. The big question was, had it changed the way he felt about her? A part of her, a cynical part, whispered, *Of course it had. How could it not?*

She scowled at her reflection. Jeff deserved more credit than that. She took a deep breath and reached for the doorknob.

Out in the hall she hesitated. She had two options: flee to the refuge of her bedroom or rejoin Jeff. He was probably still standing in the room by the deck, bewildered by her sudden exit. She decided the best refuge would be in his arms. If ever she needed a hug, the time was now.

But Jeff wasn't where she'd left him. He wasn't out on the deck either. She made a circuit of the downstairs, checking every room. No sign of him. Flutters in her midsection made her insides itch. She took the stairs two at a time and sprinted to her bedroom. From her balcony, standing on tiptoe, she could see the entire parking area.

The red pickup wasn't there. She had known it wouldn't be. Would have bet on it, in fact. It was that cynical part of her again, continually devising worst-fear scenarios. Except . . . this one had come true.

She walked over to her bed and sat down. She lay back and stared at the underside of the canopy. A strange numbness was flowing through her, anesthetizing her every emotion. Jeff was gone, gone for good, and she was too numb to feel the loss.

And by the way—a psychopath wanted to kill her.

Like she cared.

50

On the drive back to the hospital to drop Sarah off, Detective Wojanowski asked her how the talk with Livvy had gone.

"About what I expected," Sarah said. "Like hitting her between the eyes with a sledgehammer."

The detective nodded. "That's what I was afraid of."

Sarah decided to go for it. "Detective, you seem to have a lot of empathy toward transgender individuals. Does the police department have sensitivity training or something of that nature?"

The detective shook her head. "No, unfortunately. Not that some of my colleagues couldn't use it."

"So you're just compassionate by nature?"

The detective was silent for a mile or two before she answered. "My sister Janet lives in Boston, where I'm from originally. She had a child, a sweet, sensitive little boy named Andrew—Andy. Beginning when he was three, Andy insisted he was a girl. Janet took him to a psychologist, who, after a thorough evaluation. confirmed that he was transgender. Andy wanted to have a girl's name, wear girls' clothes, and attend school as a girl. Based on the psychologist's advice, Janet supported her child's transition.

"Unfortunately, her husband, John, wasn't as enlightened. Somewhere along the line he'd taken up with an evangelical church, so naturally he asked the minister about Andy. The minister convinced him that satanic forces were trying to possess his son, and he condemned transgender people as 'abominations.'" She sighed and shook her head. "He put his foot down. Transitioning was out of the question, and the matter was closed. No appeal to reason, or pleading from Janet got through to him. His position was inflexible. 'No son of mine is going to be a sissy,' he said, 'if I have any say in the matter.'

"That being the case, my sister allowed her child, who wanted to be called 'Andrea,' to transition on the sly. John was a long-haul trucker and away from home most of the time; otherwise, the deception wouldn't have been possible. When Andrea was about twelve, Janet allowed her to take a hormone blocker to prevent male puberty, which Andrea was terrified of. The clandestine situation went on for a couple more years, until one day John happened to come home unexpectedly. The bastard knocked Janet around for a while and then physically dragged Andrea to a crackpot who claimed his faith-based therapy could 'cure transgenders.'

"Needless to say, it didn't work. And so her loving father disowned her and kicked her out. She was fourteen, transgender, and on the street."

"There weren't any relatives or social agencies she could turn to?"

"I would have gladly taken her in, but by then I had left Boston to come out to Oregon and was completely unaware of the tragic events back there. Janet contacted child protective services and explained the situation, and they tried hard to find her. But Boston is a big place. They finally found Andrea in an abandoned house, badly beaten and unconscious. She died in the ambulance on the way to the hospital. My sister was devastated. Still is. She divorced that son of a bitch, but that didn't bring Andrea back."

"I'm very sorry about your niece," Sarah said. The sad truth was, she'd heard many other accounts that were just as tragic. Too many.

"Thanks. I think about Andrea a lot. All she wanted was to be who she was. She was smart and funny. And pretty. She could have done anything she wanted."

The hospital parking lot was unusually empty.

"Here we are, Doc."

Sarah got out and closed the door and then leaned in the window. "I'm really glad this case was assigned to you, instead of someone less . . . enlightened."

"Take care, Dr. Soong."

"You too."

Concealed by trees and dense brush, Chapman was satisfied with his makeshift observation post at the edge of the woods. He raised the binoculars again and surveyed the house and grounds. He'd been watching off and on, mostly on, for the past three hours. A groundskeeping crew was mowing, raking, and trimming shrubs; he counted six workers. There were signs of activity in the house as well, windows being cleaned, people going in and out.

The lady plainclothes cops, assuming the passenger was also a cop, had left thirty minutes earlier in the Chevy Caprice. It had rattled him when they first showed up. He'd been worried that they had somehow identified his next target and were there to move her to a protected location. But when the unmarked cruiser left, only the two women were in it. That told him the cops were way behind the curve, and he breathed a little easier.

Soon after the cruiser left, a departing red pickup flung gravel while accelerating down the driveway, a big guy behind the wheel. As far as Chapman was concerned, *everyone* could leave. Everyone except his quarry. Speaking of which, shortly after the pickup left, the girl—he recognized her from the photo—appeared briefly on an upstairs balcony. She looked out over the parking area and then went back into the house. He saw her for maybe ten seconds, total. Long enough to realize the photo didn't do her justice. If he didn't know, he'd never clock her as an abomination. She wasn't like the others; this one was special. It would be the best hunt yet, by a long shot.

Come outside again, pretty thing. Jimmy wants to play.

He lowered the binoculars and closed his eyes. The inside of his eyelids burned from lack of sleep. He felt himself drifting off; after a halfhearted struggle to stay awake, he gave in. He dreamed about the girl. She smiled and reached out to him. Anticipation of what he was going to do to her, taking his time and making it last, gave him an erection—

A van with "South Hills Heating & Air Conditioning" signage rumbled by, jolting him awake.

More people. It was going to be tough to catch his lovely quarry alone and unprotected. But the challenge was what made this particular hunt so stimulating.

An opportunity would present itself if he was patient. And if he'd learned anything in the joint, it was patience.

51

Jeff drove aimlessly, his mind a maelstrom of anger and confusion. The anger was directed inward, at himself. First, for eavesdropping on a private conversation, and second, for scurrying away after being caught at it. He pounded the pickup's steering wheel with his fist for what must have been the hundredth time since he'd left the Conovers' place.

"What a stupid idiot." He spat the words. "A stupid, stupid idiot."

Eavesdropping on that conversation had been a total lapse in judgment. What the hell was he thinking, to do something so invasive? It was inexcusable. And when Livvy caught him *in flagrante*, what did he do? He compounded his idiocy by jumping in the truck and hauling ass. Fleeing the scene, running out on her.

He rolled down the window and shouted to an oncoming car, "LOOK, EVERYBODY! I'M A COMPLETE IDIOT!" As they passed by, the people in the car stared open-mouthed at the crazy person yelling out the window.

What a thoughtless, self-absorbed dope he was. He should have been there for Livvy. But *no*—when the chips were down, ol' Jeffrey Mason Longcypher was M.I.A. What a prize jerk! He raised his fist to pound the steering wheel again and then suppressed the impulse.

Instead of proceeding through the next intersection, he pulled over and waited until traffic passed and then made a U-turn. He had to go back. He had to apologize, to beg Livvy's forgiveness.

In the meantime he needed to come to terms with the fact that the girl he loved was transgender. As difficult as it was to believe, Livvy had been born male. It was incomprehensible. There was absolutely nothing masculine about her. Nothing even androgynous about her, for that matter. She was as feminine as any woman he'd ever set eyes on. Nevertheless, she was transgender. That was the reality.

In the courtroom of his mind, he was both prosecutor and defendant, and it was time for the cross-examination:

Did he feel he'd been deceived?

Of course not. Livvy hadn't known. And if he hadn't found out by eavesdropping, he was sure she would have told him. He'd never known her to be anything but completely open.

Did the revelation cause him to question his masculinity or his heterosexual orientation?

The question bordered on ridiculous. He was a man. He liked women exclusively and always had. It had never even occurred to him to question these fundamental aspects of his being. End of story.

Was he concerned about what other people would think about him for being with Livvy?

If so, it would be the first time in his adult life he gave a tinker's damn (an expression he'd swiped from Pauly) what other people thought about him. And how would they know? It wasn't as if Livvy would have to wear a scarlet letter T.

Think carefully, now—was the revelation a deal breaker for their relationship?

It was the Jackpot Question.

Could it be that, deep down, the idea of being with a transgender woman made him uncomfortable on some level? Was there a dark pool of insecurity and/or bigotry roiling beneath the surface of his psyche, undetected but ready to erupt? Could he be that shallow? And be unaware of it?

Admittedly, his prior knowledge of transgender people had been meager, coming mostly from movies and television, where more often than not they were depicted as oddities. But any misconceptions he'd had were demolished by the public television program he'd watched with Livvy at the Conovers. Nothing like actual facts to shift one's paradigm. Still, he never thought he'd ever even meet a transgender woman, let alone have a relationship with one.

One thing set Livvy apart from other transgender women: She had no recollection of ever having been male. In her mind she had always been female. And, he realized, despite newly acquired knowledge to the contrary, he couldn't think of her any other way. As far as he was concerned, Livvy was a genuine, one-hundred-percent authentic woman.

His woman.

Deal breaker? Not a chance.

Only then did he remember, and he nearly drove off the road. He had been so thoroughly flabbergasted by the startling revelation, he'd completely forgotten the reason for the detective's visit: to warn Livvy that a serial killer who had murdered five transgender women might be stalking her.

She could be his next victim.

Whatever it took, he would not allow that to happen.

He stomped on the accelerator pedal and the truck shot forward.

52

Livvy lay on her bed, wondering how things could have gone so wrong so quickly. For a while it had seemed like she was making progress at putting her life back together. She still had amnesia, true, but she knew her name and where she was from. She didn't have to worry about money. She had friends, people who cared about her—Leia, Charlotte, and the Conovers. And Jeff, who had pledged his love to her and with whom she had made love.

Then along comes a devastating triple whammy, shattering her life to smithereens again. Surprise! You're transgender. Surprise! A psycho wants to kill you because you're transgender. Surprise! You've lost Jeff because you're transgender.

The weird thing about it was, she didn't feel like a transgender woman, just a woman. But then, how was a transgender woman supposed to feel?

She swung her legs over the edge of the bed, stood up, and began removing her clothes. When she was completely undressed, she padded over to the full-length mirror and stood in front of it, scrutinizing her reflection. She turned this way and that, looking for vestigial signs of maleness, residual traces of masculinity, afraid she would find some.

But the person in the mirror looked totally female. What was it Dr. Soong had said? That she was "extremely fortunate to have transitioned very young," and because of that, she was undetectable—"unclockable" was another word the doctor had used. For someone so fortunate she certainly felt miserable.

She turned away from the mirror and dressed listlessly.

It was strange. One would logically assume that her primary concern would be the serial killer stalking her. Instead, foremost in her mind was the likelihood she would never see Jeff again. The terrible realization crowded out all other concerns, like a sickening punch to her gut. She wished the numbness hadn't faded away.

After a jaw-creaking yawn, she lay back on the bed and closed her eyes.

Henry the dog paced back and forth in front of the house, stopping occasionally to stare intently at the wooded expanse beyond the parking area before resuming his patrol. He was prevented from conducting a closer investigation by an electronic perimeter fence that would, if breached, signal his collar to deliver an uncomfortable shock.

Ellie found her husband on the deck, laying out steaks on the the stainless steel barbecue's grill.

"Floyd, Henry's bothered by something in the woods. He keeps staring down there with his hackles up."

"Probably an animal of some type, maybe a coyote," Floyd said. "If if he's still on full alert after we're finished eating, maybe I'll take him down there and find out what he's so interested in."

"Also, I'm a little worried about Livvy. She's been holed up in her room since her visitors left, and she said she wasn't hungry when I checked on her a bit ago. Jeff said he'd be here for the barbecue, but then he took off as well."

"Maybe he and Livvy had a lovers' spat."

"Well, I'd better call Charlotte and Leia. Those steaks will be almost done by the time they get down here."

From his improvised hunter's blind on the edge of the woods, Chapman watched the massive German shepherd through his binoculars. The dog greatly complicated matters. It would be next to impossible to sneak up on the house with it there; getting rid of it was a priority. Shooting it was out of the question, of course. Had he known that a dog would be involved, he could have gotten hold of a quick-acting poison or tranquilizer, something efficient and silent. The question was, could he dispatch the dog silently with a knife? It could be done, but it would be tricky.

It began to sprinkle lightly. The sky to the west was clear of dark clouds, so it was probably just a brief shower. Nevertheless, any dampness would be bad if it turned colder. He stood up and walked over to the motorcycle concealed in the brush and removed a plastic poncho from one of the saddlebags. Between his heavy Carhart coat and the waterproof poncho, he'd be just fine.

The unmistakable aroma of barbecued meat wafted into his nostrils, making his mouth water. He wished he had some of it. Instead, he retrieved a package of jerky, a bag of Fritos, and a can of 7-Up from the saddlebag. He sat down on a log where he could watch the house while he ate his meager lunch.

53

Livvy woke with a start. There had been a knock at her bedroom door, or had she only dreamt it? She called out, "Yes?"

"Are you up, dear?" Ellie's voice, muffled through the door. "Jeff is here to see you."

Lucid dreaming. She had just read an article about it in *Psychology Today*. The knock at her door, waking suddenly, Ellie talking to her—they could all be elements of a lucid dream. *If so, I'll take it.* She got out of bed.

A smiling Ellie was there when she opened the door. Her smile vanished, replaced by concern. "Honey, you look terrible," she said. "Aren't you sleeping well?"

"Did I hear you say Jeff is here?"

"Yes," the older woman said, her tone conspiratorial, "and he's holding a lovely bouquet of roses. I wonder who they're for?"

Best lucid dream *ever*. "Be right down."

"I'll tell him, dear."

She darted into her bathroom and splashed cold water on her face, toweled off quickly, and inspected herself in the mirror. She looked like she'd been clubbing snakes over in Ireland. Her hair was tangled, and her eyes were red and had faint dark crescents under them. She finger-combed her hair. Nothing she could do about the eyes.

Livvy paused at the top of the curved staircase and whispered, "Oh god." She started down, and it felt as if her heart was trying to jump out of her chest. The way things were going, she wouldn't be surprised if she had a coronary right then and there. Midway down she saw Jeff standing at the bottom with a bouquet of white roses, looking sheepish.

"Hi, kiddo," he said when she reached the bottom.

"You're back." Never had the obvious been stated so succinctly.

"Yeah, I—" He held out the bouquet to her. "A guy was selling roses out of the back of his van, so I stopped and bought those."

She took the bouquet and thanked him. The roses looked like they needed water. It would give her a chance to retreat a moment and collect her wits. They badly needed collecting.

"I wouldn't blame you a bit," he said, "if you told me to just go the hell away. But I want you to know how—" The grandfather clock in the foyer began loudly chiming the quarter-hour. They remained frozen awkwardly, looking at each other, until it the chime ended, and then Jeff resumed talking. "I want you to know how terribly sorry I am about eavesdropping and then taking off. It was deplorable behavior, and I have no excuse. Other than terminal stupidity."

"But you came back."

"Kicking myself in the ass the whole way. I had to come back, Livvy. I want us to be together. No matter what."

No matter what. She bit her bottom lip, hard enough to dispel any possibility that it was a lucid dream. "I'm glad you did."

"Hey," he said, beckoning to her. "Come here."

She laid the bouquet on the bottom stairstep and went to him. He held her tightly and kissed her forehead, her cheek, the tip of her nose, and finally her mouth, in a way that left no doubt in her mind about his sincerity. If only the doctor and detective would return and tell her they'd made a terrible mistake and she should forget everything they'd told her . . .

"Listen, honey, it's not safe for you here with that nutcase on the loose. Go pack some clothes and things, and then we'll take Ethan's pickup to the airport. We can hop in Four Seven Whiskey and be on the ground in Colby a half-hour later. In the morning we'll jump in the Apache and get the hell out of Dodge for a while."

"Where would we go?"

"My vote's for Monterey. There's a bed and breakfast on the Monterey Peninsula I think you'd really like. Or we can fly to Palm Springs. Ever been there?"

She tapped her temple with an index finger. "Amnesia."

"Sorry. Anyway, we'll stay away from Portland until they catch that creep. The sooner I can get you to safety, the better I'll feel. So, honey, please . . . let's get cracking."

She nodded. "I'll let everyone know I'm leaving for a few days, and then I'll go upstairs and pack a suitcase."

He took her shoulders and held her at arm's length, locking eyes with her. "I love you, Livvy. Never doubt it."

She felt like skipping as she went off to find Leia and the others. So she did. She was an excellent skipper.

Chapman heard voices and raised his binoculars. A couple emerged from the path between the house and parking area. It was the big guy he'd seen driving the red pickup. He was carrying a suitcase. His companion was Chapman's quarry. The man stowed the suitcase in the pickup's back seat and then walked around and opened the passenger door for the girl. Before she got in, the man leaned down and kissed her.

"Shit." Chapman said. Her leaving complicated things.

The man climbed in behind the wheel and started the engine. The pickup moved down the driveway, and within seconds it passed within twenty feet of Chapman's overgrown hideaway.

Chapman ran to the motorcycle and tossed the binoculars in a saddlebag. He pulled his helmet on and swung his leg over the seat, simultaneously thumbing the engine to life.

Then he engaged the clutch, tapped the transmission into gear, and eased the motorcycle between two bushes and onto the graveled driveway. The pickup was almost to the highway, a quarter-mile ahead of him. About right.

He followed them onto 217 North, carefully maintaining a discreet distance. They turned east on Highway 26, the Southwest Sunset Highway, which terminated at I-405. I-405 merged with I-5 North as they crossed over the river on the Marquam Bridge and continued north along the east side of the river. After proceeding north on I-5 for about a mile, they exited onto I-84, the Banfield Expressway, and traveled east to Troutdale, where they took the Marine Drive exit. A sign announced, "Airport."

Hanging back in second gear, Chapman watched the pickup turn into the airport's entrance. He waited three minutes by the Bulova on his wrist and then followed them. Concealed behind a utility shed, he saw the pickup parked beside a hangar, no one in it. He spotted the pair about five hundred feet away. They were standing beside a low-wing airplane, its cockpit door open. While the girl stood and watched, the guy unhooked the tie-downs and walked around the airplane checking fuel and oil levels and inspecting various parts of the craft. Finally, both he and the girl climbed into the plane and closed the door.

In a few minutes the engine started and they began moving. The airplane turned onto a taxiway, taxied down to the end, and lined up on the runway. After a short takeoff roll it lifted off and headed east. Chapman had a sinking feeling as he watched it disappear on the horizon. "Son of a fucking bitch," he said aloud.

He turned to go, but then a fuel truck pulled up and sat idling next to a building that was sure-damn the airport office. A man in coveralls hopped out of the truck and began walking toward the office.

It was worth a shot, Chapman decided. "Hey there!" he called out and started jogging. The fuel truck driver stopped walking and waited for him.

The driver turned out to be just a kid, no more than nineteen, still dealing with acne. "You need something, mister?"

"The plane that just took off, do you know where it's headed?"

"Sure do. Why?

"I was supposed to be on it," Chapman said, adopting a pained expression. "Guess I'm a little late. Story of my life."

"Oh. They're flying to Colby, about eighty miles up the river. Jeff Longcypher operates the little airport there. But you knew that, right?"

"Right. But I'm not exactly sure where Colby is. Mind if I take a look at that map on the office wall?"

"Help yourself."

The map told him he could take the Columbia River Highway all the way to his destination. Piece of cake.

He walked back to the motorcycle (which he was becoming fond of, despite his initial scorn) and pulled the helmet over his head and fastened the chin strap. The Honda purred to life, and he aimed it at the airport's exit.

54

Jeff kissed both her eyelids and then planted one on her lips. "Up and at 'em, Covington."

Livvy yawned and stretched. "What time is it?"

"Quarter to eight. I've been up for half an hour. And I've already showered, so the bathroom's all yours. Bacon, eggs, hash browns, and fresh-squeezed orange juice will be on the table by the time you finish your shower and dress. Oops, I forgot—you don't eat bacon. I do, though."

"Everything else sounds delicious."

"Pauly's getting the Apache ready, topping off the tanks and doing pre-flight checks. I want to be in the air by nine, which will put us in Monterey a bit before one o'clock, just in time for lunch. I know a great little seafood restaurant there."

She tossed back the covers, swung her legs over the edge of the bed, and sat up. She was wearing a tank top and bikini underwear.

Jeff leaned a shoulder against the knotty pine, watching her. "On second thought," he said, "ten o'clock wouldn't be such a bad departure time."

She rose to her feet. "Go make breakfast." Aware that he was still watching her as she padded barefoot to the bathroom, she exaggerated the sway of her hips.

"Make that an eleven o'clock departure," she heard him call through the bathroom door.

It was 8:47 when they started down the pine needle-covered footpath from the cabin to the airport, Jeff with a suitcase in each hand.

"What the hell did you pack in your suitcase, kiddo? It's twice as heavy as mine."

"Just necessities—clothes, shoes, blow drier, curling iron, makeup, facial cleanser, moisturizer, sunblock, shampoo, conditioner, hair brush, hand mirror, laptop computer . . ."

"Sheesh. Good thing the Apache can carry a lot of weight."

"Tell me again about that bed and breakfast."

"You're going love it. It overlooks Monterey Bay, and the sunsets are spectacular. It's owned by a gay couple, former engineers who quit the Silicon Valley rat race before the bubble burst. It's their pride and joy."

"It sounds perfect."

"And after Monterey, we can fly to Palm Springs, or Las Vegas, or wherever we decide. The Apache has a fifteen-hundred-mile range."

"You said the Apache's a twin. So if one engine quits, we'll still have the other?"

"That's the idea. But I've never had an engine quit on me. Aircraft engines have backup systems. Besides, Pauly makes sure my airplanes are all in tiptop shape."

"Pauly seems like an interesting character."

"I don't know what I'd do without him. He knows aircraft inside and out and he's totally dependable. I don't have a moment's concern about letting him ride herd on things when I'm not around."

"You said he was a roadie for the Evil Dead?"

"Grateful Dead. A little before our time. But don't be fooled by Pauly's laid-back appearance. During Papa Bush's Desert Storm he was an F-117 crew chief. That's big juju. After Pauly was discharged from the military, he chose . . . a somewhat less structured lifestyle."

"I'll say."

"Anyway, we're outa here, you and me. Our only objective will be to have as much fun as possible."

She had to admit, she felt a childlike excitement about the adventure in store for them. Yesterday had been a miserable day overall, but she had a feeling today would be a memorable one.

"Here we are," Jeff said. "And it's a good thing, because my right arm is now three inches longer than the left."

"That must be the Apache," she said, pointing.

A twin-engine airplane was parked in front of an open hangar, parallel to it, its rounded nose pointed at them. It was white with red accents and it gleamed in the morning sun. Even though Jeff had referred to it as "the old girl," it looked new to her.

"Yep. Looks like Pauly has her about ready to go."

They stepped off the footpath onto the tarmac and walked toward the shiny craft.

Jeff set down the suitcases. "Hey, Pauly!" he called out. "Squawk ident."

From somewhere inside the open hangar came a reply. "In here."

Jeff dropped the suitcases on the tarmac, and she and Jeff walked toward the source of the voice. Inside the hangar, they spotted Pauly right away. He was sitting in a padded metal roll-around chair, an apologetic expression on his face. Duct tape was wrapped around his chest, upper arms, and the chair back, effectively immobilizing him.

"I'm real sorry, Jeff," he said. But he was looking beyond them.

They turned in unison to see what he was looking at

A man was standing there grinning at them, a blue-black semiautomatic pistol in his hand. It was pointed at them. "Welcome, folks," he said in a jocular manner. "You're just in time."

Livvy glanced at Jeff. All the color had drained from his face. He moved her behind him, interposing his body between her and the gun.

"You're James Chapman," Jeff said. "I saw your mugshot on television."

"At your service," the grinning man said, making a grand flourish with his free hand.

"What do you want? Money?"

"An airplane ride," Chapman said. His teeth were very white, the canines pointed and noticeably longer than the rest.

"Where would you like to go?" Jeff's posture seemed to become more relaxed. Slouching casually, he edged closer to a workbench.

"Mexico," Chapman said. "I got the idea just this morning, after I heard that big airplane start up out there. Slept in your storeroom, by the way. Got in late. Anyway, that's when the idea hit me. It's the perfect solution—fly to Mexico, where a man can get lost if he wants." He indicated Pauly with the pistol. "Hippie man here is going to fly us."

"Us?" Jeff asked.

"Well ... not you. Sorry." He looked directly at Livvy. "Just my guest and me."

He was taking her hostage? She felt as though she was about to vomit.

Jeff lunged toward the workbench, reaching for a half-inch thick steel rod about two feet long that was laying on top. He snatched it, whirled, and hurled it in what looked to be one fluid motion, and then he charged Chapman.

But Chapman's reflexes were lightning-fast. He dodged to the right, so instead of striking the middle of his chest, the spinning bar careened off the point of his left shoulder and landed with a clang on the cement floor. Chapman roared with pain and fired three shots in quick succession; the first two missed Jeff, but the third found its target. He dropped with a horrible slackness.

Livvy cried out and ran to him. The top right side of his head was covered in blood, wet pink hunks of flesh glistened obscenely. The unspeakable horror of it engulfed her.

"Hey, it was self-defense," Chapman said, still grinning. "He tried to kill me, so I blew his brains out. He didn't give me any choice."

She broke down then and buried her face in Jeff's shoulder, overcome by grief and hopelessness. Jeff's cinnamon scent filled her nostrils; it was as if he was saying goodbye to her. She felt a tap on her arm.

"Sit your ass down in that chair next to hippie man."

Still sobbing, she did as she was told.

Chapman reached in his pocket and took out a large nylon pull tie and made a six-inch loop. "Stick your hands in here, pretty thing. Do it now."

She complied, seeing no other choice. He tightened the pull tie on her wrists, snugly enough that there was no possibility of wriggling out of it.

Chapman stuck the gun in his waistband and walked over to Jeff's body. He shook his head slowly and clucked his tongue with mock-sadness. Then he bent down and took hold of each leg by the ankle and began dragging the body toward the open hangar door.

"What are you doing with him?" Her voice had an edge of hysteria.

"I'm moving your boyfriend where he'll be more comfortable." He winked at her and resumed dragging the body out the door and around the corner out of sight.

She looked at her fellow captive. "Pauly, he killed Jeff. Jeff's dead." *Dead.* The word had a shocking finality.

"I know, Livvy," Pauly said, almost inaudibly. "I know."

"And after we get to Mexico he'll kill us too."

"Be cool," he whispered to her.

Be cool? How could she be cool, when Jeff was lying dead somewhere and they were at the mercy of a psychopath?

Chapman reappeared whistling, absurdly, the theme song from *Jeopardy.* He took a folding knife from his left front pants pocket, opened it, and walked over to Pauly. The blade gleamed under the hangar's lights. Chapman leaned down and sliced the duct tape encircling Pauly's chest and arms and then folded the knife and put it away. The gun was back in his hand in an instant. Pauly peeled away the remaining strips of duct tape from the front of his coveralls.

"Okay, hippie man, you and this pretty thing are going to stand up and walk slowly out to the airplane." He waved the gun toward the open door. "Do it now."

She and Pauly got to their feet and began walking toward the open door, Chapman following closely. They halted next to the airplane and waited for further instructions.

"Put sweetie here in the back seat and buckle her in. Then I want you to climb in the driver's seat and fasten your own seat belt. I'll get in last. Now go."

Pauly climbed onto the left wing, opened the cockpit door, and then bent down and offered his hand to her. She grabbed it with both still-bound hands and he helped her up and into the back seat of the Apache. After fastening her seat belt securely he slid into the left front seat. Chapman hopped up on the wing and, instead of taking the front seat beside Pauly, he climbed into the back and sat down beside her, on her right.

He looked over and smiled. "Hi there, sweet thing."

She felt his hand on her thigh, just above the knee. It made her skin crawl.

Pauly closed the cockpit door and then looked around at Chapman for instructions.

"Let's get the show on the road," Chapman said. "I want to be in Mexico before nightfall."

Pauly toggled various switches and the instrument panel came alive. He started the engines next, but the one on the right sputtered to a stop within seconds. Pauly swore under his breath and tried to restart the engine, but it wouldn't cooperate. He shut down the running engine.

"What the fuck's the problem?" Chapman shouted.

"Starboard engine seems to be acting up."

"You gotta be shittin' me."

"I rebuilt the carburetor last week. Probably needs a minor adjustment. But I can't do it from in here."

Chapman made a sound like a growl. "How long's it going to take?"

"Not long," Pauly said. "Fifteen, twenty minutes."

"You better hope to hell it's not any longer. Unless you want a 9mm-sized third eye smack in the middle of your forehead."

Pauly nodded and opened the cockpit door and climbed out. After unbuckling his seat belt, Chapman reached over and unbuckled hers.

"Sweetie, you and me are going to chill beside the hangar until he gets the airplane fixed. I'm sure we'll find a way to amuse ourselves until then." He looked down at the nylon pull tie binding her hands together and took out his knife. Using his thumb and index finger, he turned her chin so that she was looking squarely at him. "If I free your hands, are you going to do anything stupid?"

She shook her head. One quick slice and the pull tie fell away.

"Let's go, sweetie." Chapman climbed out of the cabin and then reached in for her.

He still had hold of her hand after she stepped down onto the tarmac. They walked together to a spot near the corner of the hangar.

"Work your magic, hippie man," Chapman called to Pauly, who was hunched over the troubled engine.

Then Chapman turned his attention to her. She flinched when she felt his hand on her waist.

It seemed to amuse him. "'Come on, baby," he said in a wheedling tone of voice, "let's me and you get to know each other better, okay?"

"I'd rather not," she said.

He feigned hurt feelings. "Don't be that way, pretty thing. Be nice to ol' Jimmy."

She felt his hand slide under her top. She twisted away before he touched her breast, but Chapman grabbed her by the wrist and pulled her back.

"Listen here, sweetie pie, we're going to be together for quite a while, so I'll have plenty of time to warm you up." He reached around and squeezed her buttock. "You might as well relax and enjoy it."

She noticed Chapman's earlobes. Or rather, lack of them. And those savage amber eyes—the eyes of a crocodile looking at prey on the river bank. Her gaze slid down to the detailed snake tattoo on the side of his neck. It was even more repellent up close. She stifled a shudder, not wanting to give him the satisfaction.

A cold, savage fury had been steadily building in her, displacing the terror. With nothing to lose, she asked him a question: "Why transgender women?"

"It has been ordained," he said. "Thou shalt not suffer a witch to live."

She looked for an indication he was joking but saw none. "I don't understand."

That ugly laugh again. "See, it's like this: You and your kind are abominations. You are offensive in the sight of God. I am the sword of retribution and salvation."

She realized then that he wasn't evil so much as crazy, totally unhinged. Evil or crazy, he was nevertheless a cold-blooded killer. And she was absolutely certain about one thing: She was not going to climb in that airplane with him again.

No matter what it took to avoid it.

55

The return to consciousness was a gradual process. He became aware that he was lying face-down on asphalt, but he had no idea how he came to be there. He tried to turn over but succeeded only in twitching. On the second attempt he managed to raise his right side slightly before a wave of nausea and dizziness made him stop. He lay panting until it passed and then, using his right arm and leg, he found he could lift his body enough to roll over onto his back. The effort exhausted him.

After some time passed—minutes or hours, he wasn't sure—he figured he'd better assess his injuries. He couldn't feel his left arm. Or his left leg, for that matter. In fact, the entire left side of his body seemed to be completely numb. He found that he could move the limbs, but there was no kinesthetic feedback whatsoever. His left side belonged to someone else. Weird.

A confusing jumble of impressions kept intruding into his awareness, and he prodded at them until finally they coalesced: a snake tattoo, a grinning man with lots of teeth, flashes of a gun muzzle, a hopeless cry—

Then he remembered.

With his right hand he reached up and touched the right side of his face and then examined his fingers. Smeared with blood. Gingerly, he explored further. He probed just behind the hairline and felt something wet and sticky. Torn, bloody tissue. And under that, a hardness of bone. The slug had created a shallow groove in the underlying skull, from the entry point behind the hairline to the exit point five or six inches farther back, leaving behind several loose flaps of scalp. All totally, shockingly numb. One-quarter inch lower and the slug would have blown off the top of his skull.

It could kill him still. He might have a concussion with intracranial bleeding that would result in a fatal clot. Shards of bone inside his skull might be turning his precious brain tissue to jelly.

But none of those things concerned him. The only thing that mattered was saving Livvy from that monster, an objective that at the moment seemed impossible.

He surveyed his surroundings. He was lying between a trash barrel and the emergency generator. Chapman must have dragged his body there assuming he was dead. He extended his right arm and grasped the generator's base. It took great effort to pull his body toward it, but he finally managed to sit up with his back against the generator. He had double vision, and a dull ache had begun behind his eyes. But his strength was steadily returning, which encouraged him to attempt to stand up.

It was a mistake. His left leg collapsed and he went down.

Lying there, he heard two male voices, one of which belonged to Pauly, that came from around the corner of the hangar. He couldn't make out what they were saying, but the voice he recognized as Chapman's was barking orders. Soon afterward he heard an aircraft engine start; it was one of the Apache's two Lycomings.

Walking upright was out of the question, so he tried crawling. He found that he could move, after a fashion, using only his right side for motive power, like a crippled bug. It was about twelve feet to the right-front corner of the hangar. With the wounded insectoid crawl, it took him almost five minutes to traverse the distance. Then he had to rest for another five.

He risked a quick peek around the corner. The Apache was twenty feet away, parked directly in front of the hangar, its rounded nose pointed almost in his direction. Only one engine was running; the other refused to start, its propeller rotating in quick, spastic jerks. The running engine was shut down, and Pauly emerged from the cockpit. He walked around the wing to the front of the aircraft and opened the misbehaving engine's nacelle cover. Jeff couldn't see anyone else around. He wondered if he should risk trying to get Pauly's attention somehow. Between the two of them, maybe they could overpower Chapman before he shot them.

"What the fuck's the problem now?"

The proximity of the voice, unmistakably Chapman's, made Jeff freeze in mid-breath, afraid to even exhale. Chapman was just around the corner, not more than four feet from where he crouched.

"Listen, you hippie asshole," Chapman said, "if you don't get that airplane running like a Swiss watch right away ..." The distinctive sound of a pistol slide being racked completed the sentence.

Pauly's muffled answer from beside the Apache's engine was unintelligible, but his tone was conciliatory. Jeff remained frozen in place, unsure what to do next. But he had to do *something*.

"And you, pretty thing," Chapman said, "you just hang loose. Okay?"

Silence.

"Okay?" he repeated, louder.

The answer was a thin cry of pain and protest.

His tone jocular, Chapman said, "Ever been to Guadalajara, sweetie pie? No? We're going to have us a memorable vacation." After a pause, he said, "I don't think you realize just how special you are. Extra-special. You deserve extra-special treatment."

Livvy said, "Stop doing that."

Chapman's laugh was ugly. "You'll get used to it, pretty thing, I guarantee."

Jeff gritted his teeth with helpless frustration, imagining what Chapman was doing to her. Poor Livvy—at the mercy of that twisted bastard. He had to do *something*. But what? And how?

The sound of the Apache's engine turning over interrupted his frantic contemplation. He risked another peek around the corner, keeping his head low, maybe a foot above the ground. Pauly's face was visible through the cockpit window. The engine caught for a few seconds and then sputtered to a stop. On the next try it started and steadied into a smooth idle. Then the other engine started. Pauly increased both engines' RPM and synchronized them.

"HEY!"

The angry shout from around the corner startled him. At first he thought he'd been discovered, but then he saw Livvy running across the tarmac with Chapman in hot pursuit. He caught her ten feet in front of the Apache's left wing, grabbed her by the hair and jerked her to a stop. Teeth bared and one meaty hand holding her by the neck, he back-handed her with his free hand.

Livvy whirled and delivered a kick to Chapman's kneecap. It made him wince, but he quickly recovered. She followed up with hitting, kicking, clawing, and, when he grabbed her arm, biting. Chapman swore and jerked his hand back. His face contorted with fury, he lunged toward her, but Livvy managed to dart out of his reach.

Jeff feared Chapman would shoot her out of frustration. An adrenaline rush hit him, full on. It blunted the pain and gave him strength.

It wasn't a conscious decision.

Injuries forgotten, he emerged from around the corner of the hangar and lurched toward them. The twenty-foot distance seemed like a hundred yards. He had no plan beyond getting his hands on Chapman. Rage turned his vision red. A loud roaring from somewhere close by drowned out all other sound. A detached part of his mind identified its source: his own throat.

Chapman released Livvy and turned toward Jeff, his back to the still-idling engine ten feet behind him. Jeff had enough presence of mind to skid to a stop barely a yard away from the gun pointed at his midsection and raise his hands in the time-honored gesture of surrender.

"Hey now, boy. You're a hard one to kill," Chapman yelled over the sound of the idling engines. "But if at first you don't succeed . . ."

Livvy screamed.

What happened next seemed to unfold like a slow-motion movie.

Chapman suddenly roared with surprise and pain. Pauly's terrier, Jerry, had hold of one of Chapman's legs by the Achilles tendon, teeth sunk deep, savaging it as if the leg were a rodent. Frantically trying to shake the dog loose, Chapman stumbled backward and lost his balance. He flailed his arms wildly, trying to regain it, but he continued to lean back farther and farther, ever closer to the spinning propeller's aluminum blades.

As Jeff and Livvy looked on in horror, Jimmy Chapman's head and one of his forearms disappeared inch by inch, puréed in a fan of pink spray that bloodied a broad swath of the tarmac, splattered the left side of the aircraft's nose, and flew high into the air to fall as crimson rain. Chapman's headless torso, being of greater mass and protected by his heavy coat, was snatched by the propeller and tossed like a rag doll. It landed in a bloody heap fifteen feet from the aircraft.

The Apache's engines sputtered to a stop, and a shocking silence fell over the airfield.

With a glad cry, Livvy ran to Jeff and threw her arms around him. "I was sure he killed you!"

"He came close," Jeff said, his voice sounding faraway-strange to him. But Livvy was safe; nothing else mattered.

Pauly climbed down from the Apache's cockpit and ran to them. "Jesus H. Christ, man! We thought you were dead!"

"So I've heard."

Pauly looked at the misshapen mass that had been Jimmy Chapman and let out a long, low whistle. "Oops," he said.

Oops, indeed.

Jeff's head throbbed, a dull ache in synch with his heartbeat. All around the edges of his vision a gray fog seemed to be steadily expanding inward, shrinking his field of view with each passing moment. He took a deep breath. "When you get a chance ... could one of you call an ambulance?" Even the effort of speaking exhausted him. "And maybe the sheriff?"

His legs began to buckle, and he grabbed Livvy for support. Her cry to Pauly for help came from far away ...

56

The titillating events that had transpired two days earlier were of course still dominating the slow news cycle:

"Tuesday at an airport in Colby, a tiny town on the Columbia Gorge, suspected serial killer Jimmy Chapman forcibly abducted a Portland woman and a Colby aircraft mechanic, after shooting and seriously wounding the airport manager. Chapman met with a gruesome death when he accidentally fell backward into a spinning —"

Jeff pressed a button on the remote to mute the TV. He'd had enough of the local news. He definitely didn't want to listen to the entire account again.

Livvy entered the room just then with several magazines from the gift shop in the hospital lobby. She leaned down and kissed him. Then she moved her chair closer to his bed and took his right hand, the one that could feel. Above his eyebrows, his head was wrapped with in a turban-like bandage. It looked bad, but a CT scan had determined there was no hemorrhaging in his brain, and sensation was already returning to his left side.

"You look like a swami," Livvy said.

"A swami who had the crap beaten out of him."

"My hero."

"The real heroes are you and Jerry Garcia. Between the two of you, Chapman didn't have a chance."

"I can't speak for Jerry, but I was motivated by sheer desperation. At that point I felt I had nothing to lose. Then you came lurching out making that terrible roaring sound, your head covered in blood and your face all contorted . . . my god, you looked like something out of a *Walking Dead* episode."

"I like to make an entrance."

"As bad as you looked, you were a sight for sore eyes. I was thrilled you were alive."

"Barely alive, it felt like."

"Floyd and Ellie suggested that you recuperate a few days at their house after you're discharged. You're family, they said."

"That's nice of them, but I've got an airport to manage."

Livvy held up her hand. "Pauly's taking care of things at the airport, so there's no reason for you to rush back. It won't hurt you a bit to spend a few days relaxing as their houseguest. Besides, it gives me a chance to play nurse." She leaned over and gave him a peck on the cheek.

He snatched up the TV remote and unmuted the volume. On the screen was a mugshot of a familiar face.

"*. . . has been charged with criminal mischief, breaking and entering, and trespass. A spokesman for Oregon Medical Research Institute described Stingler as a 'disgruntled ex-employee.' Stingler uploaded the virus, which he named 'Staph,' to the hospital's mainframe using an operating system back door that gave him remote access. However, IT Director William Morley discovered the virus before it could be activated. Left unchecked, Staph would have done irreparable damage to the billing and patient databases and backups, Morley said. Stingler is being held on a $500,000 bond. And now the weather—*"

He muted the television again. "Payback's a bitch. Ferret-face is responsible for this entire mess. If he hadn't hacked Dr. Soong's email none of this would have happened."

"And I'd be completely unaware of certain things that I'd just as soon—"

He pulled her down to his level and kissed her, ignoring the stab of pain in his shoulder. "Don't sweat the small stuff."

"Small stuff? Jeff, I can't have children."

"We'll adopt. Or use *in vitro* and a surrogate. When we decide we want children."

"Are you asking me to marry you?"

"Who said anything about marriage? I'm offering you a job as a nanny." He tried to maintain a deadpan expression, but he had a tell: The corners of his mouth twitched. Livvy had pointed it out early in their relationship. He hadn't yet identified Livvy's tell, assuming she had one. She was good.

"No, thank you," she said. "I hate kids."

"Yeah. Me too."

And neither of them cracked a smile.

Epilogue

Karen yawned and filled two cups with coffee. Sumatran. Gil had gotten her hooked on more expensive coffee and now the brew at the station house tasted like some kind of solvent. She was setting the cups on the breakfast table when he shuffled in wearing his bathrobe, blinking at the morning light.

"There's your java, Sunshine," she said on her way to the front door. "Watch me go postal if that paperboy skipped us this Sunday." Last week there had been no Sunday paper waiting for her on the porch. It put her in a sour mood all day.

But the newspaper was there, thank God. She tossed it on the table and sat down. She always read the World, National, and City/Region sections, in that order. She slid the Sports section over to Gil, who hadn't uttered a single word yet. That was fine with her. She wasn't much for morning conversation herself until she'd had a cup of coffee.

She almost overlooked the headline below the fold: "Victims' Families Bring Class Action Suit Against Evangelical Author." The short article made her feel like applauding.

"You're smiling," Gil said. "What are you so pleased about?"

"Listen to this." Karen read aloud, "'The families of the victims of serial killer James Chapman filed a fifty-million-dollar class action suit in civil court against Richard Ronson, director of the non-profit Family Morality Council and author of *Abomination* and *Pathway To Normal*, both of which condemn transgender people in the harshest possible terms. A copy of *Abomination* was found among Chapman's possessions after his death. The plaintiffs allege that Ronson's book incited Chapman to kill their transgender daughters, therefore Ronson is complicit in the murders. Asked to comment, Ronson said, "This lawsuit is specious and totally without merit. It's a transparent attempt at extortion, as well as a vicious attack on Christianity. My right of free speech is protected by the Constitution." Legal expert Ross McCoy pointed out that the First Amendment protects Ronson only from infringement of speech by government. "It doesn't protect him from civil lawsuits," McCoy said, adding there was ample precedent for the plaintiffs' suit.'" Karen looked up. "That brought a smile to my face."

"About time one of those Christian-in-name-only bigots was held accountable," Gil said. "No telling how many violent wackjobs his hate-filled nonsense stirred up. Like pouring gas on a fire."

"Ronson's playing the victim card, of course."

"If there's any justice in the world, the families will win the lawsuit and sting that phony where it hurts."

Karen resumed scanning the news. Another article soon caught her eye: "State Senator Questioned In Ethics Probe." She looked up at Gil. "I don't know if I can handle this much good news in one day."

"Something else?"

She cleared her throat. "'State Senator Ken Culbertson, a Republican from Oregon Senate District 30, appeared Friday before the Senate Ethics Committee to answer questions about his alleged misuse of campaign funds for personal expenditures and his acceptance of expensive gifts, none of which he declared as income. The senator denied the allegations and called the hearing a "liberal witch-hunt." Culbertson's approval rating has fallen precipitously since the controversy, and political insiders are predicting he will lose his reelection bid in November. Culbertson dismissed their speculation as "liberal claptrap" but had no further comment.'"

Gil snorted. "Wasn't it Culbertson who advocated jailing transgender people and then denied it, and when a YouTube video of him saying it surfaced, he introduced a bill to make videorecording state politicians without their consent a crime?"

"The very one, and his party supported him all the way."

"Culbertson and his GOP cohorts hate videorecording like vampires hate sunlight. It's hard to deny you said something when there's a video of you saying it on YouTube." He scowled. "To hell with those fanatics; let's talk about something else. Ready for your class tomorrow, hon? This is your—what, third one?"

"Fourth. And yes, I'm prepared. Overprepared." The class was the department's Transgender Sensitivity Training. It was her brainchild. She proposed the idea, and the big badges went for it. There was a lot of grumbling, initially, from her fellow cops, but the sessions were mandatory. Nevertheless, the classes had been going remarkably well. After last week's session ended, a detective from Robbery Division thanked her and confided that his younger sister was transgender. His gratitude made Karen's day. *Too late to help Andrea, but at least I can try to make life easier for others like her.*

"It's a beautiful spring day," Gil said. "Let's take Patty to the zoo. Think she'd enjoy that?"

"Sure she would. When you're ten, going to the zoo is high adventure."

"And how does her mother feel about it?"

"I'd like it too." The zoo would be a refreshing change of pace, as far from cop stuff as you could get. But she'd have to give the zoo's snack bar a wide berth; their caramel corn was so delicious it was criminal. Now that she was at her target weight, with a thousand dollars' worth of new clothes in her closet, she wasn't about to risk falling off the wagon.

Gil laughed, one short bark. "The last time I went to the zoo was with my dad. He bought me a miniature sheath knife at the gift shop. I loved that knife."

"If you're a good boy, Special Agent, maybe I'll buy you another one."

"You spoil me, Detective."

She chuckled. He had it turned around.

It was the noon hour, and Café Yumm at Southwest 3rd and Morrison was busy. Sarah lucked out when a couple at a nearby table stood up to leave. She pounced. "Petra! Over here," she called to her lunch companion, who'd just finished paying for her order at the register.

"Good job, Sare," Petra said, depositing her napkin and silverware on the table before sitting down. "Before I forget, congrats on your third-place finish in Vegas. I'm impressed."

"Thanks. I was pretty happy with it." In four years of competing in the World Series of Poker in Las Vegas, this was the highest she'd ever placed. Texas Hold 'Em tournaments had been a respite from the demands of the practice, burnout preventatives.

"Maybe you'll win the big pot next year."

"We'll see. I might be too busy to go. Ah, here are our orders." Sarah nodded thanks at the server.

"Since when are you too busy for a poker tournament?"

"I've had a tempting offer."

"Do tell," Petra said.

"The day after I got back from Vegas, I had a visit from a lawyer with a hundred-dollar haircut and a suit that damn sure didn't come from Men's Warehouse. He flew out from Boston to offer me a job."

"What kind of job?"

"Medical director of a new foundation to be based here in Portland, the Transcend Foundation."

"Never heard of it, but it sounds impressive. Why did they come to you?"

"That's what I asked the lawyer. He didn't know. At least, he said he didn't."

"So tell me about this foundation. What do they do?"

Sarah glanced around before answering. "You're not going to believe this, but their stated purpose is to provide support for the transgender community."

Petra's eyes opened wide. "You're kidding! Did the lawyer tell you who's behind it?"

"No, it's all very hush-hush. But if the high-powered legal talent and the scope of the mission are any indication, it's extremely well financed."

"Just what kind of support do they provide?"

"The whole spectrum—counseling, medical care, legal services, and financial aid."

"I'm speechless."

"That's not all," Sarah said. "A major focus will be educating the public about gender issues."

"They'll be going head-to-head against the right-wing fear machine."

"They know that."

"So . . . are you going to take the job?"

"Definitely."

Petra smiled. "Good for you."

"Look at all the hurdles we have to overcome to become our true selves. It's a miracle anyone succeeds. Those who make it, unless they live stealth, often face unbelievable discrimination and bigotry. And I don't have to tell you how many of our sisters are beaten, raped, or killed. The Transcend Foundation hopes to change all that, and it has the resources to do it. I want to be part of it."

"That's exciting, Sare."

Sarah took another bite of her Yumm Bowl. Her life's trajectory was about to change drastically. But she was also curious who was bankrolling the Transcend Foundation.

Very curious.

The air at altitude was as smooth as a sheet of ice on a Wisconsin lake. Seen from the airplane, the Iowa landscape below resembled a quilt made of tiny green and tan patches, the rectangular symmetry occasionally interrupted by random ribbons and blobs of blue, rivers and lakes.

Jeff turned away from the view outside the cockpit and looked over at his co-pilot. "High-altitude sightseeing," he said. "Nothing like it."

Livvy laughed. "I was just thinking the same thing."

"Airspeed and altitude check, please."

She scanned the instrument panel, zeroing in on the altimeter and airspeed indicator. "Three hundred knots at twenty-five thousand feet, Captain."

"Thank you, Covington. Let's see, it's two-forty Central Daylight Time. That's Chicago off in the distance directly ahead, so factoring in an hour layover at O'Hare to refuel the plane and grab a light lunch, we should touch down at Logan in time for dinner."

The trip to Boston was the Lancair Evolution's first long-distance flight, and Jeff was delighted with the sleek craft's performance; it truly was like flying a light jet.

"I'm glad my meeting with Mr. Cavenaugh isn't until the day after tomorrow," Livvy said. "That will give us a chance to spend time with Nora. She's going to show us around. We'll see where I grew up. And I have a million questions to ask her."

"Is there any rush to get back, hon? We can stay in Boston as long as you want."

"Just so I'm back in Portland by the nineteenth for my audition."

"Right, I forgot," he said. "Ellie told me that if you don't get the chair she and Floyd won't donate another dime to the Oregon Symphony."

"I know. I appreciate their support, but I need to make it clear that I want to get it on my own, without any coercion from them, however well-intentioned it may be."

"You'll get it. Unless the conductor's deaf."

Livvy's hand found his, and they flew along in comfortable silence holding hands. The sleek craft sliced through the thin air, its turbocharged engine purring softly, the autopilot maintaining heading and altitude with inhuman accuracy. Jeff yawned, and out of the corner of his eye he saw that Livvy was doing the same.

"Want to log some time in a high-performance aircraft?" He reached out to the autopilot's panel and disengaged it. "Your controls."

She looked over at him. "Wait, are you sure? This airplane is way different than the one you've been teaching me in."

"You'll do fine."

She chewed on her lower lip, concentrating on the task. "Remind me to wear different shoes next time. It's harder to operate the pedals when you're wearing clogs."

A while later he turned to her. "What's your verdict?"

"It's a little scary. So much more . . ."

"Responsive?"

"Yes, responsive. You know, I think I like a stick better than a yoke."

"That's what *she* said."

"Just for that—your controls." Livvy released the stick and rudder pedals. When he had control, she said, "The sad thing is, that was one of your better that's-what-she-said jokes."

"This is a tough room." He re-engaged the autopilot, which immediately set about correcting the deviation from heading and altitude. Then he patted her shoulder. "Nice work, Covington."

She was a good student, a quick learner. And she had a feel for it, which couldn't be taught. She had yet to solo, but the way she was progressing it wouldn't be long.

After ten minutes of silence, Livvy said, "If I get the chair with the Oregon Symphony, I'll have to commute between Colby and Portland for rehearsals and performances. Maybe we should also have a condo in Portland. Might come in handy from time to time."

Her enthusiasm made him smile.

"Nothing fancy, though," she added. "I plan to spend every possible moment in Colby, surrounded by cedar and knotty pine."

"An heiress with simple tastes. Refreshing."

At first, when confronted with the fact that she was worth a boatload of money, Livvy's reaction was embarrassment. She acted as though she would rather just forget she had it. Yeah, right. How do you forget about ten billion bucks? Compared to that, the eight-hundred thousand he'd managed to sock away was chewing-gum money. ("But you earned your money," Livvy said. "That's the difference. It didn't just fall in your lap, courtesy of your parents' estate.")

She became more receptive to the idea when it occurred to her that she could use her fortune to, as she put it, "make the world a better place." He'd teased her about sounding like a beauty pageant contestant, but the truth was, that kind of money could make a considerable impact. Over the past three months she'd had a number of mysterious powwows with several Boston lawyers and accountants. They were "going over some investments," Livvy told him. And she hinted at something else, something in the make-world-better-place category, but she wanted to keep it to herself for a while. It was just as well; he'd just as soon not be involved with Livvy's finances. He had a flight service to run. It was enough to keep him occupied.

"Something's been bothering me," Livvy said, looking out the side window. "There's a chance that being in Boston, seeing people and places I knew before, will be a catalyst that makes my memories return. If so, I hope I don't remember *everything*, only the good stuff."

"Whatever comes along, we'll deal with it. Okay?"

She leaned over and kissed his cheek. "Aye aye, Captain."

He looked down at Livvy's slender hand. The engagement ring she'd picked out reflected her preference for elegant simplicity. But that only halfway explained her attraction to him. He was arguably simple—but elegant? Maybe she saw him as a diamond in the rough.

His co-pilot, on the other hand, was an embodiment of understated elegance. Her unassuming, girl-next-door appearance and manner sometimes made that easy to overlook, but it was undeniable. In the muted afternoon light of the aircraft's cabin she looked exceptionally lovely to him. He admired her high cheekbones, the gentle curve of her cheek, the line of her slender throat, all unquestionably, emphatically female. Any guy in his right mind would count himself lucky to be with her. And she had chosen *him*.

"You've been staring at me," Livvy said. "What, may I ask, is so captivating?"

"Those earlobes of yours, kiddo. They're exquisite."

She sighed. "Have I informed you that you are a peculiar person?"

"You may have mentioned it." He gave her a quick kiss. "But again, nobody's perfect."

Her laugh was like the ringing of silver bells.

And later, high above western Pennsylvania, Olivia Leigh Covington was officially inducted into the Mile High Club.

THE END

About the Author

T.J. McCandless is currently touring the country in a motor coach, accompanied by an obstreperous terrier. When not writing spine-tingling thrillers, McCandless enjoys exploring places that are off the beaten path, always on the lookout for intriguing locales for future novels.

www.ingramcontent.com/pod-product-compliance
Lightning Source LLC
Chambersburg PA
CBHW030628110726
47901CB00002B/368